THE BIG IF

by Sharisse Coulter

ISBN 978-0-9888378-4-3
Copyright 2015 by Sharisse Coulter
sharissecoulter.com
Facebook
Twitter

More Titles From Sharisse Coulter:
ROCK MY WORLD

Chapter 1

Getting older isn't what I thought it would be. As I enter my third decade of spinning on this ball in space, I am starting to see the tangible effects of every little decision made along the way. What was once a vast expanse, open for exploration, has narrowed to a comfortable, defined road. I don't know how to feel about that.

On the one hand, I don't miss the angst and uncertainty of my high school days, nor the parental control or curfews. I do miss how all doors were propped open with possibilities. The future could be anything I chose, which made my everyday decisions small—like tiny pebbles in the ocean—compared to the grandeur that lay ahead.

But a strange thing happened on the road to adulthood. Those seemingly insignificant pebbles created larger ripples that spread out, encircling me. It's a good circle. A great one, in fact. But if I'm honest, sometimes it feels a little claustrophobic, too. Then again, maybe my mom is right. Maybe I'm just overthinking things.

I do some of my best thinking in traffic. Inching forward without nudging the speedometer, I roll the windows down, turn up the radio and breathe in Eau de Malibu: an intoxicating combination of exhaust, salt water and something indefinable yet distinctly Los Angeles. Most people hate lurching along like this, but for me, sitting on the Pacific Coast Highway going nowhere quickly yields my most productive self-reflection.

The vibration of my phone in the cup holder puts my self-reflection on hold, and I can't help but glance at it.

Hey sexy wife, hope class was good. Can you pick up Thai if I call it in? Love you. You're the best!

I tap out a quick "K" and flip the phone over so I'm not tempted to read Seth's response.

I turn up the radio to overwhelm any further distractions. The DJ announces, "And now, Marc Justin's new single 'Cinderella'." I roll my eyes.

Tuning out the lyrics of this inane pop song, I wonder how Cinderella became an icon for women's wish fulfillment. I do that sometimes. Wonder about things usually taken for granted, things no one bothers to question, thinking about them as though I'm an alien life form seeing Earth's cultures for the first time.

In the case of the fairy tale, I've got to point out: glass high heels? Impractical and uncomfortable, not to mention dangerous. No way Cindy could dance the night away in those things. As far as I'm concerned, it's right up there with that Chinese foot-binding practice.

On top of which, if I met this alleged Prince Charming— shared an amazing connection—but the next day he couldn't recognize me except by my shoe size, I'd seriously reconsider the notion of true love. Maybe the story should be renamed "Beware of Fairy Godmothers." She's the real problem. Showing up with her magical toolbox, she pretends to be all sweet and helpful. She sets Cinderella up to trade in one form of imprisonment for another, albeit fancier one. Not cool. In both scenarios Cinderella never gets the one thing she really wants: freedom.

I smile to myself, wishing Seth were here having this conversation with me. He's always amused by my randomness. Which is great because I can't seem to help it. I've always been prone to daydreaming. Especially as a kid.

When adults used to ask, "Penelope, what do you want to be when you grow up?" I proclaimed without hesitation, "an adventurer!" I could see it all projected in high definition in my imagination. From the dangerous to the eccentric to the plain heroic, I could feel deep down in my bones that I was destined for greatness.

I pictured a life comprised of countlessly varied vignettes.

In one, I was a writer in Paris—strolling the cobbled streets, sipping un café at my neighborhood boulangerie, a handsome sophisticate at my side. We would travel and hold dinner parties, staying up too late with good friends and wine. Our lives would be rich with culture, filled with art, music, and political debate.

In another, I was a photographer—traveling the world exposing social injustices—dictators and genocides—documenting from all parts of the globe. Then I was a spy—going through life free of attachments, armed with an unwavering moral compass, quietly risking my life for the greater good. I was a superstar surgeon—taking my skills to the needy, here and abroad, making a tangible difference in their lives. I was a sailor—living with my husband and two kids on a boat, educating them through the rich tapestry of worldly immersion, surrounding them with the love and patience every child yearns for.

Noticeably absent from my myriad of daydreams was the white picket fence, suburban reality from which I came. The mundane. The norm. The standard by which I was taught to measure myself and everyone else.

No word elicits more fear in my soul than "normal." Normal is the death of adventure. I am an adventuress. I knew lots of girls who wanted to be princesses, and that's great. For them. Me? I craved the unknown. I couldn't be saddled with a corset and a tiara. Just like Cinderella, I needed freedom.

Unfortunately, my litter of siblings made it their mission to make sure I knew definitively that I was in no way special. "Mom!" my twin sisters would shout in unison, "Penelope's telling lying stories again!" I would narrow my eyes at them as our mother emerged from the back door, arms crossed, head drooping to one side as though it simply couldn't be bothered to sit up straight on her shoulders. She'd tell me, yet again, to stop lying and tormenting my sisters. I'd play along with the charade, waiting until she disappeared inside to chase my sisters down.

Despite the encouragement from my family, I never gave up my daydreams. I did learn to keep them to myself, though. And I learned to carry myself with absolute confidence—which I did—right through elementary and middle school, never questioning my destiny.

Rejections from boys I liked and mean rumors started by popular girls in high school put a couple chinks in that resolve. And then, by my early twenties, I realized that my tomboy days were numbered. It glared apparent that pretense was to replace ideals. I observed many of my previous adventuresses-in-arms lessening themselves in order for the men in their lives to feel powerful and necessary. I stubbornly eschewed these new ideals. No pretense for me. I was going to be extraordinary!

But a funny thing happens when you start down a road: it bends and curves so that you can't see what's around the next corner, let alone your final destination. Sometimes the Road to Adventure snakes along its meandering way until it winds up adjacent to normal. And when that happens, what is an adventuress to do?

I wind my little silver hatchback through Topanga Canyon—famous for a lot of naked hippie shenanigans in the 60's—where my husband, Seth, and I live in a small caretaker's cottage on a large property owned by an old patron of the arts, who only rents to musicians. He heard our indie-folk duo, Ida Bella, on a film soundtrack and offered to rent to us as long as we populated the space with creativity and artists. It suits us to be up here in the trees, surrounded by an eclectic assortment of hipsters, etherealists, creatives, and wealthy hermits.

"Hey Babe," Seth says as I shift the car into park and slide from behind the wheel. He wraps an arm around my waist, kissing my cheek as he leans across me. "Can I carry your books?" he stammers.

I shrug, trying to play the part of the shy teen, but I can't act, so I grin like the goofball I am.

"How was school?"

"Fine."

"That's it? Fine? Not 'life-changing' 'best thing that ever happened'?" he asks as we cross the short distance from the detached garage to our front door.

"Nope. Fine is all you get since you think it's stupid," I say, sticking out my tongue.

"I don't think you're stupid, though. Just songwriting classes in general." He opens the door for me, bowing to usher me inside the house. I shake my head, trying and failing to suppress a smile. "You're already a gainfully employed singer/guitarist in the best band ever. That stuff is for wannabes," he says, as though I haven't heard it before.

"I know, I know," I say, keeping my tone neutral. I don't need to hear the rest of his monologue about how music is a part of our souls, not something a textbook can break down and homogenize, blah, blah, blah. I get what he's saying. I just happen to think everyone learns differently. Plus, I like sitting in class, learning from a teacher, reading, analyzing and listening. It works for me—structure is not my enemy.

"Do you want to eat, or what?" I say.

"Are you trying to shut me up with food?"

"Yes. But if you're morally opposed, I'll eat your pad Thai," I say, waving the bag of take-out under his nose as I swish past him toward the door.

"You're generous like that."

"I am, aren't I?" I set the bag of take-out on the coffee table while he grabs plates, forks and napkins from the kitchen. He glances over as I slide my mushrooms onto his plate and grunts "thank you" with his mouth full. I flip on the TV, and we settle in to watch the Grammys.

"You cannot seriously like that guy's voice," Seth says, smacking a bottle of chili paste down onto the coffee table. I smile in defiance, knowing how much he hates Marc Justin. Not that he's met him, of course. Seth just hates everything he represents: the commoditization of art. The homogenization of music for profit. The blatant and disgusting pandering to society's lowest common denominator. Or, as he frequently put it, "making shitty music for idiots who'll buy anything they're told to."

We watch as the winner of Pop Album of the Year mounts the stage, flanked by two gorgeous girls, cleavage abounding. I groan, frustrated that the blatant female objectification is ruining my point.

"Ugh. He can't even accept an award without a bimbo on each arm?" I grumble.

"See? Unredeemable," Seth says, leaning back into the couch.

"I know, I know. I'm just saying … if you don't pay attention to the lyrics … or the dance moves … or the lack of musicianship, his voice is pretty good." My conviction can't hold up—I don't even believe myself. But I'm too stubborn to tell him so.

"That's it. I'm sorry to tell you this way, but I think we need a divorce. I cannot spend the rest of my life with a woman who thinks Marc Justin has a good voice."

"I'm sorry you feel that way. But just so you know, I get custody of the soy sauce," I say, snatching the bottle off the reclaimed wood table. I slurp noodles, wagging my eyebrows while holding the sauce in my hand, as far away from Seth as possible. He reaches for it but I pull away at the last second.

"You evil woman! Take my dignity, but not my Kikkoman!"

"Mmmm." I say, crunching down on a cashew.

"Okay, okay, I forgive you. I love you, Penelope Caruso-Byrne. Please, I want you back. May I see our baby now?"

I tilt my head from side to side, deciding whether or not to put him out of his misery. Seth leans across and snatches it away, kissing me as he returns to his side of the couch. I smile.

A typical evening off.

"Do we know who's coming tomorrow night?" Seth asks.

We've been holding Moonlight Mondays, a weekly house concert series, in the backyard of our bungalow since we moved here two years ago.

"The usuals, plus that band Josh told us about that's touring from Portland," I say.

Seth gives me a quizzical look.

"You remember. The girl plays the glockenspiel and her brother plays mandolin? They had that video you liked?"

"Oh yeah, they were pretty good."

"They'll be the only new ones, and then I think Freesia Jones might come later on, after her Hotel Café show."

"I thought she only wanted to come if we charged a cover. Why is she deigning to 'maybe' make an appearance?"

"Because she likes the new drummer from Duck Fingers."

Seth shakes his head and snaps off a dangling noodle with his teeth. We eat in silence, each making mental to-do lists.

"What about your birthday?" Seth asks.

"I already told you it's not a big deal."

"You decorate for Christmas on Thanksgiving afternoon and plan your Halloween costume in July. Turning thirty is no big deal?"

His green eyes bore into me, daring me to deny it. They look especially emerald tonight with the lamp reflecting off his glasses, picking up the green of his shirt. I love that he wears glasses. He had a hard time in high school because he wasn't athletic in a football-crazed town. According to him, he was too scrawny and weird for girls to notice him until he picked up a guitar and got on stage.

I've always been skeptical of this assessment because as long as I've known him there have been plenty of people— male and female—vying for his attention, fawning all over him. But I know what he means. My first real crush told me I looked like a lemur, with my orb-like brown eyes and unruly yellow hair.

Bearing insensitivity is the cruel test into adulthood everyone must pass, but it's bound to leave a mark. Eventually I grew into my features and it all turned out fine. Although I still flinch a little when people mention my big eyes.

I finish chewing just in time to catch a scantily clad pop

sensation lip-sync her way across the stage back to the (very slightly) older arms of Marc Justin, singing a ballad about bondage. Ah, the romance.

It's repugnant when you realize a forty-year old man is writing about sex from a sixteen-year old girl's perspective–especially when it's about being bound and gagged.

Disregarding the creepy underage S&M themes, what do these kids know about love, loss, and compromise anyway? Their parents still sign all their legal contracts, for crying out loud. What can you know about life when your mom-ager is trailing you around, dictating both your personal and professional business? But I digress.

"What are you thinking?" Seth asks.

I giggle. "How do they get people to write this crap?"

"People are stupid. Some skeezy old dude who couldn't make it on his own probably wrote that shit. And people buy it because it's packaged with a nearly naked hot girl."

I finish my noodles, smirking at how much I love Seth and our life together. We've made all our own decisions—the sacrifices and mistakes—and never given up control to make a buck. There is something deeply comforting being with the person I've grown into me with.

"Another glass?" Seth asks, waving a bottle of red wine in front of me. I shrug and he pours more into my empty glass. He tips the rest into his glass and drapes an arm around my shoulder. I snuggle into his nook, smelling his earthy smell, nuzzling closer, warm and comfortable and loved.

Chapter 2

"Have you seen the djembe, Seth?" I ask.

He pushes the broom through the seating area and points to the side of the house, which in typical 60's ranch style, L bends around the sunken backyard, creating an amphitheater effect. I set up the guitar stands and the percussion section—we don't allow full drum kits (too loud for the neighbors)—so we provide a variety of hand percussion instead. Currently, our collection includes bongos, cajon, udu, shakers and maracas, and a djembe. With all these intricately carved wooden and hide covered instruments, it looks like a world music museum and I love it.

Beneath a canopy of fairy lights, I'm overwhelmed with nostalgia. It feels like being blanketed in memories of summer evenings and I'm filled with warm fuzzies, making me wonder why any other outdoor lighting exists. The stage lights are a larger version of the same, with construction lights on either side of the performers, keeping the stage bright enough to appreciate the nuances of each performance.

"Here," Seth says, setting the djembe onstage. The large wooden goblet-shaped drum is covered with a rawhide skin, tuned by ropes that zigzag around the upper half of its body. Its name means "Everyone gather together in peace" and I can't imagine a more perfect tone to set for Moonlight Mondays.

"Looks good, Babe."

"Doesn't it?"

The fairy lights were a big splurge on my part, but after the first year of not having a well-lit space, I wanted to transform it with ambience. I'm excited to debut them and see if anyone feels the subtle (but important) cue. I adjust the Tibetan prayer flags that line the back edge of the stage. I don't fully understand their significance, but they're the only decoration Seth ever insisted on and I like that they add a pop of color in front of the ivy-covered fence. I do a visual sweep and shrug. Looks good to me.

We set out two tables, one for CDs and one for food, potluck style. I sit onstage finger picking a little progression I've had in my head all day. My solid mahogany 1935 Martin OO-17 guitar is so well-worn that it becomes translucent when the light shines directly on the pick guard. I would never take it to gigs, but I love the way it plays. There is a magical quality to the sound—a perfect writing guitar.

Closing my eyes, I focus on the melancholy chords. Without thinking, I hum a melody that flows through my body into my fingers and voice. The squeak of the back door's hinges opening derails my train of thought, as though pulled through a dark tunnel toward a distant light. I replace the guitar on its stand and straighten my t-shirt over the top of my maxi skirt.

I wave to my best friend, Lolo, who smiles back, still exchanging pleasantries with Seth. I slip on my favorite pair of flats, shaking off the lingering melancholy of the song.

"Hiieee," Lolo finger waves to me as I approach them.

"I'm gonna see if Jeff needs help," Seth says and then he's gone.

"Hi!" I say.

She pulls me into a bone crushing hug and proceeds to tell me all about their recent tour and what it was like playing her high school auditorium as an adult, speeding through a hundred words a minute.

I love Lolo and her dizzying diatribes. Next to her I feel calm. I've always felt a bit too high-strung, especially next to Seth, and it's nice to be the mellow one for a change.

She hooks an arm through the crook of my elbow as we walk to the kitchen. I pour us each a glass of wine and Lolo sips hers, leaning across the sink to look out the window.

"Oh my God! Look at the lights. They're fantastic!" Lolo says.

This is the other reason I love her. She notices things.

"You do? Seth wasn't happy when he found out how much they cost, but they really transform the space, don't you think?"

"I love them! And what does Seth know? He's been wearing the same pair of green cords for three years straight." She rolls her eyes and I smile, trying to recall if that's true.

The backyard's empty spaces fill with musicians and guests who find seating in the concrete stadium-style benches. The house buzzes with conversation and the tinkling of plates and bottles of wine, creating a murmur of anticipation that I take inordinate pleasure in having cultivated.

Starting from a couple friends getting together once in a while, to an event people ask to attend, I'm so proud of these Moonlight Mondays. They represent everything I love about music—art, community, love and inspiration.

As musicians, we're often vying for the same handful of gigs, competing for numbers needed to get showcases. Moonlight Mondays are a time to play for fun, to share an audience, and to be around people who understand us and what we do. It gets lonely without this sense of community.

Seth doesn't mind as much as me, but even as a duo, the road is isolating. Especially when we visit my childhood friends, who are all settling down with houses and kids, blending into the fabric of suburbia, with barbecues and soccer practices to occupy their time and connect them to one another. There's a look they give me—a head tilt that I imagine says, "I admire you going for your dreams, but your biological clock doesn't have a snooze button." I used to think that sort of pity was reserved for the perpetually single, but I guess the next stage is for the perpetually childless.

And the truth of it is that I do want kids. And a house. And a career. Just not in the suburbs.

Maybe my standards are too high. Like my Grandpa used to say, "Nowadays you women want it all!" His tone left no question how preposterous an idea that was, and I have to admit that in my weaker moments I see logic in his curmudgeonly proclamation.

But on a night like tonight, as I listen to Seth direct everyone to their seats and hear the first notes sounding from the stage, setting the evening's tone perfectly, I smile. Seth offers a discreet thumbs-up, pointing to the lighting and I melt a little. Surrounded by friends and fellow musicians, I am grateful for the long and twisting road that led me to this idyllic evening.

***

"That went well," Seth says as we sort the trash, recycling and compost.

"The best yet."

"You know my favorite part?"

I shake my head.

"Us," he says.

"Oh really? Of all the amazing talent here tonight you liked us the best? How magnanimous."

"That's what they call me: Mr. Magnanimous." He grins and bumps shoulders with me.

I sigh theatrically and scoop hummus from a bowl into the compost bin. I was particularly inspired by the music tonight. I'm bursting to work on my new song.

My goal is to become an equal creative partner in Ida Bella. As it is now, Seth writes and produces everything and I sing and play my guitar parts as directed. I trust him completely—he has immaculate taste and has always insisted on an intensely high standard for us both.

I know my songwriting isn't up to his standard yet and I don't want to put him in the awkward position of having to tell me so. Because he will. And while I love that he doesn't sugarcoat anything, it's also why I've kept my songs to myself. But that's about to change. I'm finishing this new song and workshopping it in class next week. When I know it's good enough, I'll play it for Seth. I'll confess to him that I want to be full partners. It's exciting to finally take the first step, and I know he'll be proud of me too.

I smile to myself as I scrub a wine glass. Seth packs his guitar in its case and tidies up the stage area. I watch him through the window, mindlessly drying the now clean glass.

Freesia Jones crosses my line of vision, talking at Jeff, who nods politely. Lolo drags him away, linking her arm in his. When Lolo reaches the point in the evening when she's ready to go, there's not negotiating with her—she doesn't care what else is happening. She spots me through the window and shakes her head in faux exasperation. I chuckle and wave, tea towel still in hand.

Freesia struts across the yard toward Seth, and from the sway of her Jessica Rabbit hips she's not offering to help him clean up. She stands a little too close and says something I can't hear through the closed window. Seth responds and she laughs, head falling back, mouth open. She puts a delicate hand on Seth's chest, as though regaining her balance and snaps her head back, her silky black hair falling around her shoulders. Calculatingly sultry. I feel like I should, but can't seem to stop watching.

Seth takes a small but noticeable step back, letting her hand fall down to her side. She shifts her weight, sticking out one hip and says something, smiling. Seth's features shift into a look I've seen a thousand times before—the polite small-talk smile, usually reserved for drunk fans at shows who mean well but end up saying really inappropriate things.

I watch Freesia try one more time to get his attention and, when he rebuffs her final attempt, she turns to leave. I finish up the dishes, grateful (and a little smug) to have the kind of husband who isn't tempted by a beautiful woman throwing herself at him. What's not to love about that?

***

"Good morning, Beautiful," Seth says, kissing the top of my head. Soft light filters into our bedroom through gauzy white curtains, backlighting his silhouette. I yawn and stretch my arms out, reviving my rested body. Something heavy shifts on the bed and I sit up. Next to me is a tray full of my favorite foods: French toast, fresh fruit, coffee and bacon.

"Happy Birthday," Seth says.

"My birthday isn't until Friday."

"Really? I'll just eat this then."

"Hey!" I slap his hand from my bacon. "Thank you. I love you," I say, leaning across the tray, lips puckered. He meets me halfway, kissing me quickly before jumping up and bounding off. He returns with a second tray for himself.

"So really, why the birthday celebration this morning?" I ask.

"Friday is going to be crazy getting ready for the show and I wanted to make sure I got some alone time with you, even if it's not on your actual birthday."

"Aren't you the sweetest guy in the world?"

"I am."

"Mr. Magnanimous."

He smiles and bites into a piece of French toast that's dripping in melted butter and syrup. I sip my tea and stab the juiciest piece of pineapple with my fork. I always eat in the same order: healthiest first, then crunchy, then sweet. That way I savor each food without mixing them together, marring their flavors. Seth thinks it's adorable (albeit ridiculous), but he humors me and never lets anything touch that isn't supposed to.

"Princess." He smiles, nakedly amused.

The week goes a lot like most weeks, apart from my birthday-breakfast-in-bed. We spend time in the studio working on a couple of new songs, play a corporate event during the week, and promote our Hotel Café show on social media, sending a new teaser video out to our mailing list. We do a couple local radio interviews too, because you never know what will bring people in.

This Friday is a showcase gig that requires a guaranteed minimum draw. If we don't reach our quota they won't book us there again. We have an ideal time slot: Friday 9pm, and we don't want to blow it.

One of the songs from our first album recently debuted as the title track on a travel documentary series for National Geographic and hopefully that will bring some extra people to the show. If the spike in iTunes sales tells us anything, it looks good so far.

It kills Seth that our music is being used for television. He says it dilutes the authenticity of the art. We made the mistake a few years back of signing up with an exclusive placement agency and pre-signed a contract for them to expedite the licensing process, which is how it ended up in the show without our direct consent.

Personally, I think music adds to the visual onscreen, guiding the emotion of the scene in a way that's as powerful as, if not more so, than listening to the song on its own. I don't bother arguing the point with Seth though. I learned long ago that once he makes up his mind, tectonic plates couldn't shift it.

That's the thing about live music, though. You never know what to expect and you just have to prepare the best you can, show up on the day, and be ready and willing to go with whatever happens.

"Do you think we should tour for the new album?" I ask Seth as we sit in traffic on our drive back from a wedding gig. He turns to look at me but I can't read his expression in the red glow of brake lights.

"I thought you didn't want to tour anymore." He says.

"I didn't mean, ever. I just wanted a home base to come back to, and new material to perform."

Seth nods his head thoughtfully as traffic lets up and we start weaving between lanes, making our way up the I-5. I'm familiar with this contemplative look of his, but it doesn't make it any easier for me to wait for his conclusions. I'm excited at the prospect of becoming a full partner, and it motivates me in a way I haven't gotten to feel before: like it's really my career too. I feel like I've been driving from the passenger seat, unable to affect the course until he makes his final decision.

***

By Friday night, I can't contain my excitement. Pitchfork magazine named us their next "Ones to Watch" and the booking guy told Seth the show is likely to sell out at the door. We've never played a sold out show before. Folk music isn't exactly rock or dance. We can't play to a club full of people drinking and partying and get them dancing. Folk music is emotional, cerebral, introspective. And though its popularity is pervasive, it's more commonly listened to in intimate moments alone, rather than with hundreds of one's closest friends.

I'm so nervous I can't even button my blouse properly. I'm going for a sophisticated bohemian look—sort of 60s Patti Smith meets Audrey Hepburn—letting pieces of my wavy blonde hair fall loosely around my face, the rest tied low in a side pony. I look in the mirror and feel like a little girl playing dress up in my mom's closet. Checking my phone, I scramble to get out the door. The time for second-guessing my wardrobe is over so I grab my guitar and a box of merch as I run to the car, where Seth is already waiting with the engine running.

He is wearing his green cords with a button down plaid collared shirt under a gray cardigan. It's an old man look but somehow he pulls it off, managing to look sexy, even. How guys do that is beyond me. It takes a lot of planning for me to look effortless, and even still, I never get it quite right.

I slap a brighter-than-usual shade of pink on my lips, making them look even fuller. It looks a little trampy in the visor mirror, but the first time I saw a color photo of myself published in a local magazine, all I saw was a mass of vanilla skin and hair, no discernible features to be found. I've learned that if I look like a hooker in normal lighting I'll look natural onstage and in photos.

My lap vibrates and I read a text from Lolo as we pull out of the driveway. "OMG! Heard the paparazzi r gonna b at the show tonight. Wonder who 4?"

"We're not forgetting anything, are we?" I ask Seth as I fidget with my phone. "I really want tonight to go well."

"Don't worry. It's going to be great."

I nod my head, settle back in the seat and take a deep

breath. Seth looks over at me and squeezes my hand.

Chapter 3

Lolo and Jeff reserved a booth in the anteroom of the bar and we sit down with them, laughing and toasting as we (or at least I) pretend not to be nervous. If we weren't performing, we wouldn't have gotten in. The always-popular venue is particularly electric tonight. The openers are onstage plugging in, and the room fills with the buzz of anticipatory banter. I've never performed for such an oddly expectant crowd before and I look over at Seth for support.

He laughs along with Jeff, impersonating something from a movie, and I am awed by his cool. Nothing permeates his confidence. It's maddening.

"Dude," a lanky kid dressed all in black says to Seth. "Uh, is this your quarter-inch?" He asks, holding the half-decapitated guitar cable that now flops around uselessly. Sure enough, I spot the bright red Velcro we put around all our cables to keep track of them.

"What the fuck, dude?" Seth says, standing up. He grabs the cable and the metal head pops off.

"Sorry. Your amp was on it when I tried to pull it out…" the kid mumbles.

"Fine. It doesn't matter. I'll borrow yours for our set," Seth says, stirring his drink.

The kid's eyes go wide and even though the room is now too loud for me to hear the rest of what's said, I can tell it isn't good. The kid slinks away and Seth turns to me. "I have to borrow an amp. I'm gonna grab Jeff's since they live close. I'll be back as soon as I can." My eyes widen in protest but he puts a hand up, cutting me off. "I'll be back in plenty of time," he promises.

Twenty minutes later, in the low din after the first band finishes, before the next act starts, the stage manager taps me on the shoulder, motioning for me to join him off to the side of the room. I follow him, heart beating a little too fast. Normally Seth handles the money and logistics side of things. I look around for him, knowing he's not back yet. I don't want to seem like I don't know what I'm doing so I put on my most business-like face.

"The second band bailed. You guys are up next, for two sets."

My mouth hangs open. I snap it shut as my mother's voice tells me not to "gape like a guppy." I blink, trying to come up with an appropriate refusal. What if Seth isn't here in time? I can't go on alone, but I don't want to be unprofessional.

"We advertised we'd be on at nine. A lot of our fans aren't even here yet." I say, trying to keep my voice from squeaking.

"It's a full house," he says, motioning to the crowd. "Nobody else is gettin' in."

I can't argue that so I nod and panic silently. I try to remind myself that Seth will be back any second. The manager relaxes his shoulders and says, "Happy Birthday." I think I mutter "thanks" but can't be sure. I check my phone and text Seth, but it won't make a difference.

I take a couple deep breaths as I open my guitar case, trying to remember the last time I've been this scared to get onstage. With Seth by my side, it always feels natural. This is terrifying. I tune my guitar for as long as I can, but there is still no sign of Seth. I'm going to have to start solo.

With the lone spotlight on me, I break out in a sweat. I wipe my hands on my skirt and clear my throat as I move the stool aside, opting to stand instead. I breathe deeply and adjust the microphone. The sound guy nods to me and I smile to the crowd. So many of them are friends and fans, people I've known throughout my life in L.A., and I am suddenly overcome with gratitude for them all. The smiling faces look up at me, oblivious to my nerves.

Lolo shouts, "Play the new one!" and fifty faces in the audience look on expectantly. I smile and try not to glare at her.

It's now or never. I fingerpick the first few bars, and after the third, my nerves fall away, muscle memory taking over. I play without looking into the audience, lost in my own world, the lyrics resonating from some deep place within me, body swaying to my own rhythm. I play all five of the songs I've written on my own, feeling vulnerable and raw. I've never tried out new songs on such a large audience and my earlier fear mingles with the excitement of something new. I sing exactly like I do at home when it's just me with the guitar. Oddly enough, it feels comfortable, like being cocooned in my own creation.

I come out of my trance to the welcome sound of applause. I smile and bow my head to the fans. Lolo mouths, "Great job!" My smile spreads, joy radiating from me to the crowd and they send it all back to me. It's the best feeling I've ever known.

I still can't see Seth and panic: a montage of terrible possibilities flashing through my imagination. There's a short intermission before our set is supposed to start and I'm determined to find him or, if he's not here, find out where the hell he is.

I navigate my way toward Lolo from the stage, eyes roving the crowd, not initiating eye contact, but smiling at those who seek me out. I feel like I'm walking a fine line between fishing for compliments and being aloof. I want to play it cool, but my heart is racing with adrenaline from excitement and fear.

The thrumming of my pulse through my bloodstream is like a drug, fueling me, making me invincible. I look around for Lolo, but lose sight of her through the crowd.

A waiter bulldozes through, knocking me off balance. I catch the edge of the bar just in time to break my fall without a modicum of grace. A warm hand covers my shoulder and I close my eyes, embarrassed that anyone witnessed my near face-plant. I open them to see none other than uber pop star, Marc Justin. His blue eyes twinkle as they light on mine, mouth twitching to reveal a perfect smile. It's arrogant and sexy, and clearly, he knows it.

My groan is stifled by the crush of momentum from the crowd at my back. I lurch off balance yet again and my hands land on his chest, barely separating our bodies. His hand moves to my back, the other resting on my waist as we sway together for a moment, the jostling crowd settling around us.

I try to speak but can't think of what to say. Marc Justin watched my set? Did he like it? He's not saying anything. Why isn't he saying anything? I frown in realization: we're not peers. He thinks what he does is above this. Above me. Condescending arrogant ass.

The crowd falls back slightly and I immediately step back. I want to get away but can't retreat more than a few inches. His hand drops from my hip and I have to avert my eyes from his intense gaze.

He looks older in person. My age, maybe? Blinded by a flash of his perfect white smile, I glance away again. He waits silently, forcing me to look at him again. He holds out a hand and I shake it in mine.

"I'm Marc."

"I know—I mean, I know who you are."

"Great set. You write those songs?"

I nod.

"That lyric in the first song, the one that went…" he says, singing my line back to me, still holding my hand in his, leaning down to my ear so as to be heard over the crowd. I bob my head, not fully registering what he's saying because I can feel the heat of his breath tickling my ear. My brain can't compute the world's most famous pop star singing my lyrics in my ear. "I wish I could have heard more."

His blue eyes sparkle, larger-than-life all-American good looks outshining a surprisingly humble demeanor. I watch his face, mesmerized by how strange it is to recognize someone I've never met before.

"I'd love to get to know the person who writes such beautiful songs. Can I take you out sometime?"

At his cheesy pick-up line I return to my senses, bristling instinctively.

I'm about to spit out a snippy retort when he's swept away by a bodyguard who appears between us out of nowhere. A gaggle of girls encircle him, closing in tighter, edging me out. They push me from the inner to the outer circle, where I am finally ejected into the bar.

"Hey! How's the birthday diva?" Lolo shouts, clearly more than a couple drinks in.

"Babe!" Seth says, kissing the side of my head. "I'd say I'm sorry, but apparently you killed it without me."

I force a noncommittal smile, trying to assess whether he's being sarcastic. His expression gives nothing away so I choose to believe he's excited for me and relax.

It's been a whirlwind of emotions and now, here with my husband and best friends, I'm happy to just enjoy my birthday. In a few minutes Seth and I will go up onstage together, perform the set we were supposed to play, and the world will revert to normal. Right?

"I- I just got asked out my Marc Justin," I blurt.

"Wha-?" Lolo asks, hands up in wide-eyed surrender.

Seth and Jeff shut up too, and Seth's mouth quirks up on one side.

"Really?" Jeff asks.

"Tell me you said yes." Seth says. We all stare at him. "What?" He looks around. "It would be hilarious. How many times have you said you wished you could teach him that women are people, not arm candy? Here's your shot."

It's true, I have said that.

"No one means what they say in hypotheticals about celebrities." I say, unsure what to think about my husband being so quick to set me up on a date with another man. Nothing about tonight is turning out how I expected.

I let the comment die in the ensuing silence, and sip an electric lime drink Lolo supplies. In under five seconds, Seth and Jeff return to their previous debate over whether some new superhero movie is the best thing ever or just capitalizing on the momentum of ... who am I kidding? I don't even pretend to listen. Lolo turns to me, effectively cutting us off from them as she regales me with anecdotes from her most recent modeling job.

I try to listen, I really do. But I want to talk about my set—go over every teeny tiny detail with her. It's horribly narcissistic, I know, but I can't stop thinking about it—how great it felt to have people listen to lyrics and music I wrote. And they liked it. I shift from foot to foot, trying to keep my focus on her words.

Lolo stops talking mid-sentence. A perceptible shift in collective focus ripples through the room. The gaggle of girls begins to move and, before I can step out of the way, Marc Justin's bodyguard slips me a business card with handwriting on the back.

Give me another shot to make a first impression. Call me. M

I stumble back, trying not to get trampled. I look at the card and then over my shoulder at my husband. When I turn around I'm face to chest with a security guard, who forges a path for me so that the next moment I am next to Marc, his body blocking us from the gaggle, Lolo on the outside with them.

"I want to see you again." He says, eyes locked on mine. I can't respond. He really commits to the schtick, I'll give him that. I don't want to be mean, but I'm not that gullible, either. Why is he bothering to talk to me, anyway?

"I'd like to talk to you about writing with me." He says, clearing his throat. He glances over my shoulder. I turn to see where he's looking and watch his security guard give him some kind of secret eye signal. I look back to Marc. He bends his face down to mine, his gaze earnest. I nod and sigh, not sure what is the appropriate level of cynicism for this scenario.

He flashes that perfect smile, eyes crinkling at the corners. "I'll have my manager set it up." I think he's going to say something else, but there's no time as he is swept into a waiting SUV that speeds off into the night. I'm left standing there with a bunch of disappointed women, feeling like I was thrust into a romantic comedy or an episode of Punk'd. Did I agree to a date or a business meeting with Marc Justin? I shake my head like a Magic 8 Ball, hoping to reveal a clearer answer: Reply hazy, try again.

As if that isn't bizarre enough for one night, it's time for Ida Bella's set. I make my way to the stage once again and squash the mental processing my head is trying to do. Seth smiles at me and we're greeted with a ludicrously supportive rush of applause from the people there for us, while the celebrity stalkers noisily move on to the next stop on their nightly crawl.

By our second song, the crowd has thinned to a more normal size, though the energy and love they send us makes me warm and fuzzy.

Chapter 4

"Are you sure you're not upset?" I ask Seth when we finally get home and start getting ready for bed.

"I'm pissed at that twerp who busted our equipment. Mostly I'm bummed I missed your set, though. Everyone said you were amazing." He pulls me to him and kisses the top of my head. I wrap my arms around his waist, nuzzling into his chest.

"I was so scared to play on my own, but once I started, I knew I was on."

"Lucky for me, you were still on when I finally got my ass back there. It was a great night, no caveats allowed."

I look up at him and he smiles down at me. I slide my blouse up over my head and reach around my back to unhook my bra. Seth raises his eyebrows, a slow grin spreading across his face.

"I'm proud of you, Babe," he says, eying my unhooked bra. "But I don't care about the show right now." He turns me around, kissing my shoulder while helping me out of my bra. He slides his hands up my skirt, rubbing the bare flesh of my upper thighs. I lean my head against his chest. "Mmmm," I groan, as his hands work inward. I relax into the rhythm that his fingers strum into me, and when I can't take it anymore I turn around, freeing him of his clothes, needing to be closer, to communicate something I can't seem to articulate.

It might not be warranted, but I'm disappointed Seth doesn't want to talk about my set or my new songs. Apart from the mention of our Ida Bella set—which was incredible, it's true—he hasn't shown any other interest. I guess I could bring it up, but it takes something away if I have to ask for it. Maybe I'm feeling guilty, needing to justify how much I loved being up there, shining in my own spotlight. Even now, hours after the show, sexually satisfied, I lay awake, listening to Seth's easy breathing. Clearly, he's not suffering from dissatisfaction.

***

The next morning Seth is already out by the time I wake up. He's recording another artist at our rented studio and I know better than to expect him home all day. I hate to admit it, but I'm relieved. I want to write today. Before I can get to that though, I need to call Lolo and get some much-needed girl perspective.

I wrap a sweater around myself and pad out to the kitchen in search of coffee. Seth left the pot on, so I pour myself a cup and sit at the little table. I see that he set out Marc Justin's phone number with an attached note:

OMG! Like, totally, you should call him! I'll be in the studio till late... Love you. S

I roll my eyes and let out an exasperated sigh. I call Lolo but she doesn't answer. I finish breakfast and slip into a little sundress. The day is too nice not to enjoy the outdoors. I grab my guitar, notepad and strappy sandals and throw them in the back seat of my car. I roll down the windows and pull my wavy hair back in a ponytail so I can see while I drive the relatively short distance to the beach. Going from Topanga Canyon to Malibu is like traveling from Neverland to Barbie's beach house, but I love it.

I can always find a food truck to get a quick bite and a patch of sand to sit by myself and tune out the rest of the world. Looking out at the ocean, I get lost in its infinite ebb and flow, its steadiness relaxing me into a meditative state.

I walk down the beach to a secluded cove only open when the tide is out, near a strip of mega mansions. I free my guitar from the case, letting my fingers explore new combinations on the fretboard, hoping to happen upon something that inspires me. I don't watch my fingers, staring instead at the vast expanse of water, rocking forward and back ever so slightly, humming to myself. As I get closer to a sound I like, I close my eyes, losing myself in the melody, the sun warming my face. A shadow blocks the light and I open my eyes.

"Pretty."

I blink and stare in stupefied silence at Marc Justin. This is either one hell of a coincidence or a serious case of stalking. He grins and motions to the sand next to me, silently asking permission to sit. I nod.

"Pen, right? Remember me?"

"Penelope," I correct. "And yes, I remember all the way back to last night."

"I think it's fate," he smirks, ignoring my sarcasm.

"You think what is fate?" I ask, scrunching my nose. Who does this guy think he is? Why is he talking to me at all? He's the most famous celebrity in the world. He should be off gallivanting with a supermodel right now.

"You writing for me," he says. "Unless you're stalking me." His shit-eating grin is probably charismatic to some, but I'm not swooning. Don't get me wrong, his lean muscular body isn't exactly rough on the eyes, but that's not nearly enough to compensate for his arrogance and every-woman-wants-me attitude.

"I thought you said writing 'with' you?" I say, lifting a brow in challenge. I choose to ignore the stalker comment, although I have to physically bite my tongue to stop from saying, "Don't flatter yourself, Pretty Boy."

He shrugs. "I haven't stopped thinking about you since I heard you sing, and now here you are playing a private show for me."

Ugh.

"What, you didn't know that I live right over there?" He motions to the other side of the bluff. I shake my head. I guess that makes it slightly less coincidental. Barely. He tilts his head, seemingly assessing my honesty, and I feel my brows rising to meet my hairline.

"Okay, okay, you don't seem like a stalker," he says.

"Gee, thanks."

"But you do know the tide is coming in, right?"

I look up and see he's right. The wet sand line has crept in and I probably would have gotten stuck here if I hadn't been pulled out of my trance.

"You like Indian food?" he asks.

"Ye-ah," I say, distracted by the two bodyguards dressed in black shirts and cargo shorts a few yards away.

"You're going to love this," he says, extending his hand to help me up. I don't take it, getting up unassisted. I wipe the sand from my dress and slide my flip-flops on. He puts a casual hand at the small of my back, ushering me around a rock. He picks up my guitar and follows a step behind me toward the main beach. We line up at the food truck parked on the far side of the parking lot.

"The chef who owns this used to run a five star restaurant in New York, but he got sick of the politics and hated that his food was only getting to a select few, so he packed it in and bought this truck. Now he parks somewhere different every day, he's only open for lunch, and nothing costs over $10. I'm kind of a stalker. So we've got that in common."

I laugh. I can't help it; the cheeky mischievous thing works on me, even though I know better. Maybe that's how he compensates for a lack of talent. I scan the menu and pick out a tandoori chicken wrap. He gets the same thing and a couple of waters. I grab my wallet but he pays before I get the money out. I tilt my head, holding out a ten-dollar bill in a here-take-it gesture. He grins and holds our food in both hands with a can't-take-it-no-hands gesture in response. I glare at him, but I have to admit I don't mind that much.

We take our food down to the beach and sit side by side. I slip off my sandals and bury my toes in the wet sand.

"Oh my God. Yum!" I say between mouthfuls. It's the best wrap I've had in my life. I don't have to tell him that though.

"Surprised?"

I give him a half smile, tipping my head to the side apologetically, mouth stuffed full. My mother would not approve of my unladylike manners.

He looks at me with one brow lifted, not saying anything. I frown, trying to figure out what he's waiting for and straighten my dress across my lap.

As I do, I feel something wet.

Sauce. All over my dress. Great.

Marc juts out his chin and swipes at a non-existent smear with his hand. I mimic his motion, wiping my face, and he busts out laughing. In his sunglasses, I catch my reflection. I've made a messy situation, much, much worse. I'm not trying to impress him, but this is ridiculous.

I see a couple teenaged girls in bikinis, creeping closer to Marc and one points and laughs at me, gesturing to her friend. I feel around for a napkin and of course, can't find one. Marc leans in and I think he's going to wipe my chin. His proximity startles me. Instead, he holds out his napkin for me to take. His finger brushes mine as I take it from him. His fans do not approve and scowl in my direction, inching closer.

The two bodyguards, who up to this point have given us space, stand between the girls and Marc. Marc is seemingly oblivious to the entire exchange. He jumps to his feet and steps in front of me. He grabs my hands in his, hoisting me to my feet like we're swing dancing.

"Can you swim?" he asks.

"Yes," I say, breathless. This is great; he thinks I'm inept at everything now.

"Can I see your phone?"

Before I can ask why, he snags it from me and tosses it to his bodyguard. I stare, open-mouthed. A squeal escapes me when he sweeps me up in his arms and sprints to the water. I'm sure my eyes are as wide as flying saucers as I'm suddenly airborne. He chucked me in the ocean!

I break through the water's surface, spluttering. I am not impressed. I launch myself at him, pushing hard on his shoulders. He goes under and a wave crashes over us both, taking me by surprise. I come up laughing and so does he. There is no end to the absurdity.

"Salt water makes everything better. Even food stains," he says.

"Jerk." I say, smiling.

He grins and holds my eyes in his. Movement in my peripheral vision distracts me and I glance away. His bodyguard holds one of the Bikini Girls back while the other flips me off and pulls at her hair. I notice at least fifteen others have joined their ranks, as well as a photographer.

"Um, Marc?" I say, flicking my eyes in their direction.

"Shit." He says, his expression hardening.

He takes my hand and gives it a squeeze under the water. It's not a show of affection, more a take-my-lead secret handshake. We speed-walk up the beach without talking for a few hundred feet. I glance over to my stuff on the beach but he shakes his head and I see his bodyguard pick up my guitar and purse. We pass the volleyball courts and the lifeguard tower, wading through the water around the bluff as the tide continues to rise. We keep walking past a bunch of houses, toward a narrow strip of beach, sandwiched between cliff and ocean.

"Sorry about that," he says, slowing his pace.

I'm not sure what to say so I keep quiet. We continue around the cliffs, nearly impassable with the rising tide, until we get to a wider strip of beach, peppered with large beachfront homes.

"Is it strange to live on the beach where anyone can just walk by and look inside your house?" I say. "I mean the idea of living on the beach is great. I just wouldn't like feeling like I was always on display."

Marc looks at me. I'm not sure what he's thinking but I suddenly feel self-conscious.

"You're interesting," he says after a few seconds.

"Uh … thanks?"

He smiles, but this time it's different. The sparkle isn't in his eyes and I can tell his mind is elsewhere. Suddenly he stops and turns to me, much too close, our bodies mere inches apart. He looks so sad that I don't want to pull away. I don't back away, but I sit on the ground, gesturing for him to sit beside me on the sand. I feel more comfortable like this and I get the impression he's about to tell me something about himself. The cool ocean breeze makes me shiver, goose bumps covering my exposed skin.

"I—," he starts, looking at me. "You're cold." He gestures to my arms. "Sorry."

"You are not. And anyway, I had fun. No apology necessary."

"See?" he says, looking into my eyes, "I like you."

"Don't you mean my songs?" I ask. His mouth twitches, but he doesn't respond.

"Stuff like that," he says, gesturing down the beach with a flick of his head, "makes me feel like I'm always on display. Like what you said about the beach house." He stands up, taking a small rock and skipping it across the water.

I don't know what to say. I wiggle my toes in the sand, waiting for him to elaborate. He doesn't. He skips another rock.

"I'm sorry," he says.

"No sorries." I say, watching him carefully. "But I am starting to get cold," I admit. "I'm going to head back." I stand up, ready to walk back the way we came.

"You can't go that way until the tide goes out. Follow me," he says, leading me, presumably to his beachfront house.

I waver momentarily, wondering if this is a good idea. He's right though, unless I want to scale the bluff, going with him is my best option. I follow him, arms crossed over my chest, shivering. He leads me around the side of a large white house with floor-to-ceiling windows facing the water. We stumble through a side gate into a beautiful courtyard, separating two halves of the house. The one on the beach side is almost entirely glass and I can see a pool table, couch, big screen TV and wet bar. Further along is a guesthouse. Marc goes around to the far side, toward the main house. Through the large windows, I can see a grand piano and a number of expensive looking guitars set up around a formal sitting area.

"Is this yours?" I ask.

He nods his assent and gestures for me to wait. I stay, weirdly obedient. I hop from foot to foot in the kitchen trying not to drip on the distressed bamboo flooring. The house is open concept, light and airy, with minimal wall décor.

There is a music area set up for band rehearsal. A surfboard-shaped table fills the corner, flanked by benches instead of chairs. A couple of real surfboards of varying sizes are propped against the wall opposite the couch in what appears to be an informal living room. The more I look around I realize that despite its size, the space looks cozy. I actually fight the urge to go flop down on the big grey couch near the fireplace.

"Here you go," Marc says, reappearing. He produces a large striped beach towel and a Hawaiian print sarong. I take the towel and eye the sarong suspiciously.

"Don't worry, it's mine." He says.

"Mmhmm."

"What? Can't a guy like sarongs? Lets in a nice breeze," he says. "I thought you might want something to wear while your clothes dry."

I give him a skeptical look and shake my head.

"Clothing is optional," he says with a smile.

"Uh-huh," I say, snatching it from him.

The wife part of me wonders if this is inappropriate, but the practical part of me wants to get out of these sticky clothes, especially since I'm going to have to walk all the way back to my car and I'd rather not chafe.

He shows me where I can change. I insist on doing my own washing. I don't need him touching my underwear. I doubt he knows how to do his own laundry anyway.

When I get back, Marc is on the phone and I step onto the deck, adjusting the halter neck I tied on the sarong. I smile at the draft on my legs. He's right; it feels good.

He sees me and mouths, "Give me a sec," before striding down a hallway. I wander back inside and pick up a Gibson guitar from a floor stand. I play the piece I've been working on, singing "da da da's" to the melody I made up. I have a verse and a chorus worked out, but I haven't come up with a second verse or a bridge yet. I start messing around with a few different chords. Maybe it's the bridge?

"Don't stop on my account," Marc says, reappearing. "I like that, whatever it was."

"I'm just messing around. I'm not really a songwriter." I say automatically.

"You could have fooled me."

"Okay, I have to ask. Did you really like my lyrics or was that just a pickup?"

He laughs, looking shocked and cheeky at the same time. "Ouch. Some people think I'm charming, you know?"

I roll my eyes so far back I nearly topple over.

"But if I were trying to pick you up I wouldn't do it with something that sophomoric."

I'm impressed with his vocabulary, which he clearly intended, if his grin is any indication. And I want to take it as a compliment, but I can't seem to reconcile the guy in front of me with Marc Justin, Man-Whore Womanizer.

"How old are you?" I ask.

"Twenty eight, but shhh, it's a secret." He says, holding a finger up to his lips.

"Seriously?"

"Why? How old did you think I was?" he asks, sitting across from me on the couch.

"I don't know," I say. I can feel heat rising to my cheeks and I know I'm blushing.

"Come on, tell me," he teases.

"Twelve," I blurt.

He laughs and falls back into the couch. "What kind of woman goes home with a twelve-year old? But I should have you repeat that to my manager."

"Don't flatter yourself, pretty boy," I say. "You trapped me with the tide; I didn't have a choice."

"You think I'm pretty?"

I play the guitar instead of answering. He stops laughing and bobs his head to the music, humming a harmony that fits perfectly with the melody I'd been singing just before.

"Okay, can I ask you another question?"

"No. Marc Justin has reached his daily question quota," he says. I narrow my eyes, but can't help smiling.

"Do you like your own music?"

He laughs so hard he snorts. "I take it you don't?"

I shift in my seat, hating the hollow sensation in my stomach I always get when I don't stop my big mouth from running. He seems miraculously unfazed by the insult.

I scrunch my nose, and can't stop myself. "No."

The smile vacates his eyes and he shrugs. "I've been doing this since I was thirteen. It's my job. I don't usually think about it in those terms."

Just a job? I've never heard anyone describe a creative career in such mundane terms.

"I was discovered in a dance troupe in Dayton, Ohio. My dad bailed six months before that, leaving my mom struggling to make ends meet. I got an opportunity and I took it." He says it so matter-of-factly that I can't fault his rationale.

"And now that you're beyond the struggling artist phase," I say, gesturing around the house, "what's your excuse?"

"My excuse for wanting to remain successful?" he asks, scooching forward on the couch.

"Yeah. Are you making the music you want to make?"

"What makes you think I'm not?" he asks.

"You're deflecting," I say.

He smiles, but doesn't give me an answer.

"Because you're smarter than that," I say, mad at myself for caving first. He inhales sharply and pulls a hand to his chest as if to say, "Who me?"

"And if you expect me to believe that you liked my lyrics, I know you know the difference between vapid crap and meaningful art." I point to the Chagall painting hanging above the fireplace.

"Vapid crap? Tell me how you really feel." He stands up

and runs a hand back and forth over the top of his head, making hair stick up at odd angles.

I feel the blood rushing to my head in embarrassment and anger, feeling like I have a responsibility to get to the bottom of this and also realizing that I overstepped in a big way. Maybe I've gleaned too much from the tabloids and feel like I actually know him—how he thinks.

Before either of us can recompose ourselves, a buff young black man, a sophisticated middle-aged woman and teenage girl with long straight blonde hair and blue eyes exactly like Marc's clatter noisily through the front door. Marc turns to them, rearranging his features to their normal affable state.

"Hey, Mom, sis, Jarrell."

Their surprise at seeing me is evident, his mother glancing from me to him, and back again, lingering on my unusual attire.

"Hi." I jump up, reaching my hand out to shake his mom's.

"Mom, Penelope. Penelope, this is my mom, Suellen," he says. We nod and shake hands. "And my sister, Casey," he says as I shake her hand. "And my boy, Jarrell." Jarrell juts a chin out in a "T'sup" gesture as he shakes my hand in a delicate grip.

"Nice to meet you all," I say. I can tell by the awkward quiet that I'm intruding, and my manners dictate that I let myself out.

"I should get going," I say, heading back toward the laundry room. "It was really nice to meet you," I say again, like the flustered idiot I am.

I escape to the laundry room, removing my still-damp clothes from the dryer. I'm not sure why I feel so flustered, but suddenly I'm shaking all over. I feel nervous and upset— caught by teacher with my hand in the cookie jar. I tug my dress on and my bra and underwear fall to the ground. I bend down to scoop them up just as Marc squats down next to me.

"Hey. I don't want you to go." He looks at me. "What's

wrong?" he asks.

Every time I feel emotional and someone asks me what's wrong, I can't help it, the floodgates open and I start crying. Which is especially annoying since I can hold it together under any other circumstances. That question just gets me every time. I don't know why.

He scoops me into his arms and holds me until I pull myself together. Luckily, I'm not actually sad so it doesn't last long. I sit down on the floor, holding my underwear and bra in my lap, feeling completely ridiculous.

"I didn't mean to offend you before," I say, because I can't think of what else to say.

"You didn't offend me," he says, looking into my eyes with the same intensity he had before. "It's just," he looks away, as though his train of thought is fleeting, "I'm not used to being around someone who calls me out on anything."

His honesty renders me speechless. I stare at him, trying to reconcile that he seems like two people in one.

"I'm surrounded by people whose job it is to tell me what I want to hear. You know Jarrell?" he says. I nod. "He's my swagger coach."

I slap a hand over my mouth to stifle a laugh, not sure if he's joking.

"You can laugh," he smirks. "It's funny. Apparently, in order to be cool I can't just walk, I have to sway my body and bob my head like a slow motion bobble head." He exaggerates the movements as he says it, and it's an impressive recreation of exactly that.

My laughter evaporates, but the smile never leaves my lips. Our eyes lock in a knowing exchange. The familiarity I felt before returns.

"Even my family has a vested interest in keeping up the status quo. I can't think of the last time someone treated me like I was just Marc."

For the first time, I take a second to contemplate what it must be like to be him. Famous. Watched. Babied. Protected. I've never been so happy to be less successful. I hug him.

Because it's the friendly thing to do. And because, in some weird way, I feel like he and I are the same.

Chapter 5

We emerge from the laundry room together and his mom and sister give me the once over, finding me wanting from the looks of it. They wander off to their side of the mansion and Marc and Jarrell do some sort of complicated handshake. I smirk, imagining how much Marc is paying for this lesson.

"We going to the game tonight?" Jarrell asks.

Marc nods.

"You bringing Layla or this bitch?" Jarrell asks, tipping his head in my direction. I wait a beat for Marc to say something and when he doesn't, I look at him instead of Jarrell.

"Ah shucks," I say, not bothering to hide my disdain. "This bitch has better things to do. Thanks for lunch," I say to Marc. He looks pleadingly at me but I can barely look at him. He didn't say anything. I should have known better than to think he had any moral substance, but he sucked me in for a minute there.

On the interminable walk along the Pacific Coast Highway to my car I chide myself for being stupid and mumble the comebacks I wish I'd thought of at the time.

***

"Marc Justin bought you lunch?" Seth asks in his best attempt at a high-pitched schoolgirl squeal.

"Yeah, and then he proved my point that he's an arrogant asshole," I say, chopping an onion in our kitchen.

"See? No redeeming qualities," Seth says, stealing a slice of cheese from the chopping board. He scurries out of my reach, knowing I hate it when he takes food off my chopping board. It messes with my system. If I'm cooking, I want it to taste right. I narrow my eyes and wag the knife in his direction. He puts up his hands in surrender, smiles, and hops up on the counter a little further down from me.

"I felt bad for him for about a half a second there," I say, still torn by the whole experience. I felt like I saw something human in him, likeable even. Then that asshole called me his 'bitch' and he let his silence speak for him.

"You're too nice. Yes, the poor beloved millionaire. Constantly bombarded by adoring fans and money," Seth says, popping a grape tomato in his mouth.

"I thought you never wanted any of that stuff anyway," I say, shooing him away from the food with my knife again.

"I don't. But obviously, he does. I don't feel bad for him."

I drop the subject because I know Seth, and I can hear him stepping up to his high horse. Rather than hear the whole spiel, I focus on chopping.

I slide the diced onions, bell peppers, pears and goat brie into the salad bowl, pull a couple salmon filets from the oven, dress the plates, and bring them over to the coffee table. Seth grabs the pasta and a couple of forks and we sit on the couch, TV already on.

It's a documentary on the increasing scarcity of potable water which I'd normally be interested in, but I'm only half paying attention. I can't stop thinking about the fact that I let myself feel bad for someone who has achieved my own professional aspirations. I mean, not exactly. I don't want to be a pop star adored by thirteen-year old girls. But the truth is that I see Ida Bella's current status as a jumping off point, not an end point. I've always been the more ambitious, though. Seth's done all the directing, which I appreciate, but I'm not even sure what he wants out of his own career (apart from me).

"Can I ask you something?"

"Shoot," he says, not taking his eyes off the screen.

"Are you happy?"

He looks at me like he's seeing me for the first time.

"I mean, career-wise. What does success look like to you?"

"Not Marc Justin if that's what you mean," he says.

"I know that," I say, trying to hide my frustration while organizing my thoughts. "But I've been thinking…"

"You?" he says, still avoiding the question.

"I'm serious. I don't think we've ever had the career conversation, apart from just let's-be-musicians-and-travel-and-play-and-stuff. It's important. This is our livelihood; we should talk about it."

He shifts on the couch so that he's facing me. He cocks his head to the side, presumably assessing how serious I am about this topic. I don't say anything and he pushes his glasses up higher on the bridge of his nose.

"On a scale of one to ten, I'd say I'm at a nine."

"So what would ten look like?" I say, hoping he doesn't ask where I am on that scale.

"Well, a ten would involve no one buying canned pop anymore. People paying attention to lyrics instead of worshipping contest-winning vocalists. And you being naked more." He smiles, running a finger from my collarbone to shoulder, kissing my neck. I'm trying to have a serious business talk with him and find out his life's goals and somehow it all reverts to sex.

"So basically," I say in a steady voice, despite his kisses setting my skin on fire, "You're telling me that your personal career goals include taking down pop music...mmmm," I close my eyes, willing myself not to get distracted, "and seeing me naked?" I'm trying to remember my point. He nods, kissing my neck, moving up to my ear, relieving me of my spaghetti strap.

"It doesn't bother you if that's unachievable?" I ask, still trying to get back on track.

"Oh, I'm pretty confident it is." He smiles and moves in, wrapping his hands under me, picking me up off the couch so that I'm straddling him as he carries me to the bedroom. He drops me gently on the bed, pulling my dress over my head. He drags my panties down—excruciatingly slowly—and I buck my hips to help him along.

When I'm fully naked he stares down at me. "Ten," he says. I can't help it. I know he's deflecting the conversation, that he hates this kind of serious talk, and I chastise myself for being weak enough to fall for it. This is just encouraging him to do it again. Am I a bad person if I have sex with him anyway?

Based on what people say, I never would have expected our sex life to improve after marriage, but that's ridiculous. It makes sense that the better you know each other, the better you can make one another feel. My husband can read my body, my every moan, and know how to take me to the edge, pulling back just in time, tantalizing me until finally, finally, taking me all the way with him until I'm shaking and convulsing and oh-so-satisfied.

We drift off to sleep, naked and sated. The bizarre becomes natural in dreaming, and as I rest, my subconscious sifts through the contents of the day, making sense of utter randomness. The last thought I actively remember is looking forward to class, working on the song I started.

Chapter 6

I arrive at the red brick building where the UCLA extension classes are held. I'm a half hour early, having given myself plenty of time to get stuck in traffic on the way down. Miraculously I didn't hit any, so I have time to grab a quick coffee from the cafe down the street.

"Large latte, please," I say. The barista doesn't look up as she taps the digital register.

"Four fifty three."

I take my coffee and settle myself onto a mostly secluded bench just down from the cafe. I pull out my guitar and notepad, trying to remember the bridge I'd been playing at Marc's house. I can't quite get it. Did it start with the minor or go up to the major 5th? I should have recorded it on my phone.

"That's not how it goes," someone says in front of me. I have a pretty good idea who that someone is, but can't begin to fathom what he'd be doing here. I shade my eyes and squint.

It's definitely him. Marc has traded his board shorts and bare chest for khaki chino shorts, a red t-shirt, a blue and white nautical seersucker blazer, a straw fedora and large black Raybans. He looks like an extra from a Molly Ringwald movie. Inwardly, I grimace.

"What, you don't like my outfit?" he says. Apparently it wasn't as well hidden as I thought.

"Now who's the stalker?" I say, wondering if Marc Justin is, in fact, following me. "No bitches on your arm today?"

"Look, I'm really sorry. I would never say anything like that," he says, sitting beside me.

"You should be. Silence is worse than ignorance." I say, debating whether or not to let my mouth run. "Do you let him call your mom and sister 'bitches' too?" I glare at him and he looks down at his feet. "You almost made me believe you were a nice guy, then proved the worst stereotype about spoiled untalented pop stars." I clench and unclench my jaw, feeling uncomfortably close to losing it. I take a deep, calming breath. "I have class," I say, walking off without looking back.

I'm relieved to see the classroom door open and head in. I slink back in the plastic chair, fuming and mumbling to myself.

As soon as I take my seat, Marc comes in and sits next to me. I'm pretty sure steam is pouring out of me just like a Marc Justin bullshit factory. I know he's not stupid. So why won't he just leave me alone?

"I am sorry," he says. The intensity in his gaze pulls me in. "My life is complicated. I told you I don't have the luxury to be myself all the time. I wasn't tricking you. That was me." I can tell he's watching me and I stubbornly refuse to meet his eyes. I'm not sure what I'm accomplishing, but it feels right not to look.

"And not everyone is opposed to my 'vapid crap'," he says with a wry smile. "Guess who's your guest speaker this week?"

I meet one famous pop star and now he's the guest speaker? What are the chances? I stare at the wall, feeling a little bad for having said that to his face, yet unable to apologize. He gets up, leaving me facing the front of the room, waiting for the rest of the students to stream in.

Marc disappears while everyone files in and Professor Sullivan starts class.

"I know we usually start with a song critique, but we're going to mix it up today. My good friend, our guest speaker, has offered to participate in the critiques as well." Sal says, while excited whispers start flittering around the room.

"Please welcome the Grammy-award-winning artist who has to-date sold over twelve million albums." Sal says, pausing for effect. "Ladies and gentlemen, Marc Justin."

The room erupts and I look around, surprised. I've heard at least half of them rip his songs apart, one actually calling him the Hitler of popular music. And now here they are, ideals be damned, wooed by a star in their midst. I sink into my chair, arms crossed, shaking my head. Sal Sullivan is friends with Marc Justin? The girl next to me gives me a not-so-subtle once-over to let me know she disapproves of me. I can't even pretend to be concerned by what she, or anyone else thinks.

Maybe it's because I'm older and learned long ago that the popularity hierarchy crumbles in adulthood. Maybe it's because I'm not starstruck. Whatever the reason, I suddenly feel like Seth, wondering why I'm wasting my time with a class that would have Marc Justin as a guest speaker to talk about songwriting. He doesn't even write his own songs!

Seth claims you can't learn songwriting in a class, and to a certain extent I agree with him, never more so than right now. I've tried to explain that not everyone is born with his innate confidence, or the ability to self-edit. I can write a thousand songs and never know if any of them are "good enough." I know that even if audiences applaud and other musicians say "good job" it doesn't mean they're being genuine.

I want the help, input and feedback from respected professionals. Like Sal Sullivan. I don't think it makes me weak. Right now, I am questioning the professional qualifications, however, if he's having Marc Justin help us learn to write good songs.

I take a deep breath and shift forward in my seat, trying to focus. Marc puts his hands together, bowing to Sal like he's a yogi or something.

"Thank you, Professor Sullivan. Or should I call you Yoda?" Sal laughs at the blatant pandering. I stifle a groan. "You have no idea what an honor it is to be here in your class. I hope your students know they are learning from the master himself."

A number of hands shoot into the air and more shout out questions. "Sure, I can ... " Marc says, flashing his trademark smile. I hear a few gasps around the room. Jesus people, have some self-respect.

"Is it true that your abs are insured for ten million dollars?" a voluptuous redhead asks. She bites her pen and leans forward in an uncomfortable looking pose, exposing maximum bare neck and chest flesh.

"What's your name? Why don't I answer that one after class?" he says, deflecting the question with hollow flirtation. Or maybe not hollow. How would I know?

"Any questions about music?"

He catches me sighing and smiles, pointing to me even though we both know I didn't raise my hand.

"Who writes your songs?" I ask.

"I co-write, usually. I like to find the most talented writers and convince them to work with me." This receives a smattering of giggles, and I narrow my eyes. He thinks he's so smooth, doesn't he?

"And when you say you co-write, how much do you typically contribute, lyric-wise?"

"Depends on the song," he says, eyes never leaving my face.

"How about your new single, 'All Up in You'?" I ask, feeling the class's attention on me.

"I didn't write the lyrics for that song. I wrote the music, though." I hear a few loud whispers of "I love that song!"

Sal interjects before I can probe further. "Why don't we save the rest of the questions for later if we have time?"

Marc nods and gives a well-rehearsed spiel about the music industry, how artists have to diversify to make a living: tour, record, merchandise, etc. I'd be willing to bet he didn't even write the speech. If he's got a swagger coach I'm sure has a speechwriter as well.

We break into smaller groups like we always do for constructive feedback.

"Penelope, can you come to my office after class? There's something I'd like to discuss," Professor Sullivan says, pulling me aside in the shuffle.

I blush, feeling the butterflies in my stomach and toes I always get when I'm in trouble. I know I didn't technically do anything wrong but it still feels like I'm getting called into the principal's office. I hope he wasn't offended by my questioning of Marc.

I nod and flick my eyes to the back of the class, where Marc is going from group to group, listening and bobbing his head in encouragement.

I'm in the group furthest from him and I play the same piece I played at his house for the group, half-listening to them decide whether it should go back to the first chord or hang at the end. A debate ensues about whether it's too indie or too pop. I stop paying attention after an argument breaks out about which current pop songs are and are not "totally derivative," Marc Justin notably exempt.

I find myself wondering, how did pop become so derided? Bob Dylan, the Rolling Stones, the Beatles—classics—all topped the popular charts. Do people believe they had better taste forty years ago? When did "pop" become a bad word?

***

"Penelope, thanks for coming," Professor Sullivan says when I stick my head in his office after class. He pushes a stack of papers off to the side of his large mahogany desk and gestures for me to come in and sit. "Please, close the door."

I do as I'm told, sitting opposite him, breathing to calm my nerves.

"As you may know, I'm on the National Music Foundation committee," he begins. "And we are committed to the Urban Arts Outreach program."

I nod. I've heard of it.

"Well, this year they asked me to find fresh talent from inner city schools to take part in an after-school songwriting program." He watches, waiting for my reaction. I'm not sure where he's going so I don't say anything.

"You're my best student," he says. I drop my gaze to my shoes, feeling my cheeks burn. "I'd like you to join me next week for a trial run at a school in South Central. Is that something you'd be interested in?"

"Wow," I say, feeling unqualified to do anything of the

sort. "What do you need me to do?"

"Teach songwriting," he says. "Chord structure, melody, the basics."

"Are you sure you don't want someone ... more experienced?"

"I saw your set at Hotel Café a couple weeks ago. If anything, I'd say you've been holding out in class," he says, the corner of his mouth tilting upward into a small smile.

I am flattered, despite my sweaty palms and blushing. He saw my show? Whoa. That's crazy cool, and also terrifying. I'm glad I didn't see him in the crowd, but I'm not sure how I could have missed him either. Was he there with Marc?

"It sounds like a great project," I say, aiming to convey certainty I don't feel. "Sure. I'll do it."

"Great!" he says, steepling his hands. He pushes his chair back and stands, handing me a business card. "Can you meet me at this address on Wednesday at 3pm? We can drive over together."

I nod automatically, unsure about this whole endeavor. He looks me over and I pull my bag into my lap, my legs bouncing of their own accord.

"Erm, you might want to wear something ... modest," he says, not making eye contact.

I look down at myself. Denim shorts. Camisole top. Not exactly scantily clad by L.A. standards. No visible cleavage, no ass hanging out. What's the issue?

"I'm not insinuating anything about your present attire," he says, clearing his throat. "Just that the kids we will be working with come from ... troubled backgrounds," he says. "I want them to focus on the music." He straightens his perfectly pressed shirt and looks away from me for a moment.

I choose not to supply my thoughts: that my wardrobe isn't the deciding factor in their attention spans. And anyway, his discomfort puts me at ease. I shake his hand and agree to meet next Wednesday.

I almost walk right into the side my own car, my mind adrift elsewhere. "Damn it! Not again," I say at the sight of the pink slip under my windshield wipers. The parking police here are out of control. If your sticker is not displayed perfectly, they ticket you. If it's expired by one minute, they ticket you. If they don't like how you parked, they ticket you. I stop and glare at the wretched thing. My parking pass is current, I'm parked between my lines; they have no reason to ticket me.

I rip it out, crumpling it between my hands with excessive force, when I notice my name written on the back. I smooth it out and discover it's not a ticket. On the back is a handwritten note.

Pen,

I was disappointed not to be in your critique group. I'd like to take you out for coffee and further discuss your bridge issues. I have some notes. Next week?

M

Is he serious? I let my head fall back, overwhelmed and frustrated. I'm sick of dissecting his intentions. I'm sick of doubting my own abilities. I'm sick of doubting my career trajectory. If he really is interested in my songwriting, that's flattering, but I'm not convinced. And I don't have time for a celebrity stalker right now.

Telling Seth about the Urban Arts Outreach program is a heavy enough weight for one day. He's not going to be happy about me spending time in South Central. He'll be worried, and then I'll have trouble not getting my Independent Woman panties in a bunch. Now this too? Marc better have his intentions on songwriting. He's in for a rude awakening if he's angling for any of my other talents.

Admittedly, I don't mind the ego boost of a celebrity stalker offering lip service for my writing, though. Even better for my ego was Sal Sullivan calling me his best student? Bonkers. That goes a long way toward easing my self-doubt. Plus, I am excited about sharing music with under-privileged kids.

Music is about connection and expression—it's the cheapest form of therapy there is. Who could benefit more than them? Whether I'm qualified or not, working with Sal Sullivan is the chance of a lifetime—one that even Seth will have to see as an unturndownable opportunity. I've never been singled out for anything like this before. I like it.

"Hey Babe. How was school?" Seth asks from the couch. He's got a guitar out and leans back to watch me as I walk in the front door.

"Great!"

"Oh? Do tell."

"Sal Sullivan asked me to his office after class. I guess he saw me at Hotel Café and he said I'm his most promising student!" I pause for dramatic effect. Seth grins. "He asked me to help him with this project for inner city kids, teaching music. I'm meeting him next Wednesday to drive down to South Central." I say, unable to contain my smile.

"Huh," he says.

I worried he wouldn't like the idea of me spending time in the ghetto, but his lack of reaction irks me even more, somehow.

"That's it? 'Huh'?"

He plays the guitar in his lap, not looking at me. I grit my teeth and stomp off to the bedroom. I don't know what his problem is, but it sure as hell isn't me.

"What's the matter, Babe?" he asks, having followed me down the hall.

"Why aren't you happy for me?"

"I am," he says.

"But?"

"But … I think … no, you know what, don't worry about it." He puts a hand up and turns to leave.

"Say it," I say, hand on hip, waiting.

"Are you sure he doesn't have ulterior motives?" he says, unblinking.

"Seriously?" He better not say what I think he's going to say.

"You know that's not what I mean," he says on a sigh.

He looks down at his shoes and shakes his head. "But of all the classes he teaches, and all the students he has, all the people he knows... You haven't even finished one semester in his class yet. How could he possibly know, like I do, what a great musician you are?"

I think it's possible my eyebrows have fused into my hairline. He took it there. He really did it. I know I shouldn't, but I can't help what's about to come out of my mouth.

"So, to be clear, you're saying he can't possibly have enough information to think I'm talented?" I say, staring at my own reflection in his glasses. He implores me to stop. I take a deep breath and he shakes his head, somehow pissing me off more. "The only possible reason he would ask me to teach underprivileged kids is if he wants in my pants? Is that really what you're saying?"

His jaw tightens and I see the effort he's making not to respond. He sucks in a breath like he's going to say something, but stops himself, exhaling his retort through flared nostrils.

I'm trying (and failing) to keep my temper under control. I am so sick of having my work constantly in question because men think that their desire or lack of desire for getting me in bed is tangled up in what I do. That somehow my sexuality itself defines me. Worse yet, I wonder if there is truth to it? There are plenty of people he could have asked, and in that one moment when I thought he was checking me out, the thought crossed my mind too. How am I supposed to know if it's a factor? I won't admit that to Seth though.

"You think he wants to fuck me?"

"Well, of course he does. He's a man," Seth says, as though speaking to a child.

"Gah!" I throw my head back, staring at the ceiling.

"I'm just asking what he really knows about your musicianship? I know you're talented. You're my wife, my partner. I love you."

"But you think I should turn him down? That I shouldn't take a huge opportunity on the off-chance he wants to have sex with me?" I say, my voice shaking in anger.

"I think you should do whatever you want. I'm just warning you to watch out for this guy."

"Thanks for the heads up."

Seth throws his hands up in a gesture of surrender and stalks out. I sink back on the bed, my breathing heavy, my earlier excitement gone.

Chapter 7

When I pull up to the address Sal gave me, I double-check the numbers. I knew he was successful, but this can't be a home address. The gilded front gate looks like it was commissioned by Louis XIV, and is easily worth more than all my worldly possessions combined. In this sprawling estate in Beverly Hills it's hard to believe we're going to see troubled inner city kids. There is a call box off the driver's side and I look for a button. I can't find one on the cold metal surface, but suddenly it buzzes and the gates grumble open.

I drive in, trying not to veer off the road as I approach the main building. I'm still not convinced it's a house. A hotel would be more plausible, judging by its size and opulence. The cobblestone drive circles around a large water fountain that bubbles softly. I feel like an intruder and park as far out of the way as possible. I tip my head back to take in the giant arched door made of railroad ties and iron, reminiscent of a castle's drawbridge.

I raise my hand to knock, but before I make contact, a suited man answers and ushers me inside. I wait in the interior courtyard. Professor Sullivan emerges, closing the interior front door behind him. He's casually dressed and seems utterly at ease waving to me. I wave back. I would never get used to living here. Not even in my most adventurous fantasies did I deign to dream this big.

"Is this your house?" I ask.

"Yeah, I didn't know what time we'd be back. I was afraid if I parked in the parking garage I'd get another ticket."

I smile.

"And call me Sal. Especially in front of the kids."

I nod and move to open my car door.

"We can take my car," he says, motioning to a black SUV.

I hear Seth's words echoing in my head and briefly war with myself.

"That's okay, I can follow you in my car," I say, twisting my keys in my hand.

"I insist," he says. "It's not safe. And I'd like to discuss the lesson plan for the day."

Judging by his tone, it isn't a request. I don't really want to waste my own gas or risk getting my car stolen anyway. South Central's reputation for gangs and violence doesn't inspire me to drive there alone. I've never been, and as a general rule I like to make firsthand impressions rather than assumptions. Although I can practically hear Lolo warning, "Girl, the ghetto ain't no politically correct playground."

"Have you worked with inner city kids before?" Sal asks.

"No, but I've done some tutoring."

"Good. But this won't be like the tutoring you've done before." He keeps his hands on the wheel and sneaks a glance at me. I try not to blush. As if I didn't feel unqualified enough.

"I have a confession," he says.

Uh-oh.

"I see something in you beyond your songwriting skills," he says.

I can't look at him. I don't want to hear the rest.

"Empathy. I've seen you in critique groups. You're diplomatic. Always aware and respectful of other's feelings."

I exhale my relief and feel an embarrassed thrill run up the nape of my neck. I look over at him. He doesn't elaborate, but I feel lighter already—I can do this.

***

We drive down a main street, slowing to a stop outside what looks like a prison. I'm struck by the disparity between the Beverly Hills mansion we left a handful of minutes ago and this high school of similar size that looks like it's been in a constant state of lockdown, housing thousands of students.

Sal steps out, removing his phone from his pocket and motions for me to stay in the car. I can't hear his conversation but a minute later he slides behind the driver's seat and we speed away.

"Where are we going?" I ask, trying to hide my nerves.

"My contact says it isn't safe to meet here today. He gave me the address of a church nearby. Can you give me directions?" He hands me his smartphone with the map loaded on the screen.

Unnamed contact? Secret meeting places? Are we CIA now? It just went from Punk'd to Alias. I'm not sure which to prefer.

We traverse the graffitied streets, past tiendas, trunk sales, and laughing kids. I follow the map's instructions, hoping not to get us lost. This isn't a place I want to ask for directions. People stare, not hiding their curiosity. The SUV thwarts our attempt to blend in. We look like drug dealers hidden behind dark tinted windows. I distract myself with the map, averting my gaze from their looks even though they can't see me.

I even appreciate Sal's advice now—I don't want to attract (extra) attention in this neighborhood. I'm glad I opted for black jeans, flats and a simple chambray top that's neither too fitted nor low-cut.

We pull into a church parking lot with a mobile medic truck taking up the far side. A handwritten cardboard sign reading "Free HIV testing" leans against it. I don't see anyone inside. A couple of other cars are parked in the lot, and I double-check the address. A padlocked chain wraps around the door handles and I can't see any light coming from inside. Across the street is an empty lot surrounded by a chain link fence. Where the other streets were filled with people, this feels abandoned.

Sal takes his phone from me and dials. "We're here," he says and hangs up. I'm beginning to feel like I've just stepped into a movie and I'm about to learn there is a bomb that needs deactivating or the whole town blows up. I trust Sal but I'm feeling less and less like the Independent Woman and more like someone who will be happy not to make the six o'clock news. Imaginary Lolo is still tsk-tsk-ing me.

A young man swaggers up to the car, hood covering his eyes, and it takes every ounce of self-control at my command to keep from screaming at the top of my gutless lungs. Or wetting my pants. Meet Marc Justin's next swagger coach. The thought provides just enough levity for me to keep it together.

Sal nods to me and gets out, following the young man around to my side of the car. My heart rate is off the charts. Sal appears calm, following our be-hooded guide across the parking lot toward the padlocked church. I can't believe I agreed to this. If I get out alive I may even admit to Seth he was right about this being a bad idea. Maybe. I close my eyes, take a deep breath, and open the door.

No one says a word as we round the building to the side entrance. The kid reaches into his pocket and pulls out a key, twisting the padlock open. He ushers us inside, pulls the doors closed with a thwump that reverberates in the large room, and locks them from inside. I don't like being locked in. Anywhere. Especially not here.

Sal puts an arm around my shoulders and gives me a squeeze. He whispers in my ear, "It's okay. It's not as bad as it looks."

I am overwhelmed with the urge to burst into tears. That would be the worst thing I could do right now. Luckily, my internal lockdown is effective, barely.

We walk around the handful of pews to a small card table, surrounded by chairs. Our students look like the United Colors of (Juvie) Benneton. No one makes eye contact or speaks. I see a beat up guitar in the corner, leaning against the wall. It only has four strings. That's not going to work.

On the way down, Sal told me we'd be going over basics today: G, C, and D chords, basic strumming. The objective was to get them interested. Give them enough to practice on their own but not so much as to overwhelm them. He warned they might take offense easily, get scared off, and might not seem like they were paying attention at all. He also assured me not to worry.

When he told me these were the kids the system forgot, I thought he exaggerated. Sitting at this dilapidated card table with them, in this neighborhood where they live, I'd say he understated.

"Everyone here?" Sal asks the kid who showed us in. He nods without looking up.

I pick up the guitar from the floor. I need to do something to distract from the feeling of eyes on me. Sal takes a new set of strings from his coat pocket and lets me set to work changing them out.

"Thanks," Sal says to me. He turns to the boys (men?) "The music program got cut last year, right?"

"Yeah, they put in new metal detectors," one of them says from beneath a ball cap. I can't see his face, just his hands fidgeting on his lap. There are a few grunts from others too.

"But you were all enrolled?" Sal continues.

Many of them shift in their seats, not answering. I'm surprised Sal didn't mention this tidbit to me on the way down. It makes more sense why he's chosen them. "How many of you know how to play?" Sal asks. A few hands go up.

"How many of you know how to tune a guitar?" he asks, circling the table. No hands go up. "How many of you have a guitar or access to one?"

Silence. "No one?" Sal says, running a hand through his hair. I finish stringing the guitar and leave the untrimmed strings to curl around at the ends.

Sal reaches out to me and I hand it off. He goes through the process of tuning, handing it off a couple times to let them tighten and test the new strings.

When it comes back to me, I unthinkingly start playing a Nirvana riff that only requires the bottom two strings. I see a couple heads perk up.

"Hey, can you teach me that?" one of them asks. I try to mask my surprise and go through it again slowly. He nods and I hand him the guitar. He gets the first couple notes right, but when he messes up he gets angry and passes it to the kid next to him like he doesn't want anything more to do with it. I shake my head and tell him to try it again. He glares at me, and the kid next to him snickers and passes it back.

He scowls, but picks it up and plays the first two notes again, looking at me expectantly. I nod and smile, pointing to the next note. He gets it and then another and another. After two minutes, he's got the lick down and is repeating it over and over. Based on his success, one of the others snags the guitar, smiling and ready for his turn to shine.

An hour later everyone has picked up the riff. If I were the ghost of Kurt I'd be proud. Or tell them to make up their own damn songs. Sal is standing in the corner, arms crossed, relaxed. It's time for us to go and Tyrone, the kid who let us in, asks me when we're coming back. Sal answers on my behalf. "Next week."

When Sal and I are safely in the car and back on the freeway heading to his house, I feel my shoulders relax. Realizing that I made it out alive, I'm better than relaxed: I feel great.

Sal is quiet, gazing straight ahead as he weaves through traffic. I'm lost in thought when we finally pull into his driveway. I move to get out of the car but he turns to me, stopping me.

"You were great," he says.

"Thanks. It was … different," I say. He frowns in concern. "Good different," I specify.

"I'm glad. Next week we'll bring enough guitars for everyone," he says, watching me carefully. I get the impression he's giving me the chance to say I'm not going back. Honestly, it's worth considering. I was terrified today. But nothing bad happened. I wasn't threatened or insulted in any way. I'm starting to think I should check my personal prejudices.

I don't know how Sal plans to get all those guitars, but clearly he has resources. I think he's a good person who wants to help. And I feel safe with him. Plus, those kids live there full time. All I have to do is make it through an hour a week. For now, that'll do.

Chapter 8

I spot Lolo as I enter the café. Her giant afro is hard to miss, but in case I do, I just have to follow the male stares gaping in her direction. She's unbelievably gorgeous and completely unaffected by the attention she receives. She's half black and half Thai with flawless mocha skin, high cheekbones and beautiful almond shaped eyes, not to mention a model's body. She is also one of the sweetest, smartest people I know, making it impossible to hate her for looking the way she does.

There are places where we might look like a misfit pair, meeting for coffee at the crack of noon. In L.A., we fit in perfectly. Angelinos don't keep time like the rest of the working world. Especially here in Silver Lake, where even hipsters are, like, not even ironically ironic. We blend seamlessly into the bohemian tapestry.

"Hey Lo," I say, plopping down across from her, my cappuccino clinking on the table.

"Hey!" she says, setting her phone down on the table. "Jeff is being such a pain in the ass." She slaps her hands on the table for effect. If it were anyone else I would ask if everything was okay, but with Lolo and Jeff this is perfectly normal. They have a roller coaster relationship—building to a passionate fight/make up crescendo only to repeat the cycle. I know this because Lolo likes to share … a lot.

"What is it this time?" I ask, dumping sugar into my mug.

"Album. Tour," she says, sighing in exasperation. "He wants all live instruments so our live show is exactly like the album. I want synthetic fills and don't think it will detract. But you know Jeff; he won't compromise at all. It's infuriating! At least Seth is coming with us for this first run. He can keep Jeff in line." Her eyes widen and she smiles as though she's just had the epiphany of her life. "You could

stop being selfish and come with us. You know you want to."
She wags her eyebrows trying to hypnotize a "yes" out of me.

"I can't. I have school. Not to mention there wouldn't be anything for me to do."

"You could be my official confidante and Sanity Keeper," she says.

I stare, silently waiting for her to drop it. She sighs in resignation.

"So? How was South Central?" she asks.

"Terrifying,"

"Well, ye-eah."

"But once I got over the fear of being raped and murdered, it was great," I say, taking a sip. "We're doing it again next week."

"And…" she says, leaning forward in her seat. "Was Seth right about your professor having the hots for you?"

"No, not at all," I say with a smug smile. "He was one hundred percent professional."

"Well, I'm glad he didn't cross any lines. I mean, gossip-wise it's boring, but I'm glad he didn't try to use inner city kids to get in your pants."

"Yeah, I'd like to think Sal Sullivan would at least be classy about trying to get in my pants."

"Ooh, but speaking of gossip … I heard you bumped into the baby pop star?" she says, arms crossed over her chest. Busted. She hates when I don't call her immediately with all gossip.

"Did Seth tell Jeff? Geez."

She's unflinching.

"It was bizarre. He's … I don't know what he is. We got food off a truck and ate on the beach and then had to hide from some stalker fans."

"Did he whisk you away on his private jet?" she asks, uncrossing her arms and leaning her elbows on the table.

"Yeah, didn't you see us fly over your house?" I say.

She sips her coffee.

"He's not what I expected. Just when I thought he didn't

seem so bad, his swagger coach comes in and starts talking about all the 'bitches' they've got going to the Lakers game. I couldn't get out of there fast enough."

"Wait up—swagger coach?" She circles her head in incredulity, afro catching up a second later. "And you were in his house? You can't gloss over these things!"

I sigh. "Yes ... briefly." I wish I hadn't said anything.

"Oooh, this is gonna be good. Spill."

"My clothes were wet and he lent me a sarong and his dryer," I say.

"I bet."

"We weren't alone long. His mom and sister came over." I drop my eyes to my frothy drink.

"So let me get this straight. A super famous celebrity bumps into you and asks you out. He buys you food, flirts with you, invites you into his house and out of your clothes, and then introduces you to his mother?"

When she says it like that ...

"It wasn't a big deal."

She cocks a brow, not believing me for a second.

"And anyway, he's a jackass."

"Okay." Lolo smirks, sipping her drink.

Uncharacteristically, she lets it go and we slip into normal conversation. I usually feel more balanced after we hang out, but I can't ignore the depth of frustration and anger I only just realized I have. I feel like a pawn. I'm angry that Seth gossiped about me to Jeff. I don't like that Lolo implied I acted inappropriately. And most of all, I hate wondering whether I'm projecting—maybe I crossed a line I didn't realize was there? That settles heavy in my stomach, making me a little nauseous.

Chapter 9

"You ready?" Seth asks, packing our guitars into my tiny hatchback.

"Yeah, let's go," I say, sliding into the passenger seat and checking my phone one last time.

We drive down the I-5 toward the LAFM radio station where we're doing a live in-studio interview and performance. I'm always nervous for these things, but particularly now, I feel unsettled. It's not the performance. On that front Seth and I are a well-honed machine. I know he would never let me humiliate myself. It's the talking part that scares me. I hate not knowing what they're going to ask and I dread being caught off-guard. Especially by the inane questions they ask. Whoever said there's no such thing as a stupid question hasn't done the music promo circuit.

I don't talk much on the way there. Seth is quiet as well, settling into our pre-show downtime as we mentally prepare. We pull into the parking lot and unload silently.

"You can wait here," says a friendly woman sitting behind the front desk. "They're running a few minutes behind, so just make yourselves comfortable."

We're familiar with the routine: hurry up and wait. I tune my guitar. We practice the song we're going to sing. It's the first single from our new album and we haven't played it out much yet.

"You okay?" Seth asks, rubbing his hand up and down my arm.

"Just nervous."

"You'll do great," he says in a voice that emanates warmth and affection. I melt into the sound, feeling better already.

This is where we're great. He knows exactly how to calm me down and inspire the confidence I lack on my own.

Without him I wouldn't have become a performer at all. Despite my middle-child need for attention, I was a total chicken when it came to getting on stage. No one in my family played an instrument. The arts were not a "serious pursuit." Classical music was okay, especially as a hobby, but we were expected to pursue the standard high-achiever professional tracks.

I met Seth by serendipity, at a movie theater where I worked the summer after college. My manager at the time complained about some guy busking out front and told me that I needed to tell him to go away or we'd call the cops. Did I mention my boss was a prick? Turns out, that prick introduced me to my future husband.

I wandered outside, mostly to hear him. I figured I'd just tell him to check out the town square where more people hung out, anyway. From the first song I heard him play I was hooked. I wouldn't say love-at-first-sight, but there was definitely a magical spark. Maybe it was the golden evening lighting, or how he seemed unaffected by his surroundings— either by the people ignoring him or the ones who dropped money into his guitar case. Whatever the reason, I stood rooted to the spot, listening to him play.

When he finished, he looked up and smiled at me. It was like he didn't see anyone else there. Since it was opening night for the most-anticipated blockbuster of the year and people were lined up around the block, it was all the more impressive. I opened my mouth to speak, not knowing what I'd say.

"Can I buy you dinner?" he asked, oblivious to the crowd around him.

"Yeah, give me just a second, okay?" I said. I marched back into the box office, chucked my nametag and apron on the desk and told my boss "I quit." Or at least that's how it goes in my memory. In reality I left an hour before my shift ended, knowing I'd get fired. But there's no need to let facts ruin a good story.

I'd never been so irresponsible. I'm not sure how I mustered the courage, but I've never regretted it. Being with

Seth felt natural in a way I never knew anything could. It was like we'd always known each other, right from that first moment. He took me to this tiny little hole-in-the-wall Greek restaurant that somehow I'd never been to in my teeny hometown. We talked in a booth until they kicked us out and then kept talking as we walked laps around the town square all night.

We've been inseparable ever since. And my parents have hated him ever since. They blame him for my going "off the rails" and subverting their clear path to my success. He ran away from home at sixteen and has no contact with his family so their disapproval has never fazed him. It makes me sad, but I'd rather be the real me—with Seth—than pretend to be anyone else for their benefit.

Seth is the one who encouraged me to perform. I started out playing second guitar and occasionally singing harmonies with him, but then we decided to go on tour and he thought we should be equal in our duo. He made me feel like I could do anything. That first show we played, at a dungeon-like bar with horrible stage lighting and about twelve people in the crowd, was the single most incredible night of my life. They applauded us. I sang the lead and played guitar. Seth was by my side. And the audience loved it. After that night I knew I could never work anywhere else. I was a musician. And for the past eight years I have been chasing my dreams with the man who encourages me to fly.

Now here we are, three albums later, inside the studio of LAFM, the taste-making indie music station, playing a song that tells the story of how we met. It's a beautiful full-circle moment.

"I just have to ask … how did you two get so adorable?" the DJ asks, after we finish the song.

Seth smiles, looking from me to her, "Thanks for having us."

"My pleasure!" she says in her chipper DJ voice. "Now tell me, it sounds like that song might be based on the two of you. Penelope, can you tell us how you met and what drew you together?"

Chapter 10

"I can't believe you're all leaving me," I say to Lolo as Jeff and Seth load up the tour van. Seth agreed to play keys and bass for Jeff and Lolo. They're doing a short Southwest run of mid-sized venues, opening for a bigger act, before ending up in Austin for a SXSW showcase slot. They're making just enough to pay Seth to play with them. On the one hand, I'd love to go and support, but I'm not keen on becoming the roadie/groupie, not to mention a financial burden. Selfishly, I'm also looking forward to some time alone to write in a quiet space.

"You can always ditch class and come with," Lolo says.

My lips twist into a one-sided smile.

"What could be better than being with everyone you love?" she says.

I narrow my eyes. "Love doesn't manipulate."

She smiles, conceding the point.

"Anyway, I'm excited about teaching the kids in South Central. No one's ever come through for them before and it makes me want to be that person."

"Boooring!" She pulls me into a hug and whispers in my ear so no one else can hear. "You sure that's all?" I nod into her shoulder and give her a squeeze.

Seth interrupts and pulls me to him, spinning me around. I lift my feet up and enjoy the centrifugal force blurring the edges of reality, focusing only on his face. He loves me. "I love you," I say, kissing him.

He nuzzles my ear. "I'm going to miss you like crazy."

These upcoming weeks will be the longest we've been apart since we met. I'm excited to have full control over the remote and enjoy my own schedule, but all my friends will be gone and it'll be lonely without them. Productive, but lonely.

***

"Sal?" I say, loading the final guitar into his SUV that Wednesday afternoon. "These are really nice guitars."

"A friend needed a tax write-off," he says.

I wait, but he doesn't offer more information. I guess when you're Sal Sullivan "nice" is a relative term. With what those instruments cost, Seth and I could live on for a year.

"Kay. That's all of them. You know where we're going?" I ask.

Sal seemed edgy and short in class earlier. I try not to take his caginess personally.

He nods. We make the half-hour drive from Rodeo Drive to Drive-By Drive in relative silence. Pulling up to the same church parking lot as last week, my shock is no less at seeing the gang signs marking territory or the deadened eyes peering out from windows covered in foil, plastic and plywood. A kid, maybe ten years old, watches us from a nearby porch, juggling a soccer ball.

On the drive down Sal told me he's advocating for the mayor to reinstate funding for public schools' music programs statewide. He hasn't had any luck getting yet. A friend of his is filming a documentary piece for the awards show depicting inner city kids choosing a life of music instead of gangs, which they're hoping brings awareness to the issue in a way that inspires action. I think it's a brilliant idea—using his celebrity and connections to affect political change.

Like last week, Tyrone struts up to the car and Sal rolls down his window. This time I smile as he approaches and the sense of foreboding is replaced with excitement.

"Is there somewhere else we can unload?" Sal asks. Tyrone juts out his chin and walks away. I presume we're meant to follow him. We pull around the building to the side entrance, parking illegally.

"Will we get a ticket parking here?" Sal asks Tyrone.

Tyrone laughs. "Nah. Cops in this neighborhood got other shit to do."

He enlists the help of a couple other guys from the class and we load everything into the small anteroom with the card table. Sal has enough guitars for everyone, plus extra strings, capos and tuners.

"Ready?" Sal asks the group. They nod. "Let's get started." Sal is on a mission today, not wasting any time. I struggle to keep up, going around the room helping everyone individually, adjusting fingering, working on strumming and generally providing encouragement. There's a focused intensity all around, a response to Sal's energy, I think. I'd feel perfectly at ease if we weren't locked inside a church in South Central.

We work on Bob Marley's "No Woman, No Cry." It's only four chords including the C and G they learned last week. We add A minor and F and, as hoped, their familiarity with the song makes it easier to pick up. They are attentive and eager, which fills me with a warm gooey feeling that what I'm doing matters.

After we finish, everyone leaves but Tyrone. He's dawdling and I get the impression he wants to say something.

"Can I help you?" I say, stepping toward him.

"Nah," he says and moves to leave. He turns back and looks at me. "Nah—it's no big deal."

"Try me."

"I was just…" he trails off, turning again to walk away. I put my hand out, lightly touching his forearm. His eyes widen and I immediately drop my hand, but silently encourage him to go on.

"I really want to practice that song."

"That's great," I say. "You're doing great, Tyrone."

"I just … I don't got a guitar to practice," he says, looking away again.

"Hang on a sec," I hold up a finger and watch him shift from foot to foot. I find Sal in the corner, putting guitars in cases. I ask him if there's one we can leave for Tyrone. He picks up the top case. We approach Tyrone, who looks like he'd rather be anywhere else.

"You gonna practice?" Sal asks, his face all business.

"Yes, sir," Tyrone says, a smile playing on his lips.

"You gonna pawn it?"

"No, sir." Tyrone says, the smile gone.

"It's yours," Sal says. Tyrone's eyes widen, a smile flickering beneath the hardened exterior. "I do have a request though," Sal continues. Tyrone's eyes harden again. "I'd like you to agree to be on camera when we bring in the documentary crew," Sal nods to Tyrone, waiting.

"You mean like, be on TV?"

"Mmhmm."

"Hell yeah!" Tyrone says. He breaks into a smile that transforms his whole face. The hard young man morphs into a giddy kid.

He plays it cool but I know Sal is relieved and happy, as am I. Tyrone will be the ideal subject for the documentary. Plus he'll be a beacon of positivity for his community. It's perfect.

Sal and I grab a guitar in each hand and head to the door to load up the car. As we step outside we're greeted by a group of men lurking about ten feet from the back of the SUV. Their relaxed demeanor is undermined by their hardened energy. The way they're standing they are effectively blocking us in, since we parked so near the side of the church. When they hear the door, they turn and move toward us. My heart hammers in my chest and I expect to pass out any second. The presumed leader reaches around to his backside, and I stifle a scream. He keeps his hand behind his back as they form a sort of pyramid, the leader the only one to speak.

"Those for us?" he says.

Neither Sal nor I say anything. It's not a question. I can't speak for Sal, but this is my first time being robbed and I for one don't know the etiquette. They don't wait, leaning in and relieving us of the cases. They turn to walk away, as though they've done nothing wrong.

My heart is still threatening to burst from my chest when the leader doubles back, invading Sal's personal space.

"I almost forgot my ride," he says, his smile revealing a golden grill that makes me think of an alien piranha. He reaches out to Sal who hands over the keys. He lets his thugs load themselves and the guitars in the car. They speed off, burning rubber donuts before leaving for good.

I stand there, open-mouthed and dumbfounded.

"Psst," Tyrone says from inside the church. "They gone?"

I can't speak … or blink, for that matter. Sal is quietly emanating rage. Tyrone takes this as affirmation.

"Man, sorry about that. That's Raphael's gang."

By his tone, I'm supposed to know who Raphael is. I don't. And I'm definitely not interested in meeting him again.

"It would have been worse if I come out. Retribution," he says, locking us back inside the church. "You gotta call someone for a ride. I'll stay till they get here. Know anyone with bulletproof windows?"

I hope he's joking. I know nothing of real life gang life, but if retribution means what it does in movies, I think he's risking his credibility and possibly his life by staying with us. Seth, Lolo and Jeff are all on tour. I turn to Sal. I'm about to start crying when he dials a number.

"Can I call in that favor?" Sal says to a muffled male voice. I can't hear the other side of the conversation, but I glean the gist and quite frankly don't care who comes to get us so long as we get out of here as soon as possible.

"Fifteen minutes," Sal says as he hangs up.

I have no idea where he's coming from, but anyone who's friends with Sal is driving farther than fifteen minutes to South Central. I settle in for a long wait and sit on my hands in a vain attempt to stop them from shaking.

Chapter 11

Fifteen minutes later Sal's phone vibrates on the card table.

"Where are you?" he asks, getting up and heading toward the door. "We're waiting for a shave and a haircut knock."

I try to say okay but only manage to bob my head in assent.

We hear the familiar knock and Tyrone goes to the door. I recognize one of Marc's bodyguards. I'm so confused. Why is he here? Do Sal and Marc share bodyguards?

"You gonna be okay?" Tyrone asks. His face is serious and he looks at least a decade older.

"Yeah, thanks for waiting with us," I say.

"Ah, it's okay," he says. "Ms. Penelope?"

I ignore how weird it is to hear him call me Ms. Penelope. "Yes?"

"Think you guys'll come back?" His jaw tightens, not quite masking his concern.

"No," Sal says. Tyrone's disappointment flashes over his features and his eyes harden. "But we'll keep teaching you."

Tyrone' head snaps up. "For real?"

"Yeah, we just need to find somewhere ... safer next time," Sal says. He puts a hand on Tyrone's shoulder and looks at the guitar. "Are you going to be able to get that home?"

"Yessir," Tyrone says, the lifeless mask returning to his face. It scares me as much now as ever, especially after having seen him as happy as a child. There is something in that look that says he's lived a life where threats are followed through. He's probably never been a kid at all.

Marc's bodyguard gets Sal and I settled in the car and I can't hide my surprise seeing Marc Justin in the backseat. I slide in next to him, desire to get far away from here trumping my shock. Sal swings himself into the far back seat and we're moving before I can get my seatbelt buckled.

"You want a drink?" Marc asks.

"Water?" Sal says. I nod. Marc's bodyguard reaches into a cooler between the front seats and hands them back to us. Marc gives me space but I can feel his assessing gaze on me. I start shivering and Marc unzips his sweatshirt, handing it to me wordlessly.

"Thanks," Sal says when we pull around the softly bubbling fountain in his driveway. "Can you drop Penelope off at home? I'll have someone deliver her car later."

I want to be indignant at the two of them sorting out what I need, but I can't muster the energy. Frankly I don't think I can drive myself home.

Marc turns to me, waiting for my answer. I nod.

"Are you sure you're okay?" he asks.

"Ye—," I start to say. I feel the familiar burn behind my eyes and tears start flowing. I sink my face into my hands. Marc pulls me to him and rubs my back while I sob and convulse. It's not the dainty kind of crying either. I try not to think about the trails of snot smearing all over his $500 t-shirt. He doesn't seem to mind and I'm so appreciative I don't even put up a fight when he automatically takes me to his house instead of my own. Right now I don't want to be alone anyway.

"Thanks," Marc says to his bodyguards. I can't hear what else he says as I go to the living room and sit on his giant couch, letting it swallow me in its warmth and comfort.

"Hungry?" he asks when he returns.

"Mmhmm," I manage to say. I'm starving, now that I think about it.

"I'll have it delivered," he says.

I don't bother asking what he's ordering.

I lay my head back on the couch for what feels like a few seconds, and the next thing I know the most delicious aroma fills the house. I must have fallen asleep. My stomach grumbles, forcing me up from the couch's clutches and into the kitchen.

"That smells incredible," I say, taking a seat at the island.

"I figured comfort food was the way to go," he says.

I smile half-heartedly. He sets out plates and silverware for us both, bringing a napkin around to me and pouring a glass of white wine. He sits next to me and lifts his glass to mine. "To your health," he says. I think I see sadness in his eyes but I could be imagining it. I'm in no state to analyze anyone else's feelings. I can't even grasp my own. I clink my glass to his.

"We have smoked gouda bacon mac and cheese, Waldorf salad, and poached salmon. Oh, and dessert. But that's a surprise."

"I don't know where you order take-out, but this is amazing." I say.

He smiles as I dig in. It tastes even better than it smells. There is nothing ladylike about the way I devour my food, barely stopping myself from licking the plate clean. I do take note that Marc has excellent manners while he eats, which I admit I like.

Good food is transformative. My mood flips 180 degrees and I have a newfound understanding for emotional overeaters. If I were regularly traumatized I'd weigh 400 pounds. Marc smiles approvingly and clears my plate. It dawns on me that he's doing it himself, not waiting for a housekeeper. I expected a spoiled pop star to have people do everything for him, but he seems comfortable in his kitchen. He takes two pint-size containers from the freezer and grabs spoons, eyeing me as he sets one in front of me. Taking a bite, he leans against the island.

Inside the container I find a gorgeous chocolate gelato, drizzled with caramel, topped with a cookie crumble. I raise my eyebrows, smiling appreciatively. I'll give him this: the boy knows food.

Standing, he waves an arm for me to follow him to the patio, which overlooks the ocean. The sun radiates shades of pink and orange into wispy clouds as it sinks below the water's edge. I'm not a fan of smog in general, but its effect on L.A. sunsets is spectacular.

We finish dessert in silence, Marc getting up to put away the leftovers, while I'm left enjoying the view. Under other circumstances, this might be considered romantic. I glance at Marc, wondering if the guy I'm with now is the real him. I no longer see Marc Justin, pop star, but Marc, a guy who helped me out of a scary situation. I could be friends with this Marc.

"Not ideal circumstances, but I'm really glad to see you again," he says.

In lieu of response, I smile. He's still on probationary terms with me, although if today is any indication, he won't be for long.

"I know you still think I'm a jerk, and I am sometimes. But there's something about you. You put me at ease. I feel like you see me." He looks down and shakes his head. "Wow, I sound so cheesy."

At least he knows it. I'm not sure I believe him, but he does seem sincere.

"Wanna go for a swim?" I ask, unable to process the confluence of emotions.

"Shouldn't we wait fifteen minutes?"

"Old wive's tale. Come on," I grab his hand, pulling him down the steps to the cold sand.

Racing into the water, fully clothed, we let our bodies collapse into the crashing waves. I dive through a large wave that washes over me, pulling the hair away from my face. The scent of saltwater and the relentless sound of crashing surf drown every thought from my mind until finally, I let go. The hardened lines of those thugs' faces ebb from my mind's eye, diluted by the ocean.

Marc body surfs a wave and crashes hard into the sand. He pops up covered in seaweed and sand. I laugh. He shrugs and then points to something behind me. A black fin breaks the surface of the water and panic grips me. I run toward shore, splashing and flailing my arms. Marc catches me by the waist and spins me around. He stands behind me, my back to his front, pointing over my shoulder. "Dolphins," he says.

Yep, I'm all courage and bravery. I shake my head in disgust at myself. No longer fearing for my life, I count five fins playing in the surf in the last seconds of light, just like us. It's completely mesmerizing. Turning around to say exactly that to Marc, I look up at him and stop myself, disarmed by the intimacy.

An unfamiliar tingle of butterflies radiates in my chest and, before my brain kicks in, I really want him to kiss me. I lose myself in time and space, forgetting that I was just mugged. Forgetting that I'm married.

I wish I could capture this feeling: being completely alive and present. My senses absorb every infinitesimal detail— lock them away in my mind, separated from everything else before and after.

Something unspoken passes between us and Marc takes me by the hand, keeping me at his side, breaking the intimacy while keeping me close. I'm not sure if I'm more disappointed or relieved.

We fall into easy banter, diving into all the topics most people avoid: religion, politics and business. He tells me more about his childhood and the underbelly of fame, and I regale him with my daydream adventures. He confides in me, and I in him. I ask where he'd like to see his career going, and he admits that he's been craving a more authentic connection to music.

"I wasn't supposed to be at Hotel Cafe that night," he says. "But I ended up stopping by. My team was trying to rush me off to make an important meeting, but from the moment I heard you, it was like everything else just fell away. Every word you sang resonated with me. I knew I had to know you. I knew I had to work with you."

"Really?" I'm having a hard time accepting that.

"I was trying to figure out how to approach you when, lucky for me, you tripped right in front of me."

I bury my face in my hands at the memory. He rests his hand on my shoulder and I look up into his eyes. I don't know how, but I know what he's communicating to me in that look, and my feet tingle in recognition of our mutual acknowledgment of something deeper than words can say. If I think too hard about it, I'll dismiss it, but in this moment, I know it's real and I let it sink in, becoming part of me.

At home many hours later, I can't stop shaking. My palms sweat, my heart races. Exhausted, I'm filled with restless energy that breaks out in gooseflesh all over my body. My appetite is gone, my mouth is dry, my stomach is cramped in knots, and though I should feel discomfort, I'm elated. Giddy. Smiling for no apparent reason.

My fingers itch to call or text him, the electricity coursing through me looking, needing, to find its counterpoint. I have to know this current leads to another electrified being. That what I experienced really happened. It is such a rarity in life to be seen by anyone, let alone a near stranger.

Even though he didn't kiss me in the water, I didn't feel rejected. It couldn't have been any other way. In fact, I've never felt sexier. He saw me for me. He acted like it was a forgone conclusion that I was the amazing person I always, in my heart of hearts, hoped and dreamt I could be. It felt like realizing my own potential through someone else's eyes. Did he feel that too? I'm awed by the power of my emotional response from one night, immediately followed by a heavy dose of guilt.

I didn't do anything wrong. No lines were crossed and nothing untoward said. There is nothing to admit, and yet I can't get his face out of my head. Apparently I'm just like the millions of tween fans around the world, sucked in by the irresistible Marc Justin.

Except that I know the way his mouth tilts up at the corners like someone I used to love. His full lips parting slightly as he contemplates something I said. I want to remember every detail of tonight and keep it locked away in a safe place. It's so rare to connect to someone like that— unprotected by emotional armor—expecting to feel exposed, and instead to feel some ancient wound healed. I feel centered. I found what I never knew I was looking for. I want to hold onto this feeling, to let it light my way the next time I feel trapped in a dark corner of self-doubt.

Chapter 12

"How was the ghetto?" Seth asks.

I recoil at the question and have to remind myself that he's just calling to check in. He has no idea what happened today.

"We got mugged," I say.

"What?"

"Yeah, some thugs took the guitars we brought for the kids and then stole Sal's car."

"Holy shit! You're serious? Are you okay? I'm coming home." Seth is in full Save-the-Day mode and I know he would drop everything and come home if I asked him to. A couple hours ago I'd have loved for him to do just that. But I'm okay now. I'd feel ridiculous if he came home to take care of me, as if there's anything he can do to change the past.

"Stay. I'm fine, really." I say. He's quiet for a bit and finally sighs. "It's not like they're going to follow me to Topanga Canyon," I say, reassuring us both.

I'm emotionally spent from the day and don't have the energy to rehash the events of the day. Or at least that's what I'm telling myself as to why I don't mention Marc. I don't want to fight or turn it into something it's not. Because it's nothing. It was a moment—a great moment—but just a moment.

"Babe," he says, and I imagine him running his hands through his hair, pacing. "I hate that I'm not there for you right now."

"I know," I say. "Thank you for that. But really, I'm okay." He expels a heavy breath. "Two weeks."

"How's the tour so far?" I ask, changing the conversation. As hoped, he regales me with stories about Jeff's crazy driving, horrible sound guys, and how much the crowds love Jeff and Lolo's new stuff. I smile, picturing them all, and feel a little left out not being there with them. Maybe I should have taken Lolo up on her offer, I think as we hang up.

Another voice deep inside assures me I made the right decision to stay. Despite getting mugged. I pluck my guitar off the floor and close my eyes, playing the first thing that comes to me. I'm not sure what it is or where it's going, but I like the upbeat melancholic sound and play it over and over.

The lyrics just pour out as soon as I start singing. I flip open my laptop and press record. In less than an hour, I've finished writing the song. A couple more practice runs and then I video a full take so I don't forget it.

Inspired by my progress, I play the song I'd been working on before, fingerpicking the bridge Marc remembered for me. Again, lyrics just flow out of me, like they'd been sitting there the whole time, waiting to be set free.

By the end of the weekend I have written five new songs. Enough for my own album, I think. I'm don't know if they're any good, but it feels great to have created something of my own. I never felt like I was missing out on anything before. I always thought of collaborating as this magical energy creative people shared, out of which something exponentially more significant than either individual bore. Maybe I'm a narcissist, but I've never felt so connected to music before. Seth and I call it "our" music, and I sing and play guitar, but it's never really felt like mine. As soon as the thought crosses my mind, I picture Seth's face. A mixture of guilt and pleasure intermingle, leaving me confused and tired.

How do I tell the man I love—the one without whom I would still be stuck in that movie theater dreaming about music instead of playing it—that I want to record an album on my own? What kind of person am I that I can't be happy as partners? But then, who knows? Maybe he'll think it's a great idea and want to use my songs for Ida Bella's next album.

Instead of obsessing over What Ifs, I distract myself with some late-night spring-cleaning. I lose myself in the menial tasks of scrubbing grout, washing and folding laundry, setting aside neglected clothes for Goodwill, and emptying and scrubbing the fridge.

Hours later, purged of guilt and self-deprecating thoughts, I sink into the couch and sink blissfully into sleep. My dreams are filled with singing dolphins and me on a raft in the middle of the ocean, swaying with the tide. There's the sound of knocking, like someone is swimming below me, wanting to climb onto my raft.

I open my eyes only to realize the knocking is real.

Chapter 13

"What are you doing here?" I ask, rubbing the sleep from my eyes as I answer the door. Glowing afternoon light blinds my sensitive eyes and I squint in retaliation.

"Well hello to you too," Marc says, stepping inside.

He comes in, making himself comfortable on my couch. I stare, open-mouthed, before finally shutting my mouth and the door.

"I wanted to make sure you weren't stranded without a car," he says, picking up my guitar and smiling as he once-overs my apron and rubber gloves, still sitting on the coffee table from my frenzy. "And to make sure you were fully caffeinated."

"Sal had my car dropped off," I say, guilty discomfort prickling the nape of my neck. It feels inappropriate for him to be here, especially with Seth out of town. Normally Seth's jackets are strewn about, along with a myriad other clues of his inhabitance, but the obvious detritus is put away after my cleaning spree. There are framed photos if Marc looks for them, but he's just looking at me. Does he know that I'm married? Technically, we have a strictly professional relationship, if we have one at all. He wants to collaborate with me on songwriting. Nothing to feel guilty about there, right? But it felt like there was a shift last night. Or maybe that's in my head. Should I tell him that I'm married? Is that presumptuous? Maybe he already knows. A quick Google search would make it pretty obvious.

"What time is it?" I ask, wracking my brain for a way to get him out of my house.

"Two thirty. Why? Got somewhere to be?" he asks, still holding my guitar.

"Yeah, actually." I lie.

He grins, not believing me for a second. Even though

he's right, it annoys me that he can tell. He waits for me to elaborate. Shit. Now I have to come up with something— something that won't interest him at all—something that will make him run back to his harem of screaming fans.

"I'm going to an open mic," I say, squashing a smug smile.

He looks like he's debating my sanity. Then, to my surprise, he nods. "Got a guitar I can borrow?" he asks.

"You want to come?" I ask, unable to hide my shock. He's one of the most famous musicians in the world. He does not want to go to an open mic. I scramble for something to dissuade him. "Won't people bother you? Will the paparazzi follow you?"

I don't know how the whole fame thing works. Seth and I only get recognized at shows, and even then not everyone knows who we are. I can't imagine what it's like for the majority of people on planet Earth to know what you look like and everything you do.

"I'll try out my new disguise," he says. "And I don't think the paparazzi are expecting me at an open mic." He holds one finger up in a "just a minute" gesture as he disappears out the front door. I stand there waiting, freaked out that I might actually have to take Marc Justin to an open mic.

I can't take him anywhere Seth and I frequent and risk bumping into someone we know. For a variety of reasons, the least of which is guilt. There's only one place I can think of that's suitable. And now I'm going to have to play my new material onstage because all of Ida Bella's songs are duets. What the hell am I doing?

"You keep all that in your car?" I laugh, shocked by Marc's transformation. He traded in his board shorts and fitted t-shirt for a pair of faded Levi's, a Coexist shirt underneath a flannel, and a wig with chin length brown hair, covering his natural dark blonde. He's wearing big rectangular glasses and beat up Converse hi-tops. If I saw him on the street I wouldn't recognize him.

"It comes in handy," he says with a shrug. "What do you think? Do I get indie cred or what?"

"Or what," I say, smiling.

Chapter 14

"Where are you taking me?" Marc asks from the passenger seat of my hatchback.

"You'll see," I smile over my shoulder, merging into the exit lane.

There is an open mic in the Valley near Encino that I remember going to when Seth and I first came to LA. We hated it because it was full of uppity college hipsters, with no real opinions of their own, regurgitating whatever they'd heard on NPR. Nothing against NPR. I just prefer people with critical thinking skills.

When we get inside I let out a breath, relieved not to recognize anyone. We write our names on the sign up sheet and Marc orders coffees while I grab a table. I snag one in the corner by the window, close enough to the door that we can make a quick escape if necessary. Marc joins me, setting our drinks on the table. I let him borrow my Taylor and he takes it out of its case and tunes up.

"What's your story?" I ask, filling the quiet.

"My cover?"

"Yeah. Give me your backstory. Your motivation."

"Grew up in San Diego. Raised Christian, went to public school. I'm taking a year off to play music before I take over my family's restaurant. I wasn't popular, but I wasn't bullied either. Pretty normal, I guess. I'm close to my mom and sister, and they both lived with me until recently. I decided I was ready for some autonomy," he says.

I bob my head, sipping iced coffee.

"How much of that is true?"

He grins in answer.

"I've never had a relationship longer than a year. I don't think women are into relationships with guys who live with their mom."

"Huh." I can't tell if it's true, but I get the feeling it is. If so, I'm surprised to hear that he wants a relationship. Based on his public persona, it seems like the last thing he'd want.

"That's it?" He laughs.

"You surprise me. Is that better?"

"You might be a good listener, but it's tough to get much out of you," he says, narrowing his eyes. "What about you? What's your cover?"

I blush and look at the table.

"I don't need one. I'm already anonymous," I say.

"No way. Make one up," he says, leaning back in his chair. "I'll wait."

"Okay ... I'm a 26-year old fashion school dropout. I tried acting, but only got cast in kid's shows. I quit after an unfortunate puppeteering experience," I say.

He tries to keep a straight face, but his chest shakes with silent laughter.

I love that I make him laugh.

"What kind of music do you play?" he asks.

"Jim Henson?" interrupts the pimple faced MC, reading from her list of sign-ups.

I chortle, recognizing the famous puppeteer's name. Marc shakes his head and raises a hand. She motions for him to come up to the stage. She whispers something to him and he nods, pointing in my direction. Unsure about something, she shifts her weight from one foot to the other. He flashes her that All-American smile of his and, even through the disguise, I can see the effect is undiminished. She blushes and nods, fixating on her shoes.

He strolls back to our table and plops down, uninterested in telling me what just happened. I want to act all cool about it, but I'm not.

"Jim Henson, huh?" I say.

He grins and puts a finger to his lips.

"What did you say to her?"

A cheeky twist of his mouth is my only answer.

"Jim Henson and Penelope Caruso?" She squeaks into

the microphone.

I narrow my eyes, studying him. Where is this going? Unsure, I'm still enjoying this absurd game of improv. Isn't that the first rule of improvisation? Everything is always met with "Yes, and?"

On stage the MC covers the microphone with her hand and whispers to Marc, "You can only play one song on her set. It's supposed to be solo acts only." He throws a lazy arm around her shoulders, whispering in her ear. She nearly convulses on the spot before skittering offstage. I shake my head. Unbelievable.

He dips his head to me and I count us in. He remembers the song perfectly, playing little harmonics and small lead riffs in a way that is complimentary and dynamic, never overshadowing my rhythm. His style is so different from Seth's. I'm used to being the one to follow Seth's lead. Marc sits back and lets me do my thing, reacting in a call-and-answer style.

With Seth, he arranges Ida Bella's songs, and we rehearse until we know every part before ever stepping onstage. I've always found comfort in that because it leaves so little to chance. What Marc and I are doing is new to me. It's organic—very in the moment.

The audience of musicians and college kids offer a golf clap that's barely audible over the espresso machine. They don't care. At all. There was a time when that would have made me self-conscious, but it's kind of hilarious. And freeing. Marc hops offstage, clapping obnoxiously loud and I bow theatrically to him, no one taking any notice of either one of us.

I fingerpick the opening bars of the song I wrote right after the mugging. Scanning the audience, I look for signs that anyone is watching. A group in the corner talks a little louder than is polite, one girl orders coffee, a few loners hunch over tables, their faces lit blue from smartphones. One by one, heads lift up and conversations diminish. By the last chorus, I perform like I'm in front of thousands, rather than tens. I lose myself in the song, coming to at the unexpected sound of applause. Genuine applause. I'm speechless.

I take my seat while Marc plays an acoustic version of one of his hit songs, changing enough of the lyrics that no one else seems to realize what he's doing. Unable to hide my amusement, I wonder why he doesn't write his own songs. He's actually a talented guitarist. And his voice is better than it sounds on his singles.

It feels like a million years have passed as we drive back home—to my home. I glance at him, wondering what he's thinking.

"I really liked that new song you played," he says.

"Thanks." I smile.

"I know you don't think I'm serious, but I'm hiring you to co-write with me for my next album."

I peek over, assessing his seriousness. I hesitate to answer.

"How about I have my manager call you to work out the details and time?" he says. I sense a little irritation in his tone, but can't quite read him.

"Okay … " I say, shifting into park and turning my body to face him. His eyes soften as they meet mine.

"I had fun tonight," he says, one hand on the door handle.

"Me too," I say, stepping out of the car.

Despite the ease we've found in conversations, our physical barriers are in full effect and we stand in the driveway, facing one another, a couple of feet between us. He goes in for a hug. I go for the kiss on the cheek. It deteriorates into a mess of awkward hugging and face dodging until I just step back and wave. Way to make things weird, Penelope.

I don't hear from him the next day but I do get a call from his manager, Chris. He sets a meeting for Wednesday at Marc's label's building. There's a writing room reserved for us. I didn't know such things existed.

Now that we're working together through official channels I relax. It provides the clarification I needed, absolving any lingering guilt. Maybe we'll be friends too, but at least now I know his interest in me is professional. I can breathe a little easier as I head to class.

Sal acknowledges me from the front of the room as the other students file in. Throughout the lecture I take notes as diligently as always, play my new songs during critique, and forget that anything is different from any other week. Almost.

Sal motions for me to join him after he dismisses everyone else. I pack up and make my way down the stadium seating to the front, following Sal to his office. He closes the door behind me and crosses the room while I sit, waiting for him to direct the conversation. Sitting on the edge of his desk, facing me, he takes a deep breath.

"How are you?" he asks, worry etched across his weathered features.

"Fine," I say automatically.

He watches me: unsatisfied, from the looks of it.

"Really, I'm okay," I say. "I was pretty shaken up but Marc helped me calm down and made sure I got home okay."

Something flickers in Sal's eyes, but I can't quite figure it out. He sucks in air and shakes his head. "I'm glad to hear it. He's a good guy."

I agree. I want to ask him more about Marc because I'm thinking they must be pretty good friends for that to be the first person Sal called. But I don't because that's obviously not why he asked me here.

"I'm scrapping the project," he says without making eye contact.

I shoot out of my chair. "No!"

"I put you and everyone else in danger. I should've known better. I let my agenda get in the way of common sense. I shouldn't have brought all those guitars. It made us a target," he says more forcefully than I expected.

"You saw the way they transformed in there. We can't give up on them. Everybody else has already." My chest heaves and my voice is tight with the threat of tears. Sal watches me and I can tell he's torn. "Let's be the ones that show up. That keep showing up." A flurry of emotions passes over his expression and I stand up taller. "What about Tyrone? You can't take this away from him," I say.

Until this moment I had no idea how invested I was. The prospect of giving up on them infuriates me. It's not fair! I won't be the next person to deny them opportunities because of where they come from.

"We just need to find a safe meeting place," I say.

"Most of those kids don't have cars. How are they going to get there?"

"What about Santa Monica?" I say. "It's not that far away. They can take the bus. Surely we can find a space that will work?" Desperation seeps into my voice.

He sighs. "If anything else goes wrong or if I think any of us might be endangered, we pull the plug. Deal?" The look he offers leaves no doubt that it's non-negotiable. I nod.

"So … do you think you'll get your car back?" I ask.

Chapter 15

The anger I felt when Sal suggested giving up on those kids sits in my chest, vibrating with the car's engine. The whole drive downtown, sitting at red light after light, I mutter to myself. It's disappointing that Sal would even consider giving up after promising Tyrone we'd be back. Didn't he see the look in his eyes? It may be irrational, my devotion to helping them, especially Tyrone, but I don't care. He wants it so badly—I can see it in his eyes. If we don't help now, what will happen to him?

I park in the garage next to the skyscraper with the Pop Rocks Records sign blazing in all its neon glory. The elevator dings and takes me to the seventh floor. The doors slide open into an all black and silver mod styled reception area. A sign below the desk reads, "Pop Rocks Records." An emaciated would-be model, maybe eighteen-years old, sits behind the semicircular desk texting while talking into her headset. She glances at me, scowls, and drops her eyes back to her phone. I approach the desk, patiently waiting directly in front of her. She has to work to pretend I'm not there, and I give her credit: she does a good job of it.

After a too long pause I give up and slouch onto a black leather bench in the waiting area. The walls are covered in framed gold and platinum records, just in case you forget what they do here. I slip my phone out of my bag to text Marc, but before I can unlock the screen, his manager appears through a door that blends in perfectly with the black leather walls.

"Penelope? Chris," he says, shaking my hand. He ushers me away from reception, typing a code into the keypad next to the door. I follow him down a long hallway of closed doors and more framed records. I nearly slam into his back when he stops abruptly outside an open door, presumably the reserved writing room.

"Thank—," I start to say. His mouth twists in a half smile as he answers his phone, disappearing down the hall. He rounds the corner and I peek inside the open door to my left. Marc gets up from a black and white leather couch, beaming. Embarrassed at the memory of the awkward kiss/hug debacle the other night, I smile and wave.

"Thirsty? Hungry?" He waves a hand Vanna White style across the impressive array of snacks, espresso machine, wine fridge stocked with waters, kombucha, tea, Gatorade, and a mini bar.

"Fancy," I say. "How about a latte?"

Marc shrugs and dips down, moving his head around as he inspects the machine, reminding me of a monkey discovering a wheel. His face scrunches in confusion and he pushes a few buttons to no avail.

"Let me try." I find espresso grounds, scoop them into the portafilter and twist it into place. I grab milk from the fridge and pour it into the silver carafe, pointing the steamer wand inside.

"Look at you. Now who's fancy?" Marc says, folding his arms across his chest.

"Like most everyone else in LA, I've been a barista," I say.

He snags a spring roll from the tray next to me, popping it in his mouth while he watches me steam and froth the milk. I pour the coffee and milk into a mug and use a rag to wipe off the wand.

The room is laid out like a lounge, with a couch and over-stuffed chairs arranged conversationally near a wall with a projector screen rolled down. The kitchen separates one seating area from another. On the other side are a couple of bistro tables with simple black plastic and chrome chairs, a ping pong table and a variety of colorful overhead lights.

I carry my latte and plant myself in a seat at the table closest to the window. Marc follows, sitting across from me as I pull out a notepad and my favorite pen. It's not one of those fancy gift-type pens or anything. I just love the way the ink spreads evenly, flowing from one letter to the next. It never leaves anything extraneous, and I like that.

"Do you have any ideas for what kind of song you want to work on? Lyrics? Themes?" I ask, scribbling a heading into my notebook. I've never co-written before so I'm hoping I can take his lead without him realizing it.

"Something catchy, for sure. I want a killer hook," he says, looking around the room, his knee jackknifing up and down.

"Okay ..." I say. No idea what he wants, I think, doodling in my notebook. "How about theme? Is there anything you want to say?"

He wrinkles his forehead, thinking. "How about a love song? Everyone loves a love song." He flashes me his registered trademark smile and leans across the table on his forearms.

To keep from laughing out loud I have to bite my lip. I don't want to hurt his feelings, but I'm getting the distinct impression that he's used to just showing up and hearing what someone else has already come up with. Maybe he makes a suggestion or two and then goes back to his entourage. Yeesh.

"Why don't I just play a little and you let me know when I'm onto something you like." I look up at him and he relaxes back into his chair, feet splayed wide.

"Sure," he says.

This should be interesting.

***

By the time I get home I'm exhausted. Songwriting is usually exhilarating for me, but co-writing is something else. It's mostly stabbing in the dark, hoping for a magical light to beam down as if to say, "Yes, this is the best song ever written!" If only.

Despite that, I'm pretty excited about the song we came up with. Marc helped more than I expected, but I felt like I was able to take the lead. And it felt natural. The song is poppier than anything I've ever written, but it's cheeky—a little fun and a little sweet. Singing together while we wrote made it sound more emotional, but I'm sure that will be produced out of the final version.

I flop onto the couch and snag the remote. As soon as I do, my phone rings. Sal's name flashes on the screen.

"Can you come early tomorrow?" he asks when I answer.

"Sure. How early?" I have no idea what he's planning, but I'm hoping this bodes well for Tyrone and the others. Sal sounds excited and that makes me smile.

Zoning out in front of the TV, I watch all the shows Seth would be appalled by. Sometimes it's nice to just turn my brain off and let someone else's problems dominate the airspace. I never have trouble sleeping with their problems on my mind.

Chapter 16

"You get your car back?" I ask Sal, as I hoist myself into a car that looks identical to the one we took last time.

He shakes his head. "Insurance."

I nod, pretending to understand. My insurance would probably send a card with a picture of a car on it. If I were really lucky, they'd offer me a ten-speed Schwinn as a replacement.

We drive down I-5 and head West, away from South Central. My pulse quickens when we get to the exit we'd normally take, flashing back to that thug pyramid encroaching on us. As we near the Pacific Ocean I calm down and watch the world speed by.

Sal stops in a residential neighborhood outside a townhouse on the beach. Offering no explanation, he just says, "We're here." I'm skeptical, but at least I don't feel threatened.

A large white bus, the kind usually toting around be-camera-ed tourists, pulls in and I see familiar figures spill out. Tyrone is first off and he swaggers over, giving me a complicated handshake that I fumble my way through. He laughs and we end it with a fist bump. It's good to see him smile.

"What is this place?" I ask Sal.

The sparkle in his eyes reminds me of a kid on Christmas morning. I'm excited and I don't even know what for. Sal leads us up the stairs to the front door.

Most likely, this is a friend's house, so I expect it to be furnished like someone lives here. What I'm not expecting is a full-blown multi-million dollar studio. I've never been inside a studio quite this extravagant before and I can only imagine how incredible this looks to Tyrone and the others.

We've entered what looks like a lounge room, with two

red L-shaped couches forming a square around an upholstered coffee table. Two beverage fridges sit on either side of the couch. A massive flat screen that's playing a surf film covers the opposite wall.

To my right is a NASA mission control sized mixing board, covered with nobs and dials, flanked on either side by speakers of varying sizes. The upper half of the wall is glass, looking into two recording booths. Each is set up with microphones dangling from the ceiling. The larger has a drum kit, the smaller being the vocal/guitar booth. Despite being right on the water I can't hear the ocean. What kind of insulation do they use?

A guy, maybe mid-thirties, dressed all in black approaches Sal, reaching out to shake hands. "Nice to meet you, I'm Gus. Want a tour?"

We follow him through to the recording rooms and he points out the piano room, where a baby grand sits in the middle of a vaulted fabric-lined area with wooden panels evenly spaced throughout. Along one wall I see a vintage Rhodes piano, an organ, and a stringed instrument I don't recognize.

The next room over is large enough for a full band to record all at once, a transparent partition set up to keep the drums from bleeding into the rest of the mix. We circle back to the front, where the recording booths we saw from the mixing board are. It would be amazing to record here, but I couldn't afford ten minutes in this studio, let alone enough time to record an album.

The South Central boys are full of "Oh's" and "Damn's" at each new turn, skipping from one area to the next. Gus stops at the vocal booth. "Wait here," he says. He tips his head toward Sal and they exit the way we came in.

A minute later we hear Sal's disembodied voice piped in through a speaker in the booth. Tyrone points to it, covering his mouth, hopping from foot to foot. I'm as caught up in the excitement as they are and we all look around with goofy grins.

"You like this?" Sal asks.

We respond with a raucous, "Hell ya!"

"How do you feel about recording a single?"

"Wha—yeah!"

"Can you play the guitar part?" Sal asks, looking at Tyrone, who bites his lips between his teeth and bobs his head in affirmation.

"Anyone got rhythm?" Sal continues, motioning to the drum kit.

A couple of hands go up.

"Vocals?" Sal says, clearly enjoying himself.

They all raise their hands and look around, shoving each other playfully.

"Here's how it's gonna go. Ms. Penelope and I are going to give each of you parts. We'll rehearse first, then record. Yeah?"

The excited chatter escalates as Sal's voice comes back on. "Oh, and I almost forgot. You okay with a camera crew?"

The boys are beside themselves. I've never seen them focus the way they do now as we go over chords, lyrics and percussion parts. I was relieved when Sal decided to keep teaching them, but he has seriously outdone himself with this.

We're in full rehearsal mode when the five-man camera crew shows up. They train their lenses on us as we work out individual parts and start piecing them together. The song Sal wrote is perfect. It has plenty of parts for everyone with a catchy blues rhythm that everyone seems to like.

When I look up, Marc is sitting at the soundboard, deep in conversation with Sal. Gus approaches and they exchange a one-arm man-hug handshake combo. I can't hear what they're saying but it's making Sal happy, whatever it is. I'm guessing he and Sal organized this little studio adventure. And I'd be willing to bet that this is his studio.

Not two minutes later, a good-looking Hispanic man in a tailored suit, followed by two smartly dressed women walk in, shaking hands first with Marc, then Sal, and finally with Gus. Unable to contain my curiosity, I join them.

Sal pulls me over, proudly introducing me to the mayor of Los Angeles. I'm flabbergasted. How did this happen? I glance over in Marc's direction. He sits with one ankle casually resting on the other knee, leaning back in the sound engineer's chair. Looking mildly amused as usual, I get the impression he's downplaying something. I wish I knew what he was thinking. Is he trying to impress me? I dismiss the possibility almost as soon as it pops into my head, but can't wipe the smile off my face at the thought.

When we bring the boys into the sound booth and set them up for their parts, Sal pulls me aside in the hall.

"I don't know how you got him to do this, but thank you."

"Who, Marc?" I ask.

"I thought we were going to have to pull the plug on the whole thing."

"Marc did this because of me?" I ask, incredulous.

Sal gives me a funny look. I'm not sure what to say. Hurrying down the hall back to the mixing board, I take a seat next to Marc, peeking over at him.

Two hours later, the kids are all heading home. The production crew has Sal doing some interview segment and Marc and I are left alone in the studio. I'm exploding with curiosity.

"I heard this was your doing," I say. "What prompted the philanthropy?"

"When you came in the other day you told me they needed somewhere to practice. I needed a tax write-off. Simple." Marc shrugs. He's not making eye contact, which I've learned means that he's embarrassed. I'm not going to let him shrug it off. It's an amazing thing he did for these kids, something they'll never forget.

"How did you get the mayor?"

"I'd tell you, but then I'd have to kill you," he says.

I stare him down. I'll wait here all night. He stares back, cracking in under a minute. Amateur.

"His daughter is a fan. I played her birthday party last year."

"Marc Justin plays birthday parties? Is it possible? A sellout with good intentions?" I ask, bringing a hand to my chest in mock-horror.

"If it helps someone it's never selling out," he says matter-of-factly.

I don't have a response to that. It's a good point.

"I'd only ever refuse if it were against my personal ethics," he says, as though considering the subject for the first time.

"Do you like playing birthday parties?" I ask, trying to wrap my head around his perspective.

"I wouldn't go that far. But I like kids. And making a kid happy, whether it's the mayor's daughter or Tyrone from South Central, is a good thing."

I ponder this surprisingly deep thought. I have heard Seth's take on selling out a million times. "Commercializing your art is selling out," he always says. "The second you create music with sales numbers in mind, you lose control and give in to the mediocrity of the masses."

I thought I agreed with him, but funnily enough, I agree with Marc too. If an hour of his time a year ago not only made one little girl happy, but also helped raise funding for a group of disenfranchised youth, allowing them to see a light at the end of their otherwise dreary tunnel, that's anything but mediocrity. Isn't that what art—and music—is meant to do? Connect us?

"Since we've got this studio all to ourselves … " he says, mischief in his eyes. My stomach clenches, waiting to see where he's going with this. He smiles and I squirm under his unflinching gaze. It's my turn to look away.

"We should record your EP here, now."

The breath catches in my lungs and I struggle to regulate the flow of air. My palms break out in a sweat.

"Just vocals and guitar," he says.

"In here? But this must cost…" I protest. He waves it off and waits for me to answer. "Right now?"

"Why not?" he says.

Sal reappears and I shift in my seat, not wanting to leave,

but feeling weird about letting my ride go without me.

"I'm all set. You want to come with me or are you sticking around here?"

I look to Marc and he nods to Sal. Sal shakes his hand and waves to me.

Marc hands me a guitar case. "I saw you eyeing this at my house."

It's the Gibson I was scared to play. I smile, running my fingers over the strings along the fretboard. He doesn't say anything else, but adjusts himself behind the soundboard. Inside the booth, with this beautiful guitar, I'm flustered by his thoughtfulness. Take a deep breath. I can't believe I'm doing this.

After an hour of laying guitar tracks, we move on to vocals.

"Try that chorus again, a little raspier this time," he says.

I listen back in the headphones, awaiting my cue, bobbing in time to the song.

He coaxes better performances out of me, take by take. He's encouraging without pandering and I feel comfortable losing myself in the songs, trusting his direction.

It's the middle of the night by the time we're finished. A whole EP. My EP. He hands me the CD and Sharpies my name across it with the date.

"You've got some great songs on here. You should be proud," he says.

"Thanks," I say, staring in awe at my name handwritten on the CD.

"How would you feel about opening for me on my summer tour?" he says.

"You can't be serious."

"Why not?"

I purse my lips, crossing my arms over my chest.

"You'd be great," he says. I can't think of where to start. Why would he want me to open for him?

"Plus, I could come out at the end of your set and we could do the song we wrote together. It would be the perfect introduction to my fans," he says. If I didn't know better, I'd say he looked nervous.

"What about the dancing half-naked girls who usually open? I hardly think your label would consider me a good replacement," I say with more bitterness than intended.

He looks down and I feel bad. Here I am insulting him after he's been nothing but nice to me. I'm such a jerk!

"I'm sorry," I say. "Can I think about it? Give you time to change your mind?" I look up at him. "You might not want me on tour, I can be a real jerk," I say, relieved to see a smile tugging at the corners of his lips.

"Come on, let's get out of here," he says. "You hungry?"

"Are you trying to make me fat?" I say and nudge his shoulder with mine. He lingers there, shoulder to shoulder, his body heat warming my skin. I shoot out of the chair, heart racing.

Chapter 17

For the next week I vacillate between touring with Marc and not. Was he motivated by my talent or wanting to sleep with me? His behavior has been friendly and professional, but men are always thinking about sex—or so I've been told.

I hated how naïve I felt when Seth suggested Sal had ulterior motives. That's not a trap I want to get caught in. But then, if the gender roles were reversed, would I have this dilemma? Probably not. That's the worst part: that I'm not sure I deserve the opportunity on merit alone.

Seth doesn't even know about the offer yet, which leaves an unsettled feeling in my stomach. With such a strong personality I need to know exactly what I want before I can handle him weighing in. For once, Seth doesn't know the best thing for me, professionally.

Touring with Marc would definitely be fun. We make each other laugh and he gets me thinking about things in a different way, which I love. It's exciting, spending time with him. That combination registers as slightly inappropriate for a married woman on my ethics meter. Even though I know nothing would ever happen.

The needle on that meter eeks over a bit more since I've never told him I'm married. After we didn't talk about it that first day, it seemed presumptuous to force into conversation later. Besides, I'm sure he knows. A simple Google search would tell him all about Ida Bella and Seth and me, the cute married duo. Okay, I'm rationalizing. I know that. I have to tell him. Eliminate the variable. But the question remains: will it change the offer?

The rest of the week and weekend blend together as I hide out at home, pretending to catch up on emails and social media promotion while actually clicking through photo albums from Ida Bella's first national tour.

We booked every show ourselves and played to more empty rooms than I can count. Paid in bar tabs mostly, occasionally selling enough CDs to cover gas, we crashed on friends' couches and floors. Some were more comfortable (and hygienic) than others. And we had the best time.

Seth made everything fun. He'd always pull over to check out the weird and interesting. We stopped at the most random places: posing in front of Meteor Crater, AZ; a giant NASA spaceship in Alabama; inside a gator's mouth in Florida; and on the roof of our car driving through a tunnel carved in an ancient redwood tree in California.

There was one show at a dive bar in Austin, Texas that stands out most in my memory. It made me realize just how lucky I was to have Seth. The stage manager double-booked the show. His exact words were, "I have a headache. I'd rather listen to you than those assholes."

The other band, a screamo rock group, instead of storming off, sat there with a handful of die-hard fans at the foot of the stage, booing us at top volume. They were so loud I couldn't hear my monitor. And so close to the stage I worried they'd rush it. I was terrified. My hands shook so much I could barely hold my guitar. My chin was doing the don't-cry-quiver, and I worried what they'd do to me if I cried, which only made it harder to keep it together.

Seth played the first chord, walked around to the front of the stage and turned his back to the audience, shielding me from them. He locked his eyes on mine and pulled me back into our bubble. In his eyes I lost myself, and we sang only to each other.

The haters didn't applaud, but they at least stopped booing. Some sort of silent exchange between Seth and the lead singer transpired. Whatever happened in that silent man-duel inspired him to go and take his minions with him.

"You were great," Seth said as though nothing were different from any other show. I wanted to jump him right then and there. I felt so safe and loved, certain that Seth would always put himself between me and harm.

I hug my knees to my chest, suddenly missing him in a painfully visceral way. Seth and I have been together for nearly a third of my life. The only reason I can even hypothetically entertain the idea of loving anyone else is that I take for granted he is part of me. Sometimes it feels like there is no difference—like we are a single entity with enough cells to make up two forms.

By Sunday night, I make my decision. I will tell Marc no. Not because of anything inappropriate or because I worry about his motives, but because Seth and I are a single entity, and Ida Bella is our baby. I cannot and will not abandon them for anyone. Either Marc and I can be friends or we can't, but either way, I don't want to keep up this façade of me as a solo artist. Who knows, maybe he'll want Ida Bella to open instead. Seth has always had my back and now I get to have his.

"Hey Babe," Seth says, checking in for the night.

"How's it going?" I say, contemplating whether to have this conversation on the phone.

"Good. But I can't wait to get home to you," he says.

Aww.

"I think we should plan a tour when I get home. Sound good?"

I close my eyes, pinching the bridge of my nose between my thumb and forefinger. I should feel relieved. That's what I wanted. Now he does too. For some inexplicable reason, I'm annoyed. It's the way he said it: like it's all his idea. Whose idea it is shouldn't matter, but it grates on me. Enough that I resolve not to tell him about Marc's invitation to tour. It's moot, anyway.

"So now you want to tour?"

"I thought that's what you wanted," he says, irritation creeping into his tone.

I'm gripping the edge of the kitchen table hard enough that sharp pain needles my fingertips. I let go and walk down the hall instead.

"Yeah, I did. I do. Let's do it." I smile, hoping to infuse

enthusiasm I don't quite feel.

"You don't sound sure. Am I missing something?"

I should have known I couldn't hide anything from him. But I don't know what to say, or why I'm so annoyed with him. Not really.

"I'm glad you want to tour. It's just that you said you didn't want to—," I sigh. Here goes. "And then Marc Justin asked me to tour with him."

Silence.

"You there?"

"He saw you play one set." I can practically hear Seth's forehead wrinkle in confusion. "And weeks later, he finds you and asks you to open for him? I don't get it."

"I've seen him a few times since then." I say, trying not to stumble over my words, making it sound like I was keeping it from him. "He was the guest speaker in my class. And he picked Sal and me up after we got robbed," I say. Seth inhales sharply and my toes tingle uncomfortably. "Also, his label hired me to write a song with him. So it's not totally out of the blue," I add, the knot in my stomach tightening. And he recorded my EP, I want to say, but don't.

"And you never mentioned any of that?" he says on a short breath. I hear the swish of fabric and picture him pacing. "You didn't tell me about him at all, even when I talked to you that night and offered to come home."

"It didn't seem relevant," I say. "We don't get long to talk and I'd rather hear what you're up to." The only sound is my pulse thumping between my ear and the phone. "I'm sure there are tons of things I don't know about your day-to-day."

"I would have told you about another woman," he whispers.

That phrase triggers me. How is it that when a man and woman work together it's automatically sexual? I enjoy writing songs. A famous singer hired me to write with him. Through a class I'm taking he saw more of my talent and based on my work, offered me an amazing professional opportunity. Why doesn't Seth think he wants me for my creative talent?

"I would have told you about another man," I say, my voice wavering. I take a deep breath. "I accepted a job writing for a major artist. He was impressed with the song we wrote and asked me to tour with him. I didn't tell you because I didn't want to be judged by you."

I can barely hear his breathing on the other end of the call. He must have stopped pacing. Neither of us says anything. Finally, he lets out a breath.

"Look, we have an early drive tomorrow. I'll be home in two days. Can we talk about this then?"

"Sure."

"'Kay. I love you," he says.

"You too."

My hands are shaking and blood rushes to my cheeks as I end the call. Maybe I don't have the right to be angry since I've questioned Marc's motives too. All I heard from Seth's wording was "There's no way it's professional," implying that he doesn't think I deserve the opportunity unless Marc desires me sexually. How could I not be offended by that?

I like Marc. He's a cool person. And maybe, possibly, if I'd been single when we met I'd like him in that way too. But I'm not and I don't. He likes my music. That's flattering. I don't think I should have to apologize for thinking so. Despite his assertions to the contrary, Seth wouldn't have done anything differently if the situation were reversed. Marc has been kind and generous, rescuing Sal and me in South Central, hiring me to write with him, offering his studio and connections for the kids. Not to mention my EP.

He helped me produce something original. I appreciate that. Isn't producing originality what Seth is always preaching? Shouldn't that apply to me too? Or … not if it hurts his ego? Ugh!

Chapter 18

The next day I go to the beach. It's cold but sunny, and I'm craving the fresh air. I want to have an honest conversation with Seth and to do that means I need to exorcise my anger and indignation before he gets home. Deliberately practicing patience, I wait for the slowest barista in Malibu to make my latte. The food truck isn't here yet, but I can't help but look over to where it usually is.

And wouldn't you know it, Marc is across the street. He's obviously been jogging, from the trailing rivulets of sweat gleaming on his skin. He spots me and waves. Leaning over, hands on thighs, he catches his breath before jogging toward me, hands out in a "What are you doing here" gesture.

"Stalking me again?" I ask.

"Hello to you too," he says, his breathing still ragged after his workout. "A girl I know told me this is the best coffee. How could I resist?"

I feel the heat rise in my cheeks. It's sweet that he remembered me saying I like the coffee here.

"Everything okay?"

"Yes," I lie.

"Are you acting weird because you haven't decided about the tour yet?"

"Maybe."

"That's okay. I can wait a little longer. Mind if I join you? I promise not to talk business," he says, crossing his finger over his heart like a third grader.

"Okay," I say, exhaling in relief. I hadn't realized I was holding my breath.

We take our lattes across the parking lot and he follows as I pick out a dry patch of sand. The So-Cal freezing 50-degree day forces most Angelinos indoors, leaving the beach abandoned. I tip my head to the sun, enjoying my favorite kind of day at the beach. In my head I'm the only person in existence, the ocean waving to me alone.

Marc leans back, relaxing into the sand and I instinctively want to stop him. He's going to get sand everywhere, even in his hair. I watch him and envy his carefree all-is-right-with-the-world attitude. I sigh. I seem to be doing a lot of that lately. After a short internal battle, I decide that this is the time to decline Marc's offer.

"There's something I need to tell you."

"Uh-oh," he says, sitting up, brushing the sand off his hands.

"I should have done it a while ago," I say, studying my coffee cup. Stop stalling! Why is saying no so hard?

His sits taller, his shoulders rigid as he watches me.

"I can't tour with you," I say. "I'm already in a band with my husband. I need to focus on that." I hold my breath and force my eyes back up to his face. He stands up and I look into his blue eyes, steeled for defense.

"Are you leaving?" I ask.

"Why didn't you just tell me that before?" he says.

"I don't know. I guess I should have." I can't look at him.

"Yeah, you should have."

He looks down at me and shakes his head. He opens his mouth like he's about to say something, and then stops himself. "I knew you were too good to be true," he says, half under his breath, as he walks away, leaving me in stupefied silence to wonder if he's right.

That wording—that sounded personal, not professional. So he just wanted in my pants the whole time? Congratulations, Seth. You were right. It was never about my talent. I can't breathe. Winded, as though punched in the gut.

The highs and lows clash in my head as I attempt to process the conflicting emotions all at once. Something else niggles at me too, something that tightens in my chest, but I don't have room for that right now. I was so wrong about everything. Now that it's over I can get back to how things were before.

I stand up, swiping the sand from my legs. I needed to simplify my life and he just helped me do that. Good riddance, Marc Justin. At least I can be proud of what Ida Bella puts into the world, even if it's not all mine.

I pick up a rock and skip it as hard as I can into the water. A wave crashes over it on the second skip and I pick up another. I can't stand still. That look in his eyes—that sadness—lingers in my mind. I shake my head to dispel the image. I'll probably never see him again. Maybe that's for the best. In fact, I'm sure it is.

Chapter 19

Leaning against the open doorway, I watch Seth, Lolo and Jeff pull into the driveway. They tumble out of the van like cartoon clowns, clumsy after so much time cramped in their seats. Despite the trip, Lolo is glowing and beautiful, talking a million miles an hour at Jeff and Seth. Spotting me, she squeals and crushes me in a hug.

It's hard to laugh and keep up with what she's saying, and I can only catch every third word or so.

"Ohmigod, you … seen … manager there … so excited … Coachella!" she says, arms and fro flailing. She's aglow with excitement and I realize it doesn't matter what she's saying. My friend apparently had the time of her life and I'm so happy for her.

Jeff stands by the van shaking his head. Catching my eyes he dips his head in knowing amusement and I smile. Dark circles line his eyes, and his shoulders slump forward like his back is tired of propping him up. He and Seth talk in hushed tones. I get the distinct impression I've been the topic of unflattering conversation.

"Want to come in? I can make something to eat," I say to Lolo. She looks toward Jeff who politely declines. I don't blame him. In his shoes I'd want to go home and sleep in my own bed too.

It takes Seth an eternity to unload his gear from the van. He hasn't said one word to me yet, not that Lolo gave him a chance. That's not the reason though. I know him well enough to know that he's still pissed and doesn't want to talk to me. I'm not exactly his biggest fan right now either (even if his concerns were merited) but I resolve to take the high road and move forward.

Emptying the last of his gear, he does the one-arm man-hug with Jeff and allows himself to be squished into a full hug by Lolo. I get pulled into the group and let Lolo's excitement electrify us all. As the van disappears down the driveway we wave goodbye, our smiles fading from view with them. Seth's shoulders are inches from mine and I'm aware of the space keeping us from touching. This is ridiculous.

I turn, wrapping my arms around his waist but it's like hugging a tree. He makes no effort to reciprocate. Fine. Let him be angry. I tried to pierce his silent armor, but it's his turn now. It's petty and ridiculous and I'm not interested in speaking to him until he can act like an adult. Okay, so maybe I'm only 99% high road.

Back in the kitchen, where I'd been making dinner before I heard them pull up, I mix the salad, pull the chicken and sweet potato fries from the oven and make myself a plate. I leave the rest in the kitchen. He can serve himself if he's hungry.

This level of discord has never existed in our relationship. We each feel entitled to an apology from the other. I don't know how Lolo and Jeff do this all the time. After fifteen minutes of not speaking, hearing each other's movements in different rooms, I'm going crazy.

I catch a glimpse of Seth's lean silhouette on his way to the kitchen and I wait for him to join me on the couch with dinner. He scarfs something in the kitchen and heads out back. The hose starts running and I peek through the window to see him watering cacti. This is ridiculous.

I hate being the mature one, but I can't take any more of this.

"Seth?"

He looks up from his watering.

"Those don't need to be watered. They're succulents," I say.

"It doesn't mean they never need water," he says, resuming his task.

Waiting for Zen Master Cacti Whisperer to say more, I stand on the top step. When he doesn't continue, I spin on my heels, letting the door thwap shut behind me.

The floorboards groan in protest of my stomping down
the hall to our bedroom. For clarity, I close that door too.
Anger courses through me, making my skin itch like I'm
molting. My fingers drum the air, restless. I need to keep busy.
Too bad I already cooked and cleaned. There's no way I'm
going out there to let Seth ignore me anyway, so I pick up my
guitar and play one of my new songs.

It's amazing how quickly it relaxes me. I close my eyes,
singing just loud enough to hear myself over the guitar. My
upper body sways in time, my toes dangle off the edge of the
bed.

When I open my eyes, Seth stands in the doorway,
watching me. I stop singing, and mute the guitar with the side
of my hand, keeping my expression neutral.

"What song was that?" he asks.

I barely control the urge to roll my eyes. That's what he's
going to break the silent treatment to ask? "It's mine," I say.

"You wrote it?"

"Don't sound so surprised. I said it's mine, didn't I?"
Defensiveness isn't productive, but I don't appreciate the
evident shock in his tone.

"It's good," he says, his voice flat.

"Thanks." I try to keep my voice as flat as his, but I can't.
I'm too filled with smug validation that he likes my song. His
critique both means the most and terrifies me the most.
Under other circumstances his compliment would have me
on cloud nine.

He exhales and steps around the bed, sitting down next to
me. I move to put the guitar down but he stops me.

"Play something else for me," he says.

I think we're still fighting, but now I can't tell. Music is
our common language so maybe it makes sense that this is
how we make up. I play him the song I wrote after the
mugging, which loosely alludes to the event itself. Mostly it's
a metaphor for being knocked off balance and losing your
center.

I close my eyes to sing because I'm not ready for his line

by line editing (which I know he's doing in his head). I project my voice fully this time and perform like I'm on stage. When I reach the last notes of the song I open my eyes and watch him. The coldness is gone and I see warmth and affection in them again. I'm so relieved I almost cry. But I don't. I wait.

"I'm sorry," he says.

"Me too."

"I never meant to make you feel like I doubted your talent," he says.

"I should have shown you my songs earlier," I say. I watch his reaction carefully and his shoulders slump forward.

"Babe, I just ... I got jealous. I don't want another man seeing a part of you that I don't," he says. "And I hated that he was there for you when I wasn't. It just brought up some insecurities I thought I'd outgrown."

"That's okay. I didn't mean to keep any of it from you. If the roles were reversed I might feel the same," I say.

He nods and takes the guitar from me, carefully setting it on the ground. He pulls me into him and we fall onto the bed, limbs instinctively wrapping around one another. I'm not convinced it's really the end of this conversation, but feel a familiar lightness between us again, and know it's going to be okay. I told Marc about Seth and I told Seth about Marc's offer. With my integrity intact I'm certain all will return to normal soon. And that's enough ... for now.

Chapter 20

Sal and I pull up to a nondescript strip mall in Santa Monica on Thursday afternoon. One of Sal's longtime friends gave us permission to hold lessons at this guitar shop for as long as we want. It seems like our best bet for a permanent solution. We step inside the cramped space. There doesn't seem to be room for all of us in here.

Scotty, the owner, grunts a hello to Sal and leads us to a humidified room in the back with a handful of chairs set up in a circle.

"This is what I got," Scotty says.

"Appreciate it," Sal says and leans his guitar against the wall.

Antique and custom-made masterpieces line the upper walls. Scotty may be monosyllabic, but he knows quality instruments. While we wait for the boys to arrive I tune up. There's no question it's a step down from last week, but I'm glad to be in a place that doesn't remind me of anything but music.

The mayor was impressed with what we're doing for the South Central kids and offered a decommissioned school bus to take the them from South Central to Santa Monica so they could continue working with us. A flash of yellow reflects in the glass window as the bus pulls into the parking lot and they disembark.

"Big star coming through! No autographs, please," Tyrone says, putting a hand up to stop the invisible paparazzi. Two of the other boys pretend to be fans and then shouts erupt, each claiming to be the real star. There are grins all around, and I notice that none of them has his hood up. I can't help myself; I smile.

Questions about what's going to happen with the documentary, how they can get gigs and make money from music start almost immediately. This level of excitement and enthusiasm for learning and writing makes them unrecognizable from that first day.

Sal and I make our way around to each of them, answering questions and working on new songs. It's easy to get lost in the lesson, and before I know it, time is up. As we're packing up to leave, Tyrone takes me aside.

"Ms. Penelope?" he says. "Can you help me with somethin' real quick?"

"Sure, Tyrone."

"Well I got these lyrics … or like, a poem," he says, shifting his weight from side to side. "And I was wondering if you could give me some, like, chords to put music to 'em?"

"May I?" I ask, reaching for his scribbled notebook. I glance through the stanzas, which are already written in standard verse/verse/chorus form. His rhymes and poignant use of metaphor are impressive. I look up at him. He's watching me with earnest brown eyes, looking like a small child seeking approval.

"You're a fantastic writer," I say. He stares at his shoes in answer to my compliment, so I change tacks.

"What kind of mood do you want to set?" I ask.

"What do you mean? Like, what kinda song?"

"Yeah. Do you want it to feel moody and dark or maybe happy and upbeat?"

"The song's about a drive by. It's not real happy or upbeat," he says.

I smile. "Sometimes it's powerful to use a different musical tone to heighten the meaning of the lyrics."

He blinks, staring at me like I've lost my mind.

"Okay, you know the song 'Pumped Up Kicks'?" I ask. He nods. "That's a fun song, right?"

"If you like that music, I guess." Tyrone says.

"Well it's about a kid getting shot for his shoes," I say, watching him carefully. I see his face register my meaning and I continue, "So by making it a fun song, it's highlighting the absurdity of the situation."

"I get it … I think. But nah, my song is just sad … and angry."

"Okay. So let's try this." We sit down with our guitars, playing with different chords and tempos until Tyrone says, "Yeah, I like that."

He records me playing it with his phone. The chords are ones he knows, but I write them down to make sure can practice on his own. As he heads out to the bus, I smile at the spring in his step. It's an amazing thing to help someone follow his passion. Working with Tyrone gives me the nagging feeling that Seth may be right: the mechanics of songwriting can be taught, but having something to say may be beyond that scope. It comes from somewhere within. I just hope I carry it in my soul, like Tyrone. Like Seth. Like anyone worth listening to.

Chapter 21

"Lo! Over here," I wave from the balcony of our favorite coffee shop. She pays the cashier and skips over to the table where I'm sitting. I watch her flit about and smile. I've missed her.

"How was the tour? I want to hear everything. Don't leave out a single detail," I say.

"Ohmigod! I wish you'd been there. It was fan-fucking-tastic!" she says, her hand on mine. Her eyes widen and light up as she tells me all about the producer who heard them play in Austin and invited them back to SXSW to perform on the main stage. "He said he loved my voice, but didn't take his eyes off my rack," she laughs.

"Did that bother you?" I ask.

"Hell no! If he makes business decisions with his dick, that's on him, not me."

"Fair point," I say, nodding. I'm jealous how easily she lets it roll off her back.

"What's up? How's your celebrity stalker?" Lolo asks with typical candor.

I throw my head dramatically onto the table, groaning. I tell her all the sordid details, from the mugging to that night at his house, to the studio, to the fight with Seth. She listens to my diatribe like the good friend she is, and then waits for me to give some indication as to what I need to hear. I can't help her. A part of me is sad I'll never see Marc again, but I feel good about Seth's response to my songs, which makes me wonder why I care about Marc at all.

"Did anything happen between you and Marc?"

"No."

"Did you want it to?"

"For one moment I thought I did," I admit, unable to look at her. "But it was after the mugging and I don't even think it was about him. Not really."

She watches me, silently awaiting her best friend
polygraph results. Despite the facts being in my favor, I do
feel like I have something to hide.

"Aren't you and Seth in the studio next week?"

"Yeah, we're doing that film soundtrack I told you about,"
I say.

"Tell him you want some of your new songs on it. Give
him the chance to show you how amazing he thinks you are,"
she says.

I turn the idea over in my mind, trying to see it from
every angle. It's genius! I never gave Seth the chance to love
my originals. He said he liked the song I played him the other
night. Maybe she's right. Maybe he will surprise me, and even
be excited that I want to contribute as a writer. It's unfair I've
never given him that chance.

By the time we say goodbye my happy state is restored. I
definitely need to spend more time with Lolo. Only a
girlfriend can put things in perspective for me when
everywhere I look the world is muddled and blurry.

Chapter 22

"What about hand percussion instead of a full kit? It's more soundtracky," Seth says as we sit down at the kitchen table to make our final notes before heading into the studio. I sip my coffee, nodding.

I give him space as he listens to the songs in his head. This is the side I've never been great at: arranging parts and intuitively understanding whether a song should be broken down and more acoustic, or which other instruments would enhance it.

"Which songs should we record?" I ask.

He names a bunch of our most popular new songs and stops at around seven tracks. I let him pause to think. It's now or never.

"What about one of my new songs? You said you liked the one I played the other night?" I say with what I hope sounds like nonchalance. I can't look at him. The thumps of my heart beat wildly in my chest.

"I'm not sure it's an Ida Bella song," he says. "The filmmakers specifically asked for Ida Bella." He studies his empty plate. "Maybe we could record it and see? We should also consider songs we cut from the last album."

I know what he's saying is logical. It's true, Ida Bella is a brand and our fans and employer have expectations, but my ego is not as understanding. I'm well aware of our band's sound, thanks. Seeing as I make up half of it, he's kidding himself if he thinks the songs I wrote wouldn't fit in with our sound. For the sake of productivity, I set that aside. If we have any chance of returning to our typical rhythm of life and work, I have to. My head pounds with the residual metronome of my pulse, my skull feeling two sizes too small.

Maybe I'm aspiring to a new kind of homeostasis. I want to pursue my passion. Writing and recording my own EP lit a spark from somewhere within a darkened part of me. It feels like something I have to do. If I don't, there will be serious spiritual consequences.

Outside of work, Seth and I settle back into our routine. We wake up, make breakfast, work, go for hikes, and eat dinners together on the couch watching TV. Since we're recording next week, we haven't scheduled any shows, which gives us a nice break. Originally Seth said he wanted our new album to catch on organically, which meant not touring or seeking press. But then on the phone he wanted to tour. Since then, he hasn't brought it up again. If I don't bring it up, will he? Part of me is afraid he only suggested it to pacify me.

Not that I'm keen to record a soundtrack while planning a tour. I'm not insane. The extra time buffers our heated emotions and provides some much needed head clearing before we go into the studio. It's a relief not to have any plans, but I find myself missing our little misfit community.

"Seth," I say, finding him in the back yard. "We haven't done a Moonlight Monday show in a while. What if we do one next week?"

"As in, five days from now?" He snaps at an unruly shrub near the back fence with dull pruning shears.

"Yeah, do you think that's too soon?"

"I'll ask around," he says, losing the battle with the shrub. He lowers the shears and wipes his forehead with his free arm. His forearm shines with sweat and I can see the outline of his lean musculature through his thin t-shirt. I nakedly admire him as he pulls out his phone and starts tapping.

I pad to the kitchen and bring out two big glasses of ice water. Handing one to Seth, I sit down at the little bistro table with mine. He sets his down and resumes his battle with the shrub. I watch him, wiping condensation from my glass, absentmindedly contemplating water's enviable ability to be containable at room temperature, escaping when it becomes too hot or cold. Smart molecules.

Chapter 23

Moonlight Mondays are always fun. I'm particularly giddy with anticipation about this one. Seth is the only one who knows I'm going to play a five-song set of my own music. We'll perform together too, but I need to introduce myself as an artist of my own to our community.

When I asked, "What do you think about me performing solo?" Seth responded with an underwhelming, "Cool." At least he didn't try to talk me out of it, I guess.

It's a new challenge; one that Sal has been encouraging me to take. He keeps telling me, "To grow as a writer, you have to put yourself out there." And there's no more out there than playing in front of friends, peers, and my husband and creative partner.

Reworking guitar parts and adjusting my inflection, I play around with tempos and strumming patterns to see if I can get them sounding more polished. I workshop the songs in class, absorbing constructive feedback, trying not to internalize the negative. Hipsters gotta hate, but sometimes they're right.

By Monday afternoon I have decorated the yard, swept the stage and seating areas, put out tables, chopped and stored veggies, made a new yogurt dip, organized serving dishes and drinks, and tuned my guitar. Seth finds me outside. His mouth twitches up at the corners as he leans against the side of the house watching me tweak the positioning of the instruments onstage.

"Looks great," he says.

"You think? I might move the stage a little to the right. It's not quite centered."

"That stage weighs a ton," he says, smirking openly. "No one has ever complained. Or noticed. It's fine."

"Mmm," I mumble, unable to focus on anything besides

the asymmetry. I use my body, pushing all my weight behind the left side of the stage. It doesn't budge. Seth is right; it's too heavy.

"Want help?" he says. I scrunch my nose and shake my head.

I sigh. Time to give it up. I tilt my face to the warmth of the sun, glowing gold through a thin layer of clouds. Breathe. Focus on the twittering of birds, leaves rustling in the breeze, and cars humming in the distance. They're just nerves. It'll be okay.

Whether people like my music or not, the point is that I enjoy making it. Who am I kidding? I want them to like it. I can't help it. I want Seth to like it. More than like, I want him to feel it.

I repeat my calming mantra as I take a shower, get dressed, and wait for everyone to arrive. Even though the Hotel Café show went well, I can't help but wonder if it was a fluke. Or worse, if they were just being nice. I've definitely been guilty of saying, "Great job!" When what I really meant was, "Good thing that's over."

We won't have as many as usual because we didn't give them enough notice, but all the regulars are coming.

Lolo and Jeff are first to arrive, and Lolo joins me in the kitchen and helps me carry the hors d'oeuvres out to the tables. We snack on chips and salsa and chat about silly things, catching up on gossip. Lolo really knows how to get my mind off of things. She's like a nurse, expertly distracting me before jabbing the needle in. Before I know it the house is full of people milling about, slowly making their way out back.

Now that it's spring it stays lighter later. The golden lights glow against the navy sky, as Seth and I take the stage to welcome everyone who came.

"We're going to try something a little different tonight," Seth says into the microphone. "My lovely wife ..." he says, motioning to me. The crowd cheers. It's nice to be surrounded by friends. "... has been busy. I leave her alone for two weeks to tour with those two," he says, pointing to

Lolo and Jeff in the crowd. Jovial groans and snickers erupt around them. "And she bails on me and starts writing her own songs." The crowd goes along with him, pretending to be horrified. I smile and Lolo nods to me. She's the only one who understands the element of truth lurking beneath his sarcasm.

"So on this Moonlight Monday, there's a new rule. We're only playing new songs," he says, smiling at their collective gasp. Everyone looks around, shifting in their seats. I can practically hear them going through their song catalogues. These are professionals who enjoy the safety that comes from playing worn-in songs. They try out new songs at home or in front of easy crowds, not in front of other musicians, offering themselves up for judgment. I am as surprised as everyone else, but I catch Seth's gaze and tip my head in silent appreciation. He knows I'm nervous and he's looking out for me.

Seth's eyes hold mine as he continues. "It's easy to get stuck in what's safe. I hope you'll all agree that sometimes the best thing we can do is leap from our comfort zones into something new. And I offer my wife, Penelope, as first for slaughter this evening." He smiles and waves me onto the stage. The greeting is less enthusiastic than usual, their trepidation palpable.

Leaning back into the stool I adjust my guitar and reset the microphone to my height. "Hmm-huh," I clear my throat and take a sip of water. I think I can, I think I can.

Before I chicken out, I play the opening notes to the first track on my EP, which I never quite got around to telling Seth about. I start out slowly fingerpicking the chords instead of strumming, singing softly. The song is a tender reflection of love and nostalgia and I like how it sounds sung quietly.

The audience is dead silent through the whole song. I appreciate their attentiveness but the absolute quiet is killing me. In my head, the song permeates space, stopping time. I really hope it's not just in my head. My heart pounds in my chest like a kick drum, driving me on. As the last note rings out, they clap. It could be genuine or polite; I can't tell.

I barrel on, playing through the fear. The last song is the one I wrote after the mugging. I'm not sure what it is about that song, but I start to see heads bobbing in rhythm, legs bouncing in chairs. The applause they offer when I finish leaves no doubt that they liked it.

The smile that overtakes my face feels like it wraps clear around my head. Relief is my primary reaction. Did I pass out? Nope. Did they boo? Nope. Not that they would boo, even if they wanted to. All in all, I'd say it was a win. I struggle to my feet, knees wobbling.

The rest of the night feels like one big musical hug. The emotional vulnerability of each performer is palpable and respected by all in attendance. Song introductions are more in-depth than usual, peppered with start-stop-starts, and heartwarming laughter as everyone tries something new. There is no judgment, just encouragement and love. It's more than I could have hoped for. What a great evening! I barely notice that Seth doesn't play.

Hearing "Thank you! Your bravery inspired me. I love your writing" from peers fills me in a way I don't know how I ever lived without. I smile and thank them for coming.

I don't usually seek anyone's approval, but the boost in confidence validates and inspires me. It turns out I needed this.

Seth and I thank everyone who came, waving them out as the night winds down. When it's just us again, I collapse on the couch while Seth takes down speakers and tables, rolls cables, and tidies up the yard. Though I appreciate his desire to keep things neat and orderly, I suspect it's less about that and more that he's avoiding me.

Since our fight, we'd been good—great—even. Or so I thought. I'd hoped we were past the weirdness, but this is classic evasive maneuvering for Seth. Something set him off tonight and I can only guess that's why he didn't play.

The big question is: does this mean I have to ask him what's wrong? There isn't enough energy left in my body to take on any of the uncharitable ideas that occur to me as to why he might be upset. I trudge to the bathroom, stripping down for a shower. Maybe this unsettled feeling will wash off me, down the drain.

Chapter 24

"I've got great news," Sal says to me after class on Wednesday.

"Yeah?" I say, slipping my bag over one shoulder.

"That footage we shot with the mayor turned into a great promo piece," he says. "I showed the Academy and they loved it. We're presenting it to the Board of Education next week."

"That's incredible!"

"I haven't told Marc yet. Don't tell him if you see him first."

"That shouldn't be a problem," I say, kicking the toes of my shoes against the ground.

"Something happen?" he asks, stuffing papers into his briefcase.

"Sort of." I feel weird sharing personal information with Sal. Especially about his friend.

He stops what he's doing and waits for me to elaborate. I guess after being mugged together we've moved beyond the typical professor/student relationship.

"He asked me to go on tour with him," I say.

"That's great."

"I said no."

"That's a huge opportunity. Why say no?"

The way he cuts through the bullshit takes me off guard. I'd been looking at it from a personal angle instead of a professional one.

"It wouldn't be fair to my band—or husband—to pursue a solo career," I say, trying to frame it in professional terms.

"Your husband doesn't want you to go?"

"He didn't say that, exactly."

"It's none of my business, but I've seen this scenario play out before. It never ends well. Do what you need to do.

Otherwise you'll resent him."

I stand there, stunned. The backs of my eyes sting and I blink the tears away. He turns toward the door, eyes averted. Something wet slides down my cheek and I know he's right. Not that it matters. Marc (justifiably) hates me now and I'd say it's safe to assume the offer expired. But that doesn't fix things with Seth.

"See you next term?" Sal asks over his shoulder. I swipe my fingers along my moistened eyes and nod. The corners of his mouth lift up into a small smile. He pats me on the back in an awkward combination of wanting to comfort and not wanting to actually touch me. I look up and smile in thanks. He nods with his whole body and walks away.

Without class to think about, I can throw myself into work. I'm excited about the soundtrack. Despite knowing that Seth and I need to revisit the topic of my solo stuff, I'm sure as soon as we start recording the recent drama will dissolve like a bad dream upon waking.

Everything I have is going into this recording. Hopefully I'll earn at least one writing credit with Seth. I'm growing as an artist and I need my creative partner to foster that, even if it means he doesn't get his way one hundred percent of the time. Compromise must exist in any partnership, especially marriage.

Seth sits at the patio table nursing a beer when I get home. He tips his head in a "hello" gesture and returns to the computer screen in front of him, tapping furiously. I grab a beer from the fridge and join him out back.

"Good last day?" he asks, snapping the laptop closed.

"Yeah. A little sad, but good," I say. "How're you doing?"

He shrugs.

This is how things have been since Monday night. Polite. Cordial. It's driving me bonkers. Seth shows no signs of wanting to talk about anything and since he's technically being nice I can't call him out. It's like a passive aggressive tug-of-war. Part of me wants to shake him and say, "Stop being so polite!" But that's probably not the best route. We'll be in the studio tomorrow. It's going to find a way to work itself out, one way or another. It always does.

Chapter 25

"Can you sing that line again?" Seth says to me from the mixing board. It's hour four in the studio and I'm squished into a tiny vocal booth that resembles a foam-encased dungeon. Even the grey peaks of the sound-reflecting pyramids covering the walls are starting to look like medieval spikes. Cables and musical paraphernalia cover every square inch of flooring. It's good that I'm not claustrophobic.

"That one was almost perfect, but I'd like a little more … soul."

"Can I get more volume in the headphones?" I say. I do it again, trying to inject more rasp into my voice.

"Good," he says when the track finishes.

This is how it's been since we started today. Concise. Polite. By this stage of our last album, I'd already cried in frustration, trying and failing to satisfy Seth's dictatorial producer style. An angry vein throbbed in his forehead as he told me to do it again. After many, many more takes and a few more arguments, we got to that magical moment where it all came together, better than we dared to hope for. This perfect gentleman routine is terrifying. I'm going to explode if he doesn't yell at me soon and just get it over with.

"Seth." I wait for him to make eye contact. He focuses on the computer screen. I sigh. "I need a break."

"Sure," he says without looking up.

I strip off my headphones and carefully navigate my way across the land mines strewn about the floor. I come to stand directly behind him, but he doesn't move. Making no attempt at subtlety, I shift my weight and clear my throat. My eyes flick to the screen. He's moving the cursor without making adjustments.

"What's wrong with you?" I say in a voice too loud for the small space.

"What do you mean?" His voice is even, but his green eyes flash dangerously. I can tell he's reining in his temper. Normally this is when I'd make a joke or try to pacify him, hoping to avoid a blow up. Now though, it's the most encouraging sign I've seen all day.

"You're being so ... polite!" I throw my arms up in exasperation.

"Polite is bad?"

"That's not what I mean," I say. It's difficult to fight against reason. "This isn't how we work," I wave my hands back and forth between us. "I know you're mad. But if you won't even talk to me—let alone fight with me—I can't just stay here and pretend everything's fine."

His face contorts as he spins his chair towards me.

"You want to fight?" he asks, eyes hard.

"No!"

"You want me to talk to you?" he says. I nod. "You're right. I am mad. Mad that my wife is moving on without me." His laser stare bores into mine, my disbelief stalled by the intensity in his tone. He stands up, eyes locked on mine. "Mad that I'm not a good enough partner. Mad that you want something I can't give you." A knot in my throat chokes my vocal chords, making speech impossible.

"That what you want to hear?" he asks, the vein in his forehead pulsing red against his pale skin.

"I'm not moving on without you." My voice cracks like a pubescent teen. The tightness in my throat moves to my jaw as I run the gamut of emotions.

"You forget how well I know you," he answers my unspoken question. "You have feelings for Marc. I can see it even if you can't. I don't want to share my wife, personally or professionally."

"That's insanely unfair. I can't defend myself against your certainty of a hypothetical. You're making my professional opportunity sexual, not me. This issue is about us—as professionals."

"Whatever you say." He shakes his head. "We were fine

until you started spending time with him. Ida Bella was fine. You and I were fine. You were happy. So excuse me if I disagree."

"And what about our tour? The one you only mentioned once!"

"Let's go! I said we should do it. It was your idea. You want to be partners, take the initiative to plan it." He stares me down, waiting for me to argue.

I clench and unclench my jaw, biting back the venomous words trying to escape. I take a deep breath.

"I started writing before I met him. And yes, I liked that he appreciated my songwriting. Or at least I thought he did." My chest heaves, trying to keep up with the racing of my pulse. "And you were happy. Nine out of ten is what you said. You never asked me where I was on that scale."

He raises his brows to imply "Well, then?"

"Four, at best."

Seth emits a choked laugh and gives me a look that says "Come on."

"I never questioned our relationship. Or you," I say, pulling back on my temper before I blurt things I can't take back. "But you dismissed the idea of using my songs. You must think they're truly awful if you wouldn't even try to help me make them better. You'll never know how much that hurts."

He flinches as though slapped. His eyes soften and he steps toward me. I raise my hands, protective of my personal space bubble. Now that I've let it run, I can't stop the flow. "While you were gone I recorded an EP. And I haven't shown it to you yet. Shouldn't that tell you something?"

"You recorded an EP?" He looks stricken. "Where?"

"At Marc's studio." I stand tall despite my moral high ground crumbling beneath my feet. "I don't know what you expect me to do. I love writing. You don't want to use my songs for Ida Bella and I respect that. Kind of. But you can't tell me not to pursue them on my own."

"You're backing me into a corner. If I say 'Let's use your

songs' now you'll always wonder if I really wanted to. And if I tell you to pass up on a huge opportunity because I don't want you to work with a guy with ulterior motives, I'm the asshole holding you back. Even though we both know there are plenty of other avenues you could pursue if you really wanted to."

Part of me sees his logic. The other part knows there's no going back. Either he and I move forward together or ... I'm not sure I'm ready to think about the alternative yet.

"At least admit that he wanted you for more than your writing. You're not that naïve." His laser gaze dares me to argue.

"He was completely professional," I say, chin raised in defiance. "And if roles were reversed, you wouldn't have turned down the opportunity."

"That's what you think? That I want to tour with some pop star?"

"What if it was someone you really respected? And they only wanted you?" I say.

"Do you respect Marc Justin as an artist?" he says, disdain dripping from every syllable.

I know it's a trap so I don't dignify it with a response.

"It's just ... different." He shakes his head. "You've never done any of this alone and I don't think you know what you'd be getting into."

"So ... I should trust you, but you don't trust me to figure things out for myself?" I clench my teeth to keep them from chattering.

His head tilts, a condescending look plastered on his face. I don't let that deter me. "Your fear is based on your insecurities, not my actions. I suggest you sort that out." I say, suddenly desperate for oxygen. I throw the door open and rush through the hall, seeking sunlight and fresh air.

I gulp deep breaths of cool salty air, throwing an arm over my eyes to soften the harsh sunlight. I pace in small circles, muttering things I wish I'd said to Seth, playing out different angles of the argument. When he comes after me I want my comebacks ready.

After a few minutes, I start to grasp the magnitude of the change I'm asking for. This isn't a fight about whose turn it is to do the dishes. This is one of those fights that can change the course of a relationship. I just hope he can see my side—and admit he's being unfair.

After ten minutes he still hasn't chased after me. Having run through my angry monologue I deflate, sinking into the adrenaline crash. The voice in my head wonders if I put myself in this position with Marc, but I shoosh it, stomping my foot with finality, reminding it that it doesn't matter anymore. What do I do now? I'm too stubborn to apologize and too angry to let it go.

I inhale through my nose, filling my lungs completely. Suck it up. I'm a professional with a job to do. If I want to be taken seriously, I need to act like one.

Seth looks up when the inner studio door opens. I stop just inside. He spins back to the screen, wordlessly.

I navigate my way back to the vocal booth and slide the headphones over my ears. The first bars play as I'm still untangling my blonde curls from the cord. I shuffle my feet, pull my shoulders back, and clear my throat. Seth restarts the song and we get back to work.

After we get the vocals and guitar laid down, I stand beside him, listening back to the track through the studio monitors. Seth bobs his head, his gaze unfocused as he listens. I peek over at him, and feel a knot tighten in my stomach.

"Why don't you respect me as an artist?" I ask. He stops the playback and spins to face me.

"What are you talking about? I respect you more than anyone in the world."

"It took you two seconds to decide not to use my songs."

He deflates. "I told you, I think they're great. They're just not right for the soundtrack."

"First you said they didn't fit our branding." I say in a voice that's almost a whisper.

"It's both." He links his hands behind his neck, looking

to the ceiling. "I just … it's business. It isn't personal."

"I don't see the difference," I say.

"I didn't want to hurt your feelings."

"Try me."

"Okay," he looks at me with assessing eyes. "I don't think your songwriting is ready yet. You have good ideas, but structurally there are issues."

I mull that over, trying to keep my ego in check. "Why say no? Why not help me make them better?"

"It's not that simple," he says, running a hand through his hair. He removes his glasses and rubs the bridge of his nose. "I feel like you're trying to change the rules between us. We've got a great thing already. Haven't I always steered us right before?"

"I've loved all our albums, if that's what you mean. But artists grow and their art changes with them. I don't understand how contributing more and expecting you to be honest with me changes the rules of our partnership. I want your respect. Simple as that. Either you respect me as your wife and business partner or not."

He lets out a whoosh of air and looks pleadingly at me. "That's not fair. I'm not saying no to you, my wife. I'm making a business decision. And until now, you always liked that I took charge. Please, just trust me." When I don't immediately answer he goes on. "Look, if a megastar songwriter pitched a great song for Ida Bella that I didn't think fit, I wouldn't use that either. Should I make professional exceptions because you're my wife? Wouldn't that be the special treatment you're trying to avoid?"

We stare at each other, neither willing to take it further, or back. I give in first and shake my head. "I need to think," I say.

His shoulders twitch like he's going to reach out for me but he doesn't. I turn and leave.

With no destination in mind, I drive West and end up on the PCH. I wind my way along the coast and spot the Indian food truck. I order a tandoori chicken wrap and shuffle down to the tide's edge, finding just the right spot to sit. The sea relaxes me and I focus on the sound of crashing waves, the roar of the ocean churning my thoughts into white noise.

Tipping my face skyward, I let my sight fill with the golden glow of the sun through closed eyelids. I inhale, filling my belly with cleansing sea air. I let go and imagine the anger and hurt leaving me on the exhale.

Before I achieve that objective, my phone vibrates in my pocket. Thank God, I think, relieved that Seth is breaking the silence first this time. Breathlessly I answer on the second ring.

"-ello?" I say.

"Penelope?" Marc says. The cordial tone he uses makes me fight the dual urges to laugh and cry. "Can we meet up? I'd like to talk to you. In person, preferably."

It's an amazing talent guys seem to have—popping up as soon as you've stopped waiting to hear from them. When you're dying to hear from them they're nowhere to be found, but as soon as you need some space, there they are. I drop the phone by my side so he can't hear my frustrated mumbling.

"I'm at the beach now, if you're home. I'll be here for another half hour." I say.

"I'll meet you there."

Marc stands next to me, hands in his jeans pockets, gaze on the crashing waves. His hair is more disheveled than usual and he looks closer to his age—a week overdue for a shave, small lines visible around his mouth, resigned posture. No megawatt smile today.

"This seat taken?" he asks, motioning to the sand next to me.

My lips tighten in a smile.

He leans back onto his elbows, gazing into the distance like he's posing for GQ Magazine. We watch the waves in silence for a while. Finally I turn to inspect his face. There's sadness in his eyes, but he doesn't seem mad. I have no idea where we stand. Part of me clings to the hope that he'll take it back and prove me wrong—prove that it was my talent he wanted. The other part of me holds a grudge that's impervious to his charms, even though I still feel bad about leading him on.

Nosiness outweighed reason, and I already regret agreeing to talk to him. I hate when that happens.

"I want to apologize for storming off last time I saw you," he says.

"You don't have—"

Marc's mouth turns up in the ghost of a smile but it doesn't reach his eyes. He continues, undeterred. "I think I gave you the wrong idea."

I chance a look at him and feel myself getting sucked into his earnest gaze. Don't. Let. Him. Do. It.

"I like you for more than your writing," he says. "But I didn't mean to make it seem like that's why I wanted you to tour with me."

"Why didn't you just say so? Why tell me now?" I ask, cynical of this apparent turn-around.

"My mom," he says on a shy smile. "I told her what happened and she said I made it sound like I only wanted to work with you because…"

"Your mom?" I simper.

"I know your answer is probably still no, but I'm asking again. Will you go on tour with me?"

I smile, blinking a silent "Thank you" to him.

"I'm sorry I didn't tell you I was married," I say.

Something shifts in his eyes. Like he's communicating something important to me but I don't understand. I'd give anything to read his mind right now.

"I'm not gonna lie," he says. "You should've told me sooner."

I drop my gaze to the sand.

"But I'm grateful I didn't know."

I glance up, curious.

"If I'd known, I wouldn't have—. I'm not the kind of guy

to go after another man's wife." It's his turn to watch me and I feel blood rush to my cheeks. I bury my toes in the sand. He continues, clearing his throat. "But I've been completely honest with you. I like you. And I like your writing." He gazes at my face with a softness I haven't seen before.

I choke on the lump in my throat and don't trust myself to respond.

"If you weren't married, I'd—" he says, looking me in the eyes. "But that's not why I want you as support on this tour."

"You're absolutely positively sure?" I squeak. Pull it together! Come on Penelope, keep what little dignity remains.

"You're undeniably talented. And yes, beautiful too. And you give me credibility with an audience I need to win over if I'm going to be taken seriously. It's good business. I want to prove that I'm more than just a pretty boy surrounded by half-naked models."

Words elude me. Momentarily. "If I reconsider, how do I know you won't change your mind again?"

"I guess you'll just have to trust me. Talk it over with your husband." He says. He stands up, keeping his eyes on me. "We leave in a month for eight weeks. I need an answer within 48 hours."

I nod. It's my turn to convey more with a look than I can with words. He smiles and disappears down the beach. I watch him go and let myself sink back, unconcerned with the sand in my hair. I've lost my appetite as well as my sense of direction.

Seth is going to love this.

***

When I get home I'm relieved to find Seth isn't back yet. It's been an emotional day and I need to get my bearings. In particular, I have to make sense of this whole business-not-personal thing. I don't think it's that simple. But why shouldn't it be? We're all adults, right?

I need to know that going on tour with Marc would be for professional reasons. He assures me he can separate the two, so if I believe him, then I just need to make sure I can do the same. I don't have feelings for Marc, despite Seth's assurances to the contrary. Still, I find it disconcerting. When Marc said he would never pursue another man's wife I have to admit my belly fluttered just a little. Was that ego or desire? I mean, sure, he's good looking. Of course he is: he's MARC JUSTIN! But even with the recent weirdness, I still consider myself happily married. I am not looking for love or affection anywhere else.

Professionally, I'm dissatisfied. When Seth dismissed my songs out of hand, I was shocked. It hurt my feelings and more than that, it made me realize a deeply ingrained inequality that exists between us. I can't tell if that solely applies to the professional realm. He was right about me changing the rules, though. He has always been the decision maker for Ida Bella and I've always been fine with that. Maybe it's not fair of me to make new rules and expect him to be happy about it.

I disagree on the songwriting front though. The songs are ready—Sal Sullivan agrees. He's making excuses not to use them. Those songs represent who I am right now and I want to perform them. Following his logic—since he doesn't want me to write for Ida Bella—I should find another outlet. Marc's offer is the best and most readily available. Isn't saying yes to opportunity the best professional decision? If Marc and Seth get to separate personal and professional decisions, so do I.

As the front door opens and Seth's keys clink in the bowl in the foyer, I take a breath, resolved in what I need to do. I stand in the kitchen and wait for him to come to me.

Chapter 26

I'll tell him after dinner, I think as Seth treks down the hall to our bedroom. The door clicks shut and I hear the shower running. I heat leftover pasta in the microwave and set out two plates. I slap some butter and garlic powder on slightly stale French bread and pop it in the broiler. It browns while I wait. The water shuts off and I set the garlic bread on a plate in the center of the table. I sit at the table, laying a napkin across my lap, fork still on the table. Footsteps reverberate along the length of the hallway and stop in the arched doorway to the kitchen.

He moves to the fridge, damp hair skimming the collar of his t-shirt, glasses steaming from his body heat. He grabs a beer and pops the top, chucking the lid in the trash. I sit quietly waiting for him to join me. He leans against the closed fridge door, taking a pull from his beer. He slides one foot up against the door and picks at the label on the bottle, not looking at me.

I take a bite of pasta and he pushes off the door. He walks right past me to the living room, snagging his plate and a hunk of garlic bread. I stop, mid-chew, eyes wide. Wow! Glad to see he's going to be mature about this.

I shake my head and finish in record time. I stomp off, letting the back door slam behind me. I flip the switch to turn on the fairy lights and sit on the stone steps, gazing at the empty stage, my head and lungs filled with unsaid things.

I work to normalize my breathing and close my eyes. It's not getting better on its own. I may as well pull off the Band-Aid the rest of the way.

"Did you mean what you said earlier?" I ask. Seth's empty plate sits on the coffee table and he takes another pull from his now naked bottle. He mutes the TV and looks at me.

"Which part?"

I choose the chair perpendicular to the couch and sit on the front edge. "About it being purely professional ... not personal?"

"Yes," he says, leaning forward, green eyes softening.

I feel a little bad, knowing he's making the wrong assumption.

"You think it's possible to keep the two separate?" I ask, needing to mislead him to get the truth.

"Absolutely." He sits up straighter.

"You're sure?" I ask again. It's important that I clarify this point.

"Yes," he says leaning forward, reaching for my hands. "I'm so glad you get it."

I pull away, making an effort to keep my voice even.

"Good, because I need to have a professional conversation with you," I say, watching his face turn from relief to confusion. He shrugs and nods his assent. "I've decided to accept Marc's offer to be tour support."

He looks stunned for a long moment, blinking fast.

"Seth?"

"So we had a fight and you just ran off to him?"

It takes every ounce of willpower I possess to acknowledge that it was a timely coincidence, and not worth ripping his head off for assuming.

"He called me this afternoon to ask me to reconsider. He needs an answer in 48 hours," I say, staring him down.

Hurt and anger flicker on his face and he pushes off the coffee table, backing into the couch.

"What do you want me to say? You're being played?"

I grind my teeth, unwilling to the take the bait. "Whether or not that's true isn't the point. A major star asked me to open for him on an eight-week summer tour. Yes, I think it's the right professional decision." I say, pulling my shoulders back, angling my chin out. "He knows I'm married. He suggested I talk it over with you before giving my decision." I wait, daring him to say I don't deserve this opportunity. I see the skepticism on his face but he doesn't speak. "I want to say yes." I sit a little taller, heart lighter, having said my peace.

"You set me up for that," he says.

"Set what up? Your double standard?" I say, my skin prickling with excess energy.

"What about our tour?" he says without emotion.

"When you want something, nothing stops you from immediately going after it. The fact that you didn't send out a single booking inquiry tells me you only wanted to pacify me," I say, putting a hand up to stop him responding. "Which is fine. But you don't want to use my songs for Ida Bella. And if I should separate what's business from personal, then I'd be insane not take an opportunity to get my music in front of thousands of new people." I say, chest heaving as I realize how fully I believe what I'm saying. "And if you don't trust me not to sleep with him, that's a different issue altogether."

"It doesn't bother you that he's a misogynistic sellout?" he says, standing up to his full height. "That's what you want to do with your talent? Sell out, just like him?"

"Fuck you," I whisper, withdrawing as though slapped.

We lock shining eyes on one another, our breathing loud from exertion. He stalks off first. Keys clink in the foyer and the front door slams shut behind him.

I'm stunned. A sense of foreboding overwhelms me, as the weight of our words force me to the floor. Confusion, anger and hurt—all swirl inside me, indistinguishable. After I've cried myself dry, I sit, staring vacantly at the couch. The voice in my head pipes in, stubbornly reminding me that I am who I am, and I am changing. Change is inevitable.

Chapter 27

Lolo plays with my hair as I lie on her lap like a child. Her couch is cozy and smells like lavender fresh laundry. After my meltdown yesterday, my eyes are puffy and my face is splotchy. I am unfit for public consumption.

Lolo called me as soon as Seth showed up at her house last night. He never came home and I was grateful to know where he went, although I should have had dibs on Lolo's house. She's my best friend—Seth only knows Jeff because of us.

When they left early this morning Jeff promised Lolo he'd text before they returned. Immediately after, she came over and picked me up. I didn't want to go, but Seth's absence left our house claustrophobic. Plus, Lolo's bossy when she sets her mind to something. I know she's dying for details, but appreciate that she's giving me some space (for now).

The thunk of bare feet on hardwood floors is unnaturally loud to my ears as I roll off the couch and slog my way to the bathroom. The reflection in the mirror matches my inner state. Ugh. I splash cold water on my face in a vain attempt to freshen up.

"Here," Lolo says, handing me a pink drink as I flop onto the couch.

"What's this?" I ask, sipping before she answers. It's tastes like drunk grapefruit.

"Better than coffee."

We clink glasses without enthusiasm. I want to tell her everything—commiserate over Seth's double standards, his unjustified distrust in me, and his antiquated ideas of male/female relationships—but I don't want to relive the whole damn thing. I still can't believe it happened.

Fiddling with her glass, Lolo seems to sense my hesitation. A flurry of expressions plays across her features before she sips her drink. Covering her bottom lip with her top teeth, she sets the glass down and faces me full on.

"I don't get it. You said no to Marc. You and Seth were going to tour and seemed good. What could have happened in such a short time?"

It takes excruciating effort to hoist myself up to a seated position. "I did say no to Marc," I say, shifting a pillow onto my lap. I look down, balancing my drink on top of the pillow. "But then Seth refused—" tears well in my eyes, my throat constricts and it takes conscious effort to take a breath. "He wouldn't even consider using my songs." I pause, trying to control my quivering chin. "No discussion. No apology. No nothing. Just 'no'."

Her expression hardens and I know she gets it.

"I needed space after our fight, so I went to the beach." Lolo's jaw twitches and I appreciate her self-control to stay quiet. "Marc called while I was at the beach and came over to apologize."

Her eyes widen and she shoots her hands out, inviting me to elaborate. I sigh.

"He admitted to liking me for more than my songwriting," I say, carefully assessing her reaction.

The look on her face says, "Duh."

"But he specified that said he wants me to tour with him because he thinks I'm talented and that I'd give him credibility with a new demographic he wants to break into. I have to give him an answer in 24 hours."

"Mmhmm," she mumbles.

I gape at her. "Whose side are you on?"

"Yours. Obviously. But you gotta admit it looks bad."

Words elude me.

"Just be aware," she says, patting a hand on my shoulder. "I say go for it. I'm all for using whatever advantages you've got. His motives aren't on you."

"Who cares if it looks bad? I didn't do anything wrong. Plus, I know Seth wouldn't say no to working with a woman who wanted him for more than his musical talent," I say, validated by the fro swaying in agreement.

I can't control Marc Justin's thoughts, actions or whereabouts anymore than I control the weather. All I control are my own.

"So ... then what?" she says, catching me in her unflinching Lolo's-getting-to-the-bottom-of-this stare.

Heat rushes to my face and I sink back into the couch. I relay Marc's apology and the highlights of our conversation. Lolo "Ahh's" when I get to the part about him having feelings for me but not being the kind of guy to go after another man's wife.

"He said he wanted me to perform the song we wrote together as a duet, as well as a few other songs to help him transition away from the pop thing," I say.

Lolo's fro bobs as she contemplates this information. "Well, he doesn't seem like a dick."

"But?"

"But come on. I'm not saying he's lying ... but any normal person would've Googled you and found out about Seth and Ida Bella. Do you really think he didn't know?" She quirks a brow in askance.

I twist my mouth to the side to say "Not sure."

"Mmmhmm," she mumbles.

"Let's say, for the sake of argument, that he did know. Does that mean I should say no?" I ask. She doesn't immediately respond. "When it's about him, Seth separates the personal and professional," I say, voice laced with sarcasm.

We sip in silence, each lost in thought. Finally, she smacks her hand down on the arm's chair and says, "Do you have feelings for Marc?"

"No," I say. Her forehead creases, requiring elaboration. "I mean, I like hanging out with him. We have fun together. And maybe if we'd met at another time I'd like him like that. But we didn't. And I don't."

"Well, that's it then," she says.

"That's what?"

"As long as you can maintain a wall between business and personal, it's an easy yes."

"Easy?"

"Most men'd sleep with most any woman, right? At least it crosses their minds?"

"Seth claims she's got to be at least a four. But yeah."

"Well, you're a ten, girl. Which means every man you meet, personally and professionally, would have sex with you. If you go turning down career opportunities based on the sex factor, Lillith Fair will be your only option. All men are created horny."

What's not to love about Lolo's simplified logic?

She studies the ice cubes in her glass. "You'd tell me if you had feelings for Marc, right?"

When I look at her the words "of course" stick in my throat.

"I mean, you said you don't, so you don't, right?"

"Right," I say, smiling. Seth's words resonate in my head, drowning out the sound of my own voice and I swallow the bitterness.

"Then you gotta do what's right for you." Lolo stands, dusting the metaphorical crumbs off. She poses defiantly, hands on her hips.

"What if it ruins my marriage?" I ask in a voice that's a coarse whisper.

"Then you'll be okay," she says. "If you can't be all of you with Seth then you're not right for each other."

Intellectually, I know what she's saying is true, but in my heart, I'm not sure I would recover if we didn't make it.

Lolo, sensing my hesitation, holds up her hands. "Okay, answer this: could you go back to the way things were before you showed Seth your songs and before he rejected them?"

I shake my head.

"No. You'd be thinking about it in the studio, on stage, and at home."

"Maybe … after a while … I wouldn't'," I say. It's a lie and we both know it. No matter how much I want to keep my hand on the rewind button, just in case, that's not how it plays out in real life. There is no going back.

Chapter 28

"Yes," I say into the phone. Marc's smile is audible on the other end.

"I'm glad you changed your mind. Your husband is okay with it?"

"I'm coming, aren't I?" I say. It's not technically a lie, but it feels like a betrayal to tell Marc that Seth and I are having problems.

"Great. My manager will send a contract and itinerary and I'll have you added to the posters and marketing materials. Do you have copies of your EP?"

"Just that one you gave me. It's rough anyway, it's not ready to be released," I say.

"No, you've gotta have merch for sale."

"I'd have to get it mastered, get artwork, order CDs ... I think it's just too much too soon."

"I'll put up the upfront mastering and production costs. I've got a designer who does amazing work. She'll mock something up for you. We can keep it simple—brand it as a 'One Night in the Studio' thing. People love that shit. Makes 'em feel like they're glimpsing behind the scenes."

"Alright, but I'll pay for it myself."

"You sure? I'm happy to help."

"Positive," I say in a steady voice, my shoulders relaxing. The sad state of my (our) bank account flashes in my mind. Never mind: I will figure something out. By the end of the tour I should at least break even. I hope. I won't allow myself to be indebted to Marc.

"Rehearsals are all this week and next," he continues. "I'd love for you to come. We need to get the transition between your solo set and our duets dialed in. Maybe get my band to learn some of your stuff too. Try it out. See what works."

"Okay," I say. "Hey Marc?" My mind fills with words

unsaid. "Have I said 'thank you' yet?"

"No," he laughs. I swear I can hear the twinkle in his eye. "You're welcome."

Hanging up I'm reminded of how quiet the house is without Seth here. The silence sounded less deafening when he was on tour. It's like the house knows he's gone and is holding its own silent vigil in his absence.

The rest of the week flies by in a frenzy of calls from Marc's manager, designer, publicist and personal assistant. It's an impressive ship he's constructed and they're all efficient and helpful. Except his publicist. She doesn't seem to like me. But maybe that's in my head.

Either way, it helps to distract me from having to deal with the state of my marriage.

The first day of rehearsals with Marc, I was so nervous. They were in the middle of a big choreographed dance number and I didn't want to get in the way. I said a quick hello to Marc's personal assistant before I found a spot in the corner to wait.

The choreographer shouted and pointed to various people, stopping and restarting them for all sorts of reasons I couldn't differentiate. It looked fine to me. It impressed me that Marc took his direction and joked with the other dancers, keeping the tone light but professional.

When he spotted me he waved me up and introduced me to everyone individually. The dancers took a break and his band stepped in so we could go over the duet first.

Making a great first impression, I forgot the same lyrics twice in a row. When Marc stopped me the second time, I was mortified, thinking he was going to tell me to get my shit together. Which is what I was telling myself.

Instead, he asked us all to do a bunch of ridiculously silly acting exercises, like having to have a seemingly serious conversation using only made up words. He led, seemingly unafraid to look like a fool. Within five minutes we were all laughing and bonding over our mutual discomfort. From then on, I knew I'd made the right choice.

Marc wouldn't let any of us leave until he was sure we'd gotten it exactly right. There's no doubt that he's a perfectionist, but I think he's hardest on himself. He talks to everyone individually, encouraging us, feeding us, and keeping the mood light even when he must be exhausted.

On top of knowing that I'd made the right choice in joining a great group of people to tour with, the fringe benefit of the crazy hours is that the days are filled with plenty of tedious tasks to occupy my brain until I lie down to go to sleep. Alone. In a bed that feels too big without Seth here.

I haven't heard from him in a week. This is the longest we've ever gone without talking, and I'm at a complete loss. Lolo tells me he's been spending all his time in the studio, but I can't bring myself to go see him. If he wants to talk, he knows where to find me. After the initial anger passed it was replaced with sadness, the nostalgia weighing heavy on my heart. But as each subsequent day passes without him taking a single moment out of his day to try to make things right or to see things from my perspective, my patience wanes. Anger is making a comeback, quickly replacing nostalgia, and the more I replay the tape in my head, the more righteous I feel. I'm starting to think there might not be anything he can say or do to make it right.

Does he even know when I'm leaving on tour? Who knows, maybe he's beyond caring—maybe he's over me. I drift into fitful bursts of tearful sleep where I dream about all sorts of weird creatures. Most want to eat me alive. When I wake up in the middle of the night I'm running, or so I think. Then I realize it's just a dream and drift back to sleep. The whole cycle repeats until daylight breaks through. Beauty sleep it is not. The bathroom mirror concurs.

At the ten-day mark I cave. I pull into the studio's parking lot, my head bursting with insightful arguments and witty comebacks I wish I'd have the nerve to say out loud. Seth is recording a guitar take when I interrupt. He looks put out, although his facial expressions are hard to read through the explosion of facial hair covering his skin. A beanie hides the greasy hair not sticking out around the edges and the fluorescent ceiling lights highlight his dark sunken eyes, magnified in his glasses. I've never seen him so disheveled. A small (okay, big) part of me is relieved that I'm not the only one who's upset.

I'm not sure what the official state of our marriage is, but at least he's not unaffected. I need to know where we stand before I go.

"What's up?" he says to me, as though I'm some random visitor.

"I—uh, how are you?" I stutter, already deviating from the script I practiced in my head.

"Busy," he says. "I need to finish three guitar parts by five."

"I won't keep you," I say, throwing my hands up in surrender. "I just came to say goodbye. Tour starts in two days."

"Have fun."

I turn to go, shaking my head and mumbling to myself, dropping enough f-bombs to give my mother a stroke.

I make it all the way to my car before I let out a guttural yell that frightens a stray cat in the parking lot. It stares, wide-eyed and wild and shoots under a dumpster. Great, I'm too scary to even pursue my inevitable future as a cat lady.

***

It's the last day of rehearsals and Marc and I run through the three songs—including the one we wrote together—we'll do at the end of my set. His band will back me up on half my set and stay for the songs Marc I will do together.

The choreography for his show, which I expected to be horrified by, is actually pretty great. The dancers are still over-sexualized for my taste, but there is no question they are extremely hard working. And I seem to be the only one bothered by that side anyway. Marc is enthusiastic and diplomatic, working them hard to get it right. It's obvious everyone respects him.

Despite things with Seth, I'm giddy with excitement. This is a huge opportunity—much bigger than I realized—and I get to satisfy a part of myself that's been emerging from the shadow of my insecurities. I'm a lucky girl. I just wish Seth could see it that way.

The open suitcase taunts me as I stand over the bed, trying to figure out how to fit everything I need for eight weeks into this one bag. As an opener, I get a single bunk on one of the buses. I've been asked to pack as sparingly as possible. I never thought of myself as high maintenance, but now that I'm staring at everything in my Must Take pile, I cannot imagine how this mound of fabric will ever be contained. Ugh!

In procrastination, I scurry around the house doing menial chores, watering plants and making notes for what I'll need Lolo to do while I'm gone. I'm not assuming Seth will or won't do anything, so I'm choosing to count on Lolo.

The bed, groaning, still obscured by clothes when I return, scoffs at me as I start rolling items up one by one, stuffing them down to fill every square millimeter. Something rustles in the living room as I smoosh a shirt into an open crevice. Before I can check it out, I recognize the sound of Seth's footsteps on the hardwood floors. I suck air in through my teeth, debating whether I should just keep packing. I peek my head into the hall and catch him looking at me.

His emerald eyes bore into me. It's been so long since he's done more than yell or grunt at me that I feel like a skittish stray animal, awaiting the inevitable blow up. He's shaved since I saw him at the studio. His dark hair is damp and his eyes gleam with intensity behind his black-rimmed glasses. He looks like my Seth.

A wave of homesickness rips through me and I fight the urge to run to him, throwing myself in his arms. He takes a step in my direction and I hear myself inhale sharply. Taking long strides down the hall, he doesn't take his eyes off me. He doesn't hesitate as he wraps his arms around me, kissing me, twisting his fingers in my long hair, keeping my head level with his.

I should feel angry or confused or ... something. Instead of thinking anything at all, I respond to this deep animal instinct that pulls me to him, my body pressing hard against his as I slam into the wall. He moves his mouth to my neck, immediately connecting to that spot that sets my skin on fire, sending tingles down my limbs. My hands move under his shirt, sliding up his smooth chest and pulling it up over his head.

He pulls away from the wall, lifting me up, so that I have to straddle him to stay connected. My head falls back in ecstatic anticipation as he carries me to the bed. There's only a slight pause as he raises a brow at the mess and half packed suitcase. I shrug as he tosses me onto the bed. With one swipe, he removes the mess from the bed, suitcase thumping to the ground.

I moan softly as he takes my left leg in his hands, kissing my naked ankle, massaging my calf. Without warning he throws my leg aside, and I let out an "Ah!"

Climbing onto the bed between my legs, his hands run up my thighs and under my skirt. I ground my heels and rise into bridge pose so he can take down my skirt. Eyes wide, he stops. I smile. I'd forgotten that I'm not wearing underwear. It seemed expedient not to have to do laundry again.

He groans approvingly and hikes the thin skirt above my hips, leaving me exposed. Pulling my upper body toward him, he slips my shirt up and over my head, kissing pieces of bare skin along the way.

"Mmm." I gasp, letting my breasts fall to the side, uncontained. Seth cups the right one and slips my nipple in his mouth, twisting it between his lips and tongue. The wetness of his tongue on my dry skin sparks a new round of desire, making me arch my back, yearning to get as close as possible.

Sensing my desire he keeps his own body just out of

reach, teasing me with hands, lips and tongue. My skin is so sensitive I don't think I can stand another sensation. When he goes for my other nipple I buck him off, flipping him on his back, pinning him between my legs. Holding his arms above his head I use my tongue to trace his collarbone. I trail kisses up his neck to his ear, pulling his earlobe with my teeth, moaning softly into his ear. I feel his excitement as our bodies communicate their mutual desire.

We torture each other in delicious ways, battling for control over the other's pleasure. Our bodies are our weapons, and we wield them with practiced knowledge of our opponent's weaknesses, exploiting them at every opportunity. When the fight has reached the point of no return, we undulate in unison, allowing the waves of desire to wash over us, crashing to the floor, spent.

Panting, my eyes closed, lying on Seth's sweat moistened chest, I listen to the rhythm of his pulse as it slowly returns to an even thump, thump, thump, thump. Tenderly, he strokes my arm with his thumb. I wrap an arm around his taut stomach and he turns to my wild curls, kissing the top of my head. Every detail of this moment absorbs itself in my memory, from the smell of him—soap, sweat and fresh laundry—to the twittering of birds through the open window. The sun warms my skin in the bright room, the slight breeze enough to give me goose bumps.

Seth rolls over and gets up, pulling me to my feet. He squeezes my ass and I swat his. The elastic waistband of his boxers snaps against his skin as he turns and smiles to me over his shoulder. We may not be speaking, but perhaps this a better way to communicate—for now.

He pads to the kitchen, and I follow, dressed only in the skirt that never came off. He arranges a block of cheese and a baguette on a plate, filling a glass of water, and motions his head toward the back door. I open it and let him step through, both of us sitting at the small table. It's a new sensation for me, exposing my naked breasts to the elements like this, and not altogether unpleasant.

I break off a hunk of bread and slice off a piece of brie. It melts in my mouth and, inadvertently, I let out a small moan of pleasure. Seth stops chewing to look at me. He shakes his head and I smile, reading his mind.

Everything takes on a surreal quality, like we're in a movie. My senses are alive. Seth seems to feel it too, closing his eyes to revel in the taste in his mouth and (I'm assuming) the memory of satisfaction.

His fixes another piece of bread with cheese and focuses his green eyes on me. "So ... tomorrow?"

"Yep," I say.

"You excited?" He studies his plate.

"I am," I admit. He takes a long sip of water. "A little nervous too."

"Need me to hold your hand?" He laughs, a sad smile lingering in the silent beat that follows.

"Yes," I say, straight-faced.

His mouth twists into a nearly full smile. He sighs and drops his gaze to the plate. "I appreciate you saying that."

"I mean it."

"I know you do." He takes my hands in his. "But we both know that won't do any good." He rubs his thumbs along the tops of my hands. His eyes are soft, the sharp angles of his face and lines around his mouth less pronounced than usual. He looks tired.

"The thing is ..." he starts. I get the feeling this is a practiced speech he's about to give. "You have to take this opportunity." He holds my gaze. "You're right. Change is inevitable. I wish I could take back—" he closes his eyes, wincing.

I squeeze his hand, not trusting my voice. He clears his throat.

"I'm not saying I'm totally okay with it," he says, eyes wide. There is an unfamiliar intensity in his eyes. I shake my head, offering a wry smile. "But you need to explore this new side of yourself. You were right. I wasn't supportive. I can't take it back, but I won't hold you back. If I do, you'll resent me and I'll lose you anyway." He scans my face for a reaction.

I desperately want to say he's wrong, but I can't. I have changed. He's right; I have to go. It feels like I've swallowed a rock and my eyes sting with tears. A sad smile haunts his face and he pulls my hands to his lips, kissing them, the warmth of his breath lingering on my skin. To dam up the tears I close my eyes.

"Thank you," I say. He dips his head down to my hand, kissing my ring finger before pushing his chair back to go.

By the time I follow him to our bedroom, he's fully dressed. I wrap my arms around his waist, our bodies breathing in unison. I look up and touch my mouth to his, deepening the kiss, threading my hands behind his neck, pulling him closer. He angles his head back, breaking contact, and closes his eyes. With a deep breath he walks out.

Like a zombie, I make the bed and start packing all over again. I can't think about what Seth meant when he said he was afraid of "losing me anyway." I'm terrified that he's giving up on us, petrified by the freedom he's given me, but worse still is the knowledge that I need it.

By the time I've rolled every item of clothing into neat little tubes and miraculously found a way to zip up the bag, the sun is no longer streaming in. The air is cold and I close the windows. I crawl under the covers, falling into the first deep sleep I've had since Seth left the first time. I don't even think about the fact that I'm on his side of the bed. At least not for long.

Chapter 29

Lolo gives me a ride to the tour bus departure area. She knows I saw Seth yesterday and I'm grateful she hasn't asked me to rehash it all. It's not an option to be a blubbering mess today.

She glances at me as she shifts the car to park. We lock eyes and I know she's thinking I need to be careful in my current state. I know she's right. The trunk pops open and I step out of the car. Hoisting my guitar and suitcase from the trunk I turn to face her. She purses her lips in a "What can I say?" expression. The hug I squish her in is so tight it makes tears spring to my eyes, threatening to ruin my reputation with my new colleagues. The unusual display of affection takes her off-guard, but she squeezes me back, our boobs smooshing together in pillowy protection.

"Call me lots," she says.

I nod.

I wave goodbye and take the first steps toward my new adventure.

Marc and his manager, Chris, are standing next to the front bus deep in conversation. The dancers stretch against and load gear into the second bus. The third bus, identical to the other two, must be for his band, and me. I recognize Guy, the bass player and Joe, the drummer, who wave as I make my way toward them.

My suitcase rolls and jumps along behind me until a big guy with a lanyard around his neck relieves me of it, loading it into one of the empty lower compartments. He eyes the guitar in my other hand and I freeze, deliberating whether or not I trust its safety underneath the bus. I don't like the idea of it being stuffed in this little metal sauna, but it doesn't seem fair to take up so much space in the main cabin, either.

Since I still haven't made up my mind about the guitar

when Marc waves me over, I carry it with me.

"Here, let me take that," Chris says, grabbing my guitar and loading it inside the trailer behind Marc's bus before I get a chance to protest. He smiles at the expression on my face. "Don't worry. It'll be perfectly safe. It's temperature and humidity controlled." When he opens the back of the trailer I see the familiar black and chrome gear racks used to transport all manner of musical accoutrements.

"Ride with me?" Marc says.

"Is that going to make everyone hate me—being friends with the boss?"

"It's more of a traveling business meeting. No friend stuff at all." He grins.

"Well, good. Can I check out my bunk and stuff first?"

Introducing me to the handful of people I haven't met yet, Marc gives me the tour. The bunk is a simple, two-and-a-half-foot-high space, not quite six feet long, covered with a heavy velvet curtain. Pulling it back, there's a shelf above one end with a fold down TV and wireless headphones. I have a small window with a shade and an outlet. When you get right down to it, I guess that's all you need.

"Five minutes, everyone!" Chris says, leaning out of Marc's bus door.

As we head back to his bus, I'm relieved I wasn't the only one invited. Chris, his manager, and Beth, his tour manager, are also here. He wasn't kidding about this being a meeting.

They may look identical from the outside, but it couldn't be more different inside Marc's bus. It's spectacular. Decorated in a similar aesthetic to his house in Malibu, with white walls, silver subway tiles in the kitchen area, and grey leather couches, it has an upscale beachy vibe. The up-lit track lighting gives the impression of spaciousness, providing such even lighting it feels like we're outside, even with the blinds drawn. The tinted windows have curtains that are pulled to the side, but look heavy enough to be used as blackout shades.

Marc catches me looking around and I drop my eyes to

his.

"Home sweet home," he says.

"Wow," I breathe.

"Grab a seat," he says, motioning to the diner style table. "We'll start the meeting once we get on the freeway."

As I sit down across from him, goose bumps erupt on my neck and arms. It's finally hitting me: I'm on tour! With an international superstar! To perform my original songs! Grinning like a maniac I should probably be embarrassed for myself, but I can't help it.

Marc flashes me an odd look and glances over his shoulder to Chris, who is sitting on the couch with Beth. They sit side by side, scrolling through their phones, their faces all business.

Ida Bella has been on tour multiple times, and we've done well enough to make some profit, but we've never toured on anything approximating this scale. Probably only a handful of people ever have.

The first time out, Seth and I were in our little hatchback, ducking under guitar cases, sleeping on sofas and chasing down checks at the end of the night.

Beth hands me an envelope with my first week's worth of per diems, explaining that it is supposed to cover my food expenses, but that hotels and transportation are exempt. Any extras are up to me.

"There will be food backstage before every show," she says, looking to me for visual confirmation of understanding. "The band and dancers will finish everything, so don't wait till after your set if you can stomach eating before."

Chris holds a clipboard and scans down the page, pen in hand. "I've got ten boxes of CDs and four of shirts," he says.

I nod, confirming my merchandise and sign off on my starting numbers. "We're running all merch together, tallying at the end of each night." He looks to me expectantly. Not sure what I'm supposed to say, I nod again. He hands me another paper to sign, agreeing to be paid within thirty days from the last performance date. I make an effort to appear thoughtful and professional, but I feel like I'm in high school drama class, pretending to be a grown up.

Logistics sorted, I settle into my seat, looking out the window. The big diesel engine roars to life, setting the bus to vibrate. Marc faces me, and wags his brows, as if saying, "Ready?"

I smile. The first stop isn't far. Two hours South to San Diego is where I will play my first ever stadium show. The big L.A. show will be our finale and I'm kind of relieved not to have all my friends at this first show. The road crew is already at the venue, building the hydraulic stage, setting up sound and lighting. Contemplating the full scope of what a superstar tour entails, I feel naïve. There are so many moving parts that it'll be good to get the kinks out before playing for my biggest fans and harshest critics.

We rattle and roar our way onto the freeway, finally settling into a predictable rhythm.

"Press conference is at five," Beth says, her eyes on me. "Are you prepared for questions?"

"I've done interviews before, if that's what you mean," I say.

"Support isn't usually with Marc in the press room," she says in answer to my unasked question. "He insisted you should be but I don't want to throw you to the sharks unprepared." Her tone is sweet but I sense that she's holding something back.

"I'll be fine," I assure her.

"Great," she taps something on her phone. "Your sound check is at three, until three thirty. You need to finish by exactly three thirty."

"No problem," I say.

"Doors open at seven, and Marc starts at nine. There is a local opener at seven thirty, followed by Penelope at eight fifteen." She quirks a brow at the three of us, making sure we're listening.

I'm not positive, but I think Marc smothers a smile as Beth tries to turn her sneer into a smile. I give a curt nod and look away, afraid to piss her off.

She and Chris return to their phones, occasionally checking something with the other. The city slips by in a blur as we barrel down the carpool lane. I look up and catch Marc watching me.

"There's one thing that's been bugging me," he says.

"Yeah?"

"What made you change your mind? About the tour, I mean?"

"You were right. It's an amazing opportunity."

He narrows his eyes like he doesn't believe me.

"And Seth? Is he okay with you coming?"

I don't remember telling him Seth's name. Although at this point he's had access to all my business details. Not to mention Google. Still, it sounds weird hearing him say Seth's name.

"He had his reservations," I say, trying to be as honest as possible without betraying Seth. "But he knows this is something I need to do, for me. And he supports me."

"Good." Marc gazes out the window. A flurry of emotion passes over his face. I drop my eyes to my hands, heat prickling my cheeks. Unable to look at him, I fixate on the horizon.

In the green room later, minutes from my performance, I inspect my reflection in the mirror. My long hair is more wavy than curly and I fluff the roots with my fingers, hoping to give it enough volume to compensate for my feeling of inadequacy. Smoky eye makeup is caked on heavier than usual because the stage lights are so intense. In this mirror, my brown eyes are huge, and my already pale skin looks ashen. My legs bounce up and down and I take a deep, steadying breath before I dab on red lipgloss with my finger. Baring my teeth, I check for spinach or lipstick. Satisfied that I'm not going to (obviously) make a fool of myself, I stand up, smoothing my dress.

I'm overwhelmed by the sudden realization that I wish

Seth were here. He always knows how to calm my nerves. I have to flex my fingers by my sides in order not to call him. This is something I have to do on my own. One, two, three, I count as I breathe as deeply as my dress allows. Closing my eyes, I block out every other sound and focus on what I need to do.

The door opens and I nearly slam into Beth who's waiting right outside my green room.

"Let's go," she says, shuffling me toward the stage.

I hesitate for a split second as I catch a glimpse of the packed arena. They're going to hate me, I think, looking over my shoulder. Beth rolls her eyes. "Go!" she says, shoving me into the light of the stage.

The spotlight glints off the chrome microphone as I pause to take in the moment, holding my guitar, looking out at the largest crowd I've ever seen. The lights are so bright that the arena is silhouetted in the fading day's light. The low hum of human voices and smattering of polite applause comforts me, humanizing the inhuman scale. As I pick the first notes of the first song I'm encouraged by a smattering of teenage girls in the front row who stop talking to listen. Building into the chorus, focusing solely on the sound of the guitar, I close my eyes to sing. By the second verse, my nerves are completely gone. The mediocre applause is short-lived as I go right into the second song, feeling confident that at least I won't puke.

They'll go bananas the second Marc joins me for our duet. This penultimate solo song is my last chance to make an impression on my own. I give myself completely over to the song, speeding up a little more than I intended. I glance down at the front row and smile at the upturned faces, swaying in time, clapping along. Their excitement boomerangs off them, back to me, filling me with a kind of energy that makes the existence of anything outside this moment irrelevant.

As expected, Marc comes onstage and the crowd goes bonkers, drowning us out with their applause. It's so loud it reverberates through the stage and my entire body. I look to

Marc and put my hands together, joining their applause. "Marc Justin!" I say. The thundering raucous rolls through the stadium and he beams at them.

"Let's hear it for Penelope Byrne!" he says, putting his hands together, instigating cheers for me.

I bow, hands together in Namaste.

"Think she'll let me play one more with her?" he asks them.

He knows exactly what he's doing, I think, impressed by his calculating introduction—guaranteeing they'll love me.

He winks to me and I start the song, his band taking my lead. It goes better than we've ever rehearsed and when I leave the stage, we smile to one another in silent congratulations. I float all the way back to the green room. I slip a backstage pass around my neck so I can catch Marc's show from the front and see if I can help at the merch table.

It's everything I'd expect from a pop concert: screaming teeny boppers, hydraulic stage elements, half-naked dancers. Marc sings and dances, emanating a deceptively effortless star quality packaged in All-American good looks. He leans over the edge of a jutting catwalk stage, high fiving the outstretched hands of squealing fans that jump and shout, nearly passing out from excitement. Some are even crying. The whole time his choreography is flawless. Through multiple wardrobe changes and a tempo breakdown, followed by a steady build into the finale. They call him back for a spectacular encore, complete with pyrotechnics. Don't get me wrong, I still hate the songs, but no one can argue that Marc Justin isn't a professional.

Chapter 30

"Next question from our KGFM listeners is for you, Penelope," the DJ says, looking to me and gesturing that I should move closer to the microphone. As quickly and quietly as I can, I reposition myself.

"Is touring with Marc Justin the best thing ever?"

I laugh, watching the DJ as he motions to someone on the other side of the glass. "Totally. Two weeks in and I'm starting to get my sea—I mean, bus—legs under me." I raise my brows to the DJ, silently asking if I need to expand for time or keep it short. He waves royally with a hand, indicating that I wrap up as he moves back toward his microphone.

The caller squeals, "Ohmigod, he's like, so dreamy!"

The DJ smiles to me, shaking his head at the caller. "I want to thank Penelope Byrne for hanging out with us this morning. You can catch her in Savannah at the MLK arena tomorrow night with Marc Justin. The show is sold out, but stay tuned for your chance to win tickets. Will you play a song for us before you go?" he asks.

"I'd love to. This song is off my new EP. It's called 'If I Don't Break.' I hope you like it." I play the song, hunching like Quasimodo to keep my guitar close to my mouth so both are audible through the one microphone. When I finish, the DJ nods to me and pushes a button to reactivate his mic.

"Thank you Penelope, that was really great! This is KGFM, your station for new music."

I watch him, waiting until they mute my mic. Stabbing the button, he slides his headphones off and reaches out to shake my hand. I thank him, handing over a copy of my EP and the envelope of tickets for his listeners to win.

"Thanks for these," he says, waving the tickets in a salute. "Give Beth my best." I manage a close-lipped smile.

If I've learned anything these past two weeks it's to keep

my head down and do what I'm told when it comes to Beth.
For the most part, that's worked well enough, but she
intimidates me and I can't dismiss the feeling that she doesn't
like me very much.

As has been the norm, I get the less popular station while
Marc is at the top 40 one. Today he's down the hall since
both stations are owned by the same company and housed in
the same building. I could have done both shows, as Marc
keeps suggesting, but Beth said she wanted to "let me
concentrate" on my performance this morning. I'm neither
ungrateful nor saying that I deserve the same coverage as
Marc, but he wanted us to play our duet on the air. She
insisted I'd be better off doing my own press. Which is
obviously bullshit since co-billing with a celebrity on a Top
40 station is infinitely better exposure. Instead of saying so, I
smile and play my part, acknowledging the power dynamic.

Marc, true to his word, has been the consummate
professional, leaving me to initiate contact with him, treating
me with the deference and respect he does all his employees.
A couple of times I thought I caught him watching me, but
he played it off like he wanted to talk to me, or was looking
beyond me at something in the distance.

This interview is the only thing on my itinerary today and
I plan to play tourist, making the most of the rest of my day
off. There's a bus that will take me downtown where I'll get
to wander aimlessly, exploring one of the nation's oldest cities.
This is my first time in Savannah, so I opt to start near the
river. The weather is perfect for a leisurely stroll along
cobbled streets that are lined with trees dripping with Spanish
moss.

At the bus I swap out my guitar for a bus map, grab my
purse and slip on comfy shoes. I choose denim capris, Toms
and a cotton tank top. On second thought I stuff a cardigan
in my purse and head out to the bus stop.

I take a seat on the bench beside the marker, checking
emails on my phone. Seth and I have only exchanged a
handful of texts and emails since I've been gone, all surface

stuff—mostly logistical issues about the house and bills.

I miss him. I'm still not sure where we stand, and I try not to think about it too much. A part of me feels guilty because when I'm not thinking about him, I am happy. For the first time in my life I feel independent, and it makes me realize how much I've changed since we first met.

I stuff my ear buds in, cranking some new music recommended to me by Marc's lead dancer, Miguel. It's the kind of music you can't help but dance to and I don't try to stop myself bopping around on the bench. I close my eyes, loving the anonymity of public transportation in a never-before-seen city.

A black SUV pulls up to the curb in front of me, idling. Without looking at the car I sense that it's much too close, parked illegally in the bus lane, and my neck prickles with fear. The back passenger window rolls down and I stifle a scream. When I see Marc's cheeky grin I chuck my map at him.

"Jerk! You scared the crap out of me," I say.

"Get in," he says, chuckling.

"I'm taking the bus." I cross my arms and lean back into the bench.

"Come on, don't make me explore all by my lonesome," he says, cocky charm dripping from every syllable.

"Seriously?"

He grins. "Please, can I tag along?"

"Fine."

He opens the door for me and I slide in beside him. It's just us. No Chris, no Beth.

"Where to?" his driver says, looking into the rear view mirror at us. Marc gives him an address and I shoot a sideways look at him.

"I thought you were tagging along with me?"

"Just one stop…" he says.

I widen my eyes, challenging him.

"I'm starving and I know a great place. My treat?"

I glare, but nod. I'm starving too.

"I promise, after brunch I'll follow you wherever you

want to go."

"Pinky swear?" I say, holding out my hand, pinky extended.

"Oh, I forgot we were six years old."

I don't budge and he shakes his pinky with mine, smirking. I consider it a done deal. No one goes back on a pinky promise.

Twenty minutes later we arrive at a house that looks like it was built before the Civil War. Its opulent columns and stately façade scream Old Money. The front garden is immaculately kept, as are all the neighboring properties. The plaque on the front gate reads: Built 1805, National Historical Preservation Society Member.

We walk side by side up the pathway to the front door. I can't tell if this is a private residence or a museum. It's definitely not a restaurant. Unsure whether to knock or walk right in, I let Marc lead. He opens the door, taking a step back to let me in first.

Inside is a spectacular marble foyer with double winding staircases, the likes of which were almost certainly in Gone With the Wind. My gaze is drawn upward to the gilded ceiling from which drips a crystal teardrop shaped chandelier. I'm not typically impressed by materialism, but the sheer volume of bling is enough to render me immovable. Marc elbows me playfully, and pulls me by the hand so that I follow him.

The back porch turns out to be a restaurant, after all. Apparently it's not the kind of place where signs are required. A young hostess smiles as we approach, her porcelain skin and bright eyes exquisitely beautiful.

"How many?" she asks.

"Two, please." Marc says. He leans in a little closer to her and her cheeks flush pink. "In a discreet area, if it's not too much trouble."

Ugh.

Once he flipped the charm switch she didn't stand a chance, skittering off to talk to a manager. I pity her. She must have a fan club of her own with those stunning looks, but I guess even that isn't enough to make her impervious to Marc Justin's charms.

She bounds back and ushers us to a table for two on the far side of the wrap-around deck, facing the gardens. The table is mostly obscured from view by a large column.

"Thank you." We say it at the same time and he smirks at me.

"Now that you have me here what do you plan to do with me?" I say, in my best Southern Belle accent.

A dangerous glint flashes in his eyes and I look away. What was I thinking?

"I plan on feeding you the best meal of your life," he says.

"I can get behind that," I say, flipping my hair.

He grins and turns his menu over, inspecting the specials.

"Since you hijacked my tourist day, I get to ask you questions about yourself."

"That's how this works?"

"Yep."

He offers a lopsided smile in response.

"Besides eating, what do you do for fun?" I ask.

"I play music."

"That's your job. There's gotta be something you do just for fun."

He smiles, eyes darkening. My hand goes to my face, and I shoot him an exasperated look.

"I do enjoy eating well," he says. "I also surf. And read. And spend time with people whose company I enjoy." He settles back in his chair.

"What do you read?" I ask, ignoring that last bit.

"Non-fiction mostly—biographies, history, memoirs—anything that interests me."

I don't try to hide my surprise.

"What, you didn't think I could read?"

"Not that you couldn't ... " I smile.

"After a show it helps me calm down enough to sleep." He sips his water, never taking his eyes off me. I nod, understanding the comedown he's talking about.

"What's the deal with the skank flank?" I blurt.

"The what?" He snorts loud enough to illicit a couple head turns from nearby tables.

"The bare-assed girls you accessorize with, even when you accept awards," I say, daring him to deny it.

"Marketing," he says. "Women like a man who is desired by other women. It's a scientific fact." He says it so matter-of-factly I almost don't know why I questioned it. Almost.

"So why aren't they touring with you now?"

He flashes me a smile and looks down, suddenly very interested in his menu. My cheeks feel hot and I bundle my hair in a ponytail, wishing I could calm my heart rate. I don't know what to say.

"Do you like it?" I ask.

"What? Being surrounded by beautiful women?"

"No. Manipulating your audience."

"I don't think of it like that," he says, furrowing his brows in contemplation. "I'm just climbing the corporate ladder, same as anyone. Plus, as far as I know, the models I hire don't mind the paid gig."

"What happens when you get to the top of the ladder?" I ask, not buying the I'm-just-like-everyone-else schtick.

"I do something else," he says. "I got into this to support my family. And I'm proud that I've been able to do that." His expression turns serious. "From a young age it was my responsibility. My mom and sister sacrificed a lot for me and my success is as much for them as myself." He doesn't look at me and I get the impression he'd prefer to drop it. For some reason, I can't.

"If you're not at the top, you're pretty damn close. Why keep going?" I say, trying to follow his logic.

"There's always a new mark to hit. I'm goal-oriented, what can I say?"

"Huh." I take a sip of lemon infused water, watching his face.

"What's that 'huh'? You think I'm shallow?" He smiles, but it's forced.

"No. I just wondered if climbing that ladder is making you happy?"

"Happiness is a luxury."

"A luxury money affords?"

"Are you happy?" he says, locking me in his gaze.

Good question. At any other point in my life I could have answered easily. At this moment in my life's journey, I'm questioning my marriage, career, and self, so nothing is clear-cut. The fact that I feel happy here with him while everything in my life is in such disarray is also disconcerting.

I thought Seth was being jealous and insecure saying I had feelings for Marc, but I have to admit that I'm questioning it myself. There is no other logical reason for me to grill him, spend so much time with him, or think about him as much as I do.

"I'm in the vicinity of happy," I say.

"What does that mean?"

"It means I'm in a transitional phase. Change is painful and scary, but necessary. I like where I'm going, but I don't feel settled enough to say 'yes, I'm happy.' Does that make sense?"

"It does."

After brunch—which is amazing, as promised—we head down to the riverfront. We meander in and out of little boutiques and tourist traps along cobbled streets. Marc answers a call while I explore a tiny bookstore. On the cluttered front table is a single copy of "Jim Henson: The Biography." He may have it already, but I buy it anyway.

The canopy of Spanish moss-covered trees shades us as we make a game of who can spot the most historic markers. I'm not sure who started it, but we stop at each one. Pretending to read, I look for the next one out of my peripheral vision before he sees it. I'm competitive: what can I say? It's the easiest game ever since nearly every building we pass is of some historical relevance.

It reminds me of being a kid—running from marker to

marker—so excited about life that it's impossible to walk; I have to run. Marc doesn't hold back either and we sprint from block to block, scaring the bejeezus out of the leisure Sunday strollers.

In the fading golden light we pass through a park where senior citizens walk their dogs, fathers and sons play catch, and young lovers lay out picnics on the grass. It's so idyllic it makes me want to cry. I glance at Marc, who watches the boy and his dad.

"A small token—to say thanks for hijacking my day." I hand him the book, wrapped in brown paper.

He looks confused, ripping the paper off. As he sees the title, his expression shifts, revealing a vulnerability I've never seen before.

"It's perfect."

I smile, happy to have found something for the guy who has it all. He pulls me into a massive bear hug. I squeeze him back and he pulls me closer, kissing the top of my head. I melt into his warmth. We stand there, in the middle of the park, locked in an embrace for what feels like an eternity, our bodies communicating words we won't speak.

Chapter 31

In the chorus of my second song, I experience a brief out-of-body experience. Basically, I freak out. I'm playing Madison Square Garden! This has been my dream since I saw Paul Simon with Ladysmith Black Mombazo when I was ten. That concert is what got me into music in the first place. Dad listened to Paul Simon and Simon & Garfunkle all the time, so I was already familiar with the songs, but something about the combination of his lyrics and melodies with the booming resonance of those African voices created a magical experience that resonated in the deepest part of me. I'd never felt music that way before. I wasn't just hearing it. It was tangible, physical. I remember scanning the faces in the crowd, wondering if they were feeling what I did.

In that moment I knew that if I could affect people like that at any point in my life, it would be a life well lived. Standing beside my dad in this very space, my life spread out before me with a certainty I've never felt so acutely before or after. Months later, the memory faded to an otherworldly remembrance—more a feeling that stuck with me and shaped me. And now, here I am, watching myself perform on the same stage. There is nowhere I'd rather be.

Beth knocks impatiently on my green room door.

"Someone here to see you. He's not on the list. Says he's your dad," she says, clearly annoyed to be my messenger.

"I'll be right there," I say, slipping a clean tank top over my head. My parents have never come to any of my shows before and I haven't spoken to them since I started this tour. It's probably someone trying to get backstage to see Marc.

As I round the corner, heading toward the wall of security lining the backstage entrance, I spot a familiar salt and pepper headed figure and immediately pick up my pace to a jog.

A head pokes around the side of the hulking mass of a

man who is blocking passage and I shout, "Daddy!" I tap the giant on the shoulder. "Please put my father, Ed Caruso, on the list."

The security guard doesn't look pleased, giving my dad a long once-over before taking down his ID details and handing him a laminated card attached to a shoestring necklace. Being the opener isn't enough of a calling card to thwart Marc Justin's uber security. Dad mutters, "thanks" and then smothers me in uncharacteristic affection. His eyes shine and I can't help but feel like that ten-year old girl again.

"You wrote those songs?" he asks, his pride obvious.

"Yeah, " I say, beaming.

"Thatta girl."

He squeezes his arm around my shoulders and kisses my hair. "Can I take my daughter out for a meal?"

"I would love that. Do you want to stay for the rest of the concert or go now?"

"It can't get any better, but I always like seeing concerts here. Did you know this is my favorite venue?"

I nod.

After Marc's encore, we go backstage to my green room.

"Hang on a sec, Dad. I just need to grab my purse," I say, leaving him to wait in the hall.

There's some mumbling outside and I hurry up, hoping no one is giving him a hard time for being backstage. When I open the door I'm surprised to see Marc and Dad shaking hands, Dad congratulating Marc on an "entertaining" show.

"Would you like to join us for dinner?" Dad asks Marc.

Marc looks to me and I shrug as if to say, "Up to you."

"I'd love to, Mr. Caruso."

"Please, call me Ed."

It strikes me as both sweet and a little unnerving how well they take to one another. Maybe it's a similarity in upbringings, both sons of single mothers who learned to take care of their families early in life. They're both from Ohio, with good Midwest manners, and they're both foodies.

"Do you mind if I make a restaurant suggestion?" Marc asks my father. "There is a place I've been dying to try. You like scallops?"

My dad's eyes go wide and they launch into a discussion about fishing methods and preparation. I tune out and wave to Beth, who smiles her sour smile in response. I'm starting to wonder if that's just the way she looks and not indicative of her attitude. Maybe I'm projecting.

I trail them down the long corridor to the exit, where Marc's car is waiting.

"I have a car," Dad says.

"Ed, sir, if you don't mind, I would like to get you drunk enough to tell me embarrassing stories about Penelope. And I wouldn't want you to drive after." Dad's face lights up. I roll my eyes and slide in the backseat, stuffed between the two of them.

When the car comes to a stop outside a hotel, we take an elevator to the top floor and walk the final flight of stairs. The restaurant is on a rooftop, looking out over the twinkling city lights. From this height we're spared the heat of street level, enjoying a cool breeze and a faint salty smell to the air.

A maître d' welcomes Marc with a hand over handshake and ushers us to a corner table, covered on two sides by a gauzy partition that floats in the breeze. The view overlooks the city, which is miraculously quiet from here. I sit across from Marc, next to my father, inspecting the menu as they chat about food, music and cars.

Marc orders a white wine, meant to bring out the flavors in the scallops, which he admits to only knowing about because he read an article on the chef's recommended pairings in an in-flight magazine. Dad approves and we cheer to good food, good music and good company. In a weird way I feel like I'm home from college, introducing my new friend to my dad.

It occurs to me that my dad has never been this jovial around Seth, and I get a sudden pang of indignation and guilt. Dad hasn't asked about Seth yet but I'm sure it will come up before night's end. I don't relish the idea of telling him we're taking a little time apart. I'm not sure which reaction I dread more: approval or disappointment.

The food is amazing, of course, and my dad is enamored ... and a little tipsy. Dad talks Marc's ear off and I appreciate that Marc obliges affably. I sip my wine and gaze out at the city, imagining all the different lives lived in this tiny geographic space.

Marc asks my father if he's coming to any more of our shows as we head toward his hotel. I ask Marc if he can arrange for someone to drive Dad's car back for him. Of course, it's no problem. Thanking him, I wave goodnight, assuring him I can take a cab back after I say goodnight to my father.

I walk Dad up to his room and go in, surprised by how small the room is.

"Where's Mom?"

"Your mother couldn't make it. She had to babysit Heather and Geoffry for your sister," he says, averting his eyes.

"Is everything okay?" I ask, hoping that in his tipsy state he might be loose-lipped.

"She sends her love."

I try not to dwell on his obvious lie. He probably didn't even tell her he was coming to see me.

"How's Seth?"

"Good," I lie, scanning the room with my eyes. The artwork is the awful generic kind typical in hospital waiting rooms.

"Penelope Ann Caruso," he says in his don't-lie-to-me voice.

I let out a whoosh of air, plopping down in the small armchair next to the bed. "I'm not sure. Everything was great until ..." my voice trails off.

"Until what?" he says, his voice gentle.

"I started taking this songwriting class and I sort of loved it." I watch him smile proudly. "I wrote some songs that Seth didn't want to put on our album." Dad's face contorts in anger. "And then Marc and I wrote a song together and he offered me this opener's slot as a solo act, and I took it." I look down at my hands, unsure what else to say. "Daddy, it's such a mess," I blurt, tears rolling down my cheeks.

Dad is not the type to fall for tears. He lets me collect myself, not offering any opinions.

"Does Seth know you have feelings for Marc?"

My mouth drops open. I can't believe he just said that. And so matter-of-factly. Why does everyone keep saying that? I mean, yes he's attractive. And we get along. And flirt a little. But that doesn't automatically mean I have feelings for him, does it?

Dad cocks his head in my direction, letting me sort it out. Realization dawns slowly. Pieces of the last few months filter through my mind's eye as the focus shifts, becoming clear in a way I never imagined. All these seemingly disparate elements form a connect-the-dots puzzle that makes it unbelievably obvious how ignorant of my own feelings I've been. Seth must have seen the same thing Dad sees. It breaks my heart. I never meant for any of this to happen. I didn't realize it was happening at all.

For a long time we just sit together in silence. Finally, I get up to leave.

"It's good to see you happy, sweetheart," Dad says.

"Thanks, Dad," I say, collecting my purse. "What makes you say I'm happy?"

He just smiles, hugs me to him and kisses my head.

"It's in the details. Happiness isn't the product of perfect circumstances. It's the journey of being our truest selves," he says into my hair.

I pull away, shocked at his sudden inner guru. He smiles.

"I saw that on Pinterest," he says with a shrug. "That's you and your songwriting. I can hear it in your music."

Chapter 32

"You riding with me?" Marc asks as we grab coffees from a truck stop.

It's nearly sunrise and we're heading into the Midwest, marking the halfway point of the tour. I'm wearing my usual pajamas—cotton shorts and a loose t-shirt. The temperature is at least ninety degrees without the sun and I can only imagine how much hotter it's going to get, not to mention the humidity. The curls on my head are growing by the second, looking like I should be in an 80's hairspray commercial.

In the parking lot where all three buses idle, I'm comfortable enough with the dynamics of band members and staff now that I hop on his bus without hesitation. For one thing, Marc's bus smells better. In this heat, those dancers and musicians in a confined space smell pretty ripe.

This has become our norm: drinking coffees together, me riding with him until we get to the next venue. In all our conversations I like that he's not judgmental and rarely gets defensive. He hears new opinions and contemplates them, making up his mind when he feels he has enough of the facts.

After the conversation with my dad, I can't stop second-guessing intentions, his and mine. The old When Harry Met Sally conundrum comes to mind: can men and women ever really be friends?

"I want to show you something," he says, leading me up the steps to his bus.

I make myself comfortable on the couch and blow on my coffee.

"Stevia?" he asks, handing it to me without waiting for my response. I dump two packets in the travel mug that has somehow become "mine." It's silver with a resonator guitar etched into the side. I picked it out once and now Marc always gives it to me.

Holding up one finger he motions for me to wait, and disappears into his room. When he emerges, he's holding an acoustic guitar I've never seen before.

"I want your honest opinion on this song I'm going to play tonight, okay? It's a little old-timey and I know it doesn't really suit my sound, but I don't care," he says, wiping his palms on his board shorts.

"Kay..." I say.

The diesel road train roars to life, snaking through smaller city streets toward the main freeway. It jostles us around and I set my mug in a cup holder so I don't spill on his new guitar.

Once we hit the freeway the rocking becomes more rhythmic. Marc picks up his guitar, clears his throat, and wipes his hands again.

The song is beautiful. A story of unrequited love, told from the perspective of a sea captain to his muse, the beautiful siren. By nature they cannot be together, but he loves her from afar. I don't recognize it, but it sounds like it could be an old Irish folksong.

"That's really pretty," I say, clapping. "Is that a traditional song?"

"No," he says, brows furrowed. "I wrote it."

"I'm a little jealous. It's great," I say.

He turns his head toward the window then looks back to me. "I wrote it for you."

"Oh," I say, understanding dawning. "I—," I don't know what to say to that. I blink rapidly, trying to formulate a coherent thought.

"Don't worry about it," he says, looking down at his guitar across his lap. "I just wanted you to hear it first. Before I played it tonight."

A myriad of emotions vie for my attention, and the one I latch onto is surprise. Surprise that he's adding it to his set. That he wrote it for me. That he thinks any of those things about me.

"You're playing that tonight?" I say, wishing I could be cool and articulate, instead of incapable of having an emotional conversation. I know that's what he wants—what he deserves. And I can't give it to him.

The lines of his face tighten and he gets up, turning to the kitchen.

"I'm sorry," I say, following him to the kitchen, putting my hand on his shoulder. "You just … took me off-guard. I don't know what to say."

He turns to face me, my hand still on his shoulder. He steadies his gaze on mine and kisses me. I'm not as surprised by the kiss as I am by the feeling that rips through me. It's not a gentle kiss. It's full of passion, and my body responds immediately, intensely. The urgency in his kiss makes my heart race. It's as though the tension that's been building inside him couldn't be contained any longer. In my brain I know this is not okay. I'm married. But my hormones don't care. They're blocking the message to my brain.

He wraps his hands around the small of my back, pulling me closer. As my body fuses into his, my legs give out like I'm in some silly rom-com. He catches me, holding me to him, our bodies as close possible, fully clothed. He tastes like peppermint and coffee, his soft lips are simultaneously firm and gentle, and somewhere in my muddled brain I register the smell of his shaving cream.

Pulling away slightly I take a much needed breath. Molten with desire, his dazzling blue eyes draw me in and I'm shocked by the naked emotion he's allowing me to see. I try to see myself in this situation objectively. The rules of my marital separation are vague, to say the least. It's almost definitely a terrible idea, but I know what I want to do right now. I'm just not sure what comes after.

As I start to pull back again, Marc picks me up, setting me down on the table, where he slides his hand along my torso, running a thumb across my nipple, which hardens below the thin cotton of my t-shirt. He keeps his body just out of reach and I have to put my hands behind me to balance on the table. He explores the curves of my body with one hand, his eyes drinking me in.

At my bare knee, he starts the journey up my thigh and my hormones take full control of my body. I arch my spine, tipping my head back in pleasure. His mouth finds my neck and I let go of the table, encircling his neck with my arms.

With his arms wrapped around me, he leads me with his body walking on my behalf to the bedroom. As I'm deposited onto the soft bed, I feel a sense of déjà vu, but then his lips are on me again and I'm lost. I've only ever been with Seth. Marc's hands are different, his pace slower, more methodical. I should feel nervous, but it feels natural—the mere physical extension of an emotional intimacy that's always existed between us.

He seems intent on exploring every inch of my body. I try to undo his button and fly, but he pulls out of my reach. The bus bounces and jerks below us, but we hardly notice. With a forefinger he slides the shirt off my shoulder, kissing the dip in my collarbone and repeating the action on the other side. He pulls my shirt up over my head, running his hands down my back and over the curve of my hips. A growl escapes his lips, reverberating through me, my skin answering his call with goose bumps.

I tug the pillowy flesh of his bottom lip with my teeth, a small "ah" trapped in my throat. His tongue invades my mouth once again, the sound of my desire blending with his. Desperate to feel him inside me, I writhe beneath him.

I'm naked and he's shirtless, his perfect chest pressing against mine, our lips locked in a passion that feels unbreakable. He raises his head to look at my face, running a finger along the side of my jaw, all the way to my mouth. I kiss his finger and suck it into my mouth, circling my tongue around the tip.

"Fuck," he groans, and presses his forehead to mine. He rolls to the side, disengaging. He rubs a hand along the length of my torso, grabbing my ass and pulling me to him. Our bodies pressed together, chest to chest, I feel an intangible shift.

"Is everything okay?" I ask, inadvertently glancing down

toward his shorts.

He shifts me enough that I can feel my answer. He kisses me gently and sucks in a deep breath.

"You know how I feel," he says. "I want you. And I want to know you won't regret this." He rests his head on one hand, elbow propping him up. I mirror his action.

I don't want to have this conversation right now, and I hate that he's the one to bring me to my senses.

"I don't share well," he says, looking into my eyes. "I want you for myself."

Staring into his obvious desire, I fall onto the pillow, throwing an arm over my face.

"Honestly, I don't know the rules," I admit. "I feel like I'm torn between two different planes of existence."

His chest rises and falls more quickly, but he stays quiet.

"Seth and I have been together for so long. He's wrapped into all my adult memories," I say, searching his face for understanding. "Recently something in me has changed. I'm not sure Seth understands it, or if he has any interest in the new me."

"Do you want him?"

"I love him," I say, closing my eyes. "But I can't tell if that's past or present tense. Does that make sense?"

A vague headshake lets me know he heard, but his face is masked, creating a distance that makes my chest actually, literally hurt.

"And you," I say, running a finger along his jawline. "Bring out this whole other side of me," I kiss his bottom lip. "You excite me in ways I never knew I'd been missing." His navy eyes darken and he kisses my hand. "You're spontaneous. And open." He kisses me from wrist to inner elbow. I continue, a little shaky. "You're generous and loving. You're the kind of guy I always imagined I'd be with."

"But?" He stops kissing me and my skin yearns for his mouth. "Not the guy," he says on a sigh.

Rolling away, he flops onto his back, holding me to him. I lay my head on his chest, my hair wavy and loose down his arm. We stay in this position so long we fall asleep.

When I wake up, he's no longer next to me. I sit up and slowly get dressed. From the bedroom I spot him sitting fully clothed on the couch. He's staring out the window. The edges of his hair glow in the sunlight, his shoulders are broad and muscular, and I fight the urge to wrap my arms around them. I don't move. It's not fair of me to do anything at all until I figure out what I want. A small, but not insignificant, voice in my head wants to know if he wants me for me, or if it's the challenge that really excites him.

Chapter 33

Marc has been avoiding me for five excruciatingly long days now. The closest I get to him is onstage, where he is still the consummate professional, introducing me to his audience, singing our duet and flashing that trademark smile for the sake of the show, which breaks my heart a little more every time. But as soon as we step offstage, he slips away before I can get his attention. And he hasn't played the song he wrote for me, either. I don't know why, but that makes me saddest of all.

I can't stop thinking about him—the feel of his lips on mine, his buttery skin over taut muscles, the warmth of being wrapped in his arms—it consumes me. It blends waking and sleeping hours into one interminable queue as I wait for him to break the silence. I know it's on me to figure out what I want, and theoretically I appreciate the space to do that without pressure. Realistically, it's torture. Every time I think I've made a decision to be with Marc, I think of Seth.

Seth, who has loved and grown with me my entire adult life. Can I picture my life without him? He is part of me—a big part—and no matter how much I change, a part of him will always be blended into the fabric of my being. I can only imagine his horror at my describing him that way. No one wants to be the sentimental side of that equation.

The tumble of nostalgia and desire make me dizzy. I want to duck my head under covers and wake up to discover someone else has sorted my life out for me. Until that happens, I lie here in my bunk, bouncing through to the next city, vaguely registering the unexplored landscape as it slips away.

"About damn time!" Lolo says when I answer my phone. I haven't been able to bring myself to speak to her (or anyone) since that day on Marc's bus. I wouldn't know where to begin.

"I'm so sorry, Lo."

"What's wrong?" she says, dropping the angry façade.

"I don't want to talk about it."

"Hmph. At least tell me about the tour. What's it like playing to sold out stadiums across the country?"

"It's ... amazing," I admit. I tell her all about my favorite shows so far, including the surprise visit from my dad.

"Your dad came to see you? What did he say?" She knows how long it's been since I've spoken to them. She's never even met my parents and we've been best friends for six years.

"He came out to dinner with me and Marc."

"Hang on ... Marc met your dad?" she asks, her tone accusatory.

"It just happened. They met backstage when I was getting my purse and my dad invited him to dinner—"

"Hold up. Your dad invited him? He's never even done that with Seth, has he?"

"No." I rub my temple with my free hand.

"So ... is there a you and Marc?" she asks, keeping her voice low. I assume Jeff must be within earshot.

"Lo," I say, the backs of my eyes burning. I swallow hard. "I don't know what's happening to me."

"Oh, Sweetie."

"Seth and my dad were right," I sniff. "I do have feelings for him." I take a couple breaths. Lolo sits quietly on the other end.

"My life is a mess," I say, trying to keep from blubbering incoherently. "I'm not speaking to my husband—don't know if he wants to be married to me anymore," I take a shaky breath. "And now I have feelings for someone else, which makes me despicable, even to myself." I squeeze my eyes shut tight and drape an arm over them. "I feel like I'm choosing between who I've always been and who I might become."

"That's some deep shit," she says. "What about Marc? Has he made a move?"

"Kind of," I hedge. I tell her about the song and the almost sex, finishing with how he stopped and told me he didn't want to share.

"Wow," she says, letting it sink in. "What are you gonna do?"

"No idea. You want to decide for me?"

"Shit," she muses, more to herself than to me. That about sums it up.

"Are you happy?" I ask suddenly.

"Yes," she says so quickly I know it's instinctive.

"How do you know?"

"I choose it, every day."

Hanging up, I feel infinitesimally better. The big life questions will be answered at some point, but for now I need to focus my attention on work. If I'm going to retain even a shred of self-respect, I am going to do exactly what I came on this tour to do: be a solo artist. The only things I can control are my own actions, and I intend to.

It's that time of afternoon before sound check when the bus is empty, and everyone is outside enjoying a little free time before the show. I flip open my laptop and check my email. I get a bunch of messages about marketing tips and penis enlargement, one from a fan who saw me in Atlanta, and a message from a well-known producer who got my name from Chris, asking permission to release a remix of one of my songs. It's the kind of thing that would normally send me into an indecisive spiral, but right now it's the easiest decision on my plate. I say yes. Why the hell not?

What I really need right now is fresh air. I want to hike up a mountain. Unfortunately, the Midwest isn't exactly mountainous. Parked in a flat parking lot, in a flat town, there isn't enough time or space to get my desired perspective.

In lieu of a nature hike, I change into workout clothes and running shoes, pull my hair back into a messy ponytail, and jog around the arena's enclosed parking area. It's roughly double the size of a track and heat waves radiate off the asphalt as I make my way around and around, making it hard to get enough air in my lungs. After a few laps I'm dripping sweat and breathing hard. I double over, hands on thighs, and work to steady inhales and exhales. I stand, bringing hands to the top of my head, unable to fully catch my breath. Seeking reprieve from the heat, I climb the ladder attached to the back of the bus, hoisting myself onto the roof. When I'm at the top I gulp air that's at least a few degrees cooler than street level and close my eyes.

"Hey," Marc's voice floats to me, soft and soothing. I open my eyes to see him lounging on a towel on top of his bus. So much for perspective.

Chapter 34

Unable to speak, I stare, expecting him to disappear like a mirage. Since acknowledging that I have feelings for him, I haven't figured out how to act or what to say. There's no such thing as normal. He offers a sad smile, which I return. I pause, contemplating sitting down, but it feels silly. I can't sit there and not talk to him, but I'm not ready to talk about it either. So I take the cowardly climb back down the ladder, hopping off the last rung, landing hard on the ground.

"Wait up," Marc says, jumping down with ease.

I wait, unable to walk away from him. An internal battle wages inside my head that I hope is not apparent on my face. He stops when he's near me, close enough that I want to touch him, but not enough to indicate that he wants me to.

"How are you?" he asks, his brows wrinkling. He looks from me to his feet and back again.

I want to spill my guts, to tell him how much I miss him, how conflicted I feel, but I don't. It's not fair. He's been honest and upfront with me and I won't be the girl who leads him on. I wouldn't be able to forgive myself.

Beth, trailed by two insanely attractive models, approaches us as I open my mouth to say something. She smiles at Marc and flicks her eyes my way.

"Ready?" she asks Marc. He nods and looks back to me, apologetically. Or at least I think so. I could be imagining it. The models laugh and flick their hair, linking their arms in his as they walk off together, and I'm left feeling sucker punched. Beth follows them, phone glued to her ear, and glances my way with a pitying expression. If she wants me to feel pathetic, it's working.

***

Tonight is our final Midwest show. This morning, in Marc's hometown of Dayton, Ohio, they've organized a parade in his honor. I'm excited to head to the Northwest tomorrow—our last run—before our return home. A lifetime seemingly separates where I was when we left from who I am now. Despite the uncertainty waiting for me at home, I'm looking forward to getting off this roller coaster.

Marc and I have settled into a friendly coolness that is an improvement over the freeze out, but still unsatisfying. Now that I'm aware of my feelings, the emotional distance combined with close physical proximity is excruciating.

As tour support, I'm not required to attend the parade or meet-and-greet. I'm going anyway. I miss my friend and want to see his big homecoming. His mom and sister are here and I expect a lot of other people who have known him a long time will be around too. Partly I'm hoping to uncover something unredeemable that will break the spell, solving my dilemma once and for all. The other part is hungry for information, anything to give further insight to the inner workings of this person I can't stop thinking about.

I look out my bunk's small window and watch Marc get into the backseat of a black limo, the sunrise reflecting off its hood. I check the clock on my phone, relieved my alarm won't sound for another hour. I pull the blanket over my head, falling back to sleep to the sounds of snoring and the white noise of the generator, grateful for air conditioning.

When my alarm goes off an hour later, it's dead quiet. I'm alone in the bus. It's eerie. I've been constantly surrounded by people for more than a month. Having this time and space to myself—something I'd normally relish—feels lonely. I've gotten used to the din of activity, even though I've mostly been on the outside.

Thwap! Thwap! Thwap! Comes an open fisted knock on the door of the bus.

"Why aren't you ready?" Beth says, not bothering to hide her frustration.

"Ready for what?"

She rolls her eyes. "You have five minutes until we leave. I sent you the updated itinerary this morning. You're on float six."

"Five minutes," she says, stomping off, already on another call.

I salute to her disappearing silhouette, mumbling snarky comebacks, as I throw together an outfit I hope is parade worthy and dab on a little makeup. In an effort to tame my hair, I wet my hand and scrunch it but, as always, my curls have a mind of their own. Today they've opted for puffy waves. Oh well: it'll have to do.

I've chosen a navy blue romper with little yellow anchors, paired with my usual Toms. The goal is to be able to sit or stand above a crowd without having to worry about flashing anyone. I hold up the strapless top with one hand as I sprint across the parking lot. Beth stands beside the van door and I'm certain she'd love nothing more than to leave me stranded here.

"Ready," I pant, breathless.

She looks me up and down and says, "That's everyone. Let's go." She takes a call and settles in shotgun. I slide the van door closed behind me.

We wind through Rockwellian neighborhoods of perfectly-spaced suburban homes and oak tree-lined sidewalks where kids ride bikes and mothers jog behind strollers, waving at neighbors. For the first time I see what my father meant about old-fashioned American values. They exist here in this flat oasis, away from the skyscrapers and oceans, kept in a bubble—cocooned from outside influences.

The junior high school parking lot is packed with floats varying in size, shape and extravagance. Men and women in colored polo shirts and clipboards rush around, checking things off their lists and shouting directions to stragglers.

I approach a float decorated like a coral reef with Poseidon holding a trident poised regally over the bow. A young girl, maybe ten years old, folds little pieces of blue tissue paper into tufts, sticking them to a small bare spot above a wheel well.

"Hi," I say so as not to startle her. "Nice job, it looks

great."

She smiles politely but doesn't respond, returning to her work. I take the hint and make my way down the line, heading toward a bossy looking woman in a yellow polo. There's a haughty air about her that tells me she'll know where I can find float six.

"See that pink donut?" she says, pointing to my three o'clock. I nod. "It's two floats back from there."

I thank her and head toward the giant donut. Before I get more than a handful of steps, I see Marc. He's dressed in slacks, a button up shirt and vest. His short hair is slightly less messy than usual and he's standing beside his mom and sister.

The three of them are talking to a man in a navy polo, holding a comically large scepter. He's either the mayor or the oldest prom king in history. Marc is smiling and respectful but I can tell he isn't really listening to whatever the man is saying. His mother, on the other hand, is overflowing with enthusiasm, shaking hands and beaming at her son.

"This way, honey," a giantess in a yellow polo says to me, pulling me toward a float draped in large butcher paper posters reading, "Class of 2017" and "Save the Music Program!" A few teenagers throw bits of bagel at people walking by, erupting in fits of laughter when they hit their target: a balding middle-aged man whose skin looks like he's spent the last twenty years under fluorescent lighting. They huddle together as the poor bastard shakes his head and wanders off. I raise my brows inquiringly at the giantess, unwilling to out-and-out question her sanity, but hoping she's mistaken. I didn't sign up to babysit.

"Beth put you with the choir," she beams. "She said it was your pet cause." She gives me an "Isn't that sweet?" look and I bite back the choice words I have in mind for Beth. "They're good kids. Might want to sit toward the back though, just in case." She pats me on the shoulder before heading off in the other direction.

I'm not sure how the back is going to be any safer, but the risers at least give me something to duck behind.

Watching Marc and his mom again, I fight the urge to text him. A teenage girl who wasn't involved in the bagel throwing catches me looking in his direction. Uninvited, she sits next to me on the top riser.

"He's so hot," she says knowingly.

"Are you a fan?"

"Nah, I don't really like pop music?" she says, ending the statement with a questioning lilt. "I prefer indie folk." She gives me a once over and I hold my breath, feeling like I've been catapulted through time back to the worst years of my life. Unlike my junior high school peers, she seems approving and turns her head from me to Marc. "He's hot enough to make an exception, though."

How old is this kid?

"What's your favorite band?" I ask. This girl makes me realize that I'm officially old now. I cannot discuss Marc's hotness factor with a kid, even if I agree. Especially because I agree.

"I doubt you've heard of them," she says in an imperious tone.

"Try me."

"Ida Bella?"

"I've heard of them," I say, smiling.

"You have? Wow. Almost no one's heard of them!" Her face lights up and I try not to cringe. "I'm completely obsessed. I love that one song about the daisy that wants to be a rose," she says, singing the chorus for me.

I argued with Seth to keep that off the album. I said I thought it was trite and childish. He said it was whimsical. I smile, suddenly wishing I could call him.

She looks at me, inspecting me more carefully. "You know, you kind of look like her?"

"Like who?" I feign ignorance.

"Penelope," she says. "I'm Emily, by the way," she says, putting a hand out.

I shake her hand and say, "I'm Penny."

"Woah, crazy coincidence!" she says, eyes wide.

The giantess announces our imminent departure via bullhorn and Emily shoots up, jumping down a couple of stairs. She turns back around. "Nice to meet you, Miss Penny. See ya!" She bounces off.

Another woman in a yellow polo finds me and informs me that I'm supposed to hold the "Ohio State Champions Choir" sign and wave to people. Arguing would be futile so I nod and smile and remind myself that I do, in fact, want to save the music.

The parade makes its way down Main Street, lined with smiling faces, hands waving excitedly. Zombie-like, we wave back. The kids behind me on the float sing snippets of the year's most popular hits, blending hooks and choruses into one unending mega medley. They rib each other and laugh and I have to admit, I'm a little jealous of their rapport and free-spiritedness.

We reach what I think is the end of the line, where the floats come to a stop. Ours continues on, driving around the others. As we circle into the town square, two classic cars are parked in front of a large statue standing at attention atop a large water feature. A red ribbon is tied around the fountain and I catch movement out of the corner of my eye. I turn to see Marc with his mother and sister and the two models from before, following the mayor to a podium mounted in front of the fountain.

"Good morning folks!" the mayor booms. "What a great parade. Let's give a hand to everyone who helped build floats and donated their time to organize this event," he says, clapping and grinning as everyone follows his lead.

"And now, help me welcome back our prodigal son with keys to the city!" He motions to Marc, who raises a hand over his head, waving like he just won Wimbledon.

"Thank you Mayor," Marc says into the microphone, addressing the crowd. "What a great parade." He glances over at the mayor, who is beaming. "I was lucky enough to grow up in this wonderful town, but now to be welcomed home like this— It's an honor ..." he says, holding a hand to his chest. Sighs and "awws" fill the crowd. "Thank you!" He says to raucous applause.

The mayor hands him a monstrously oversized pair of scissors and Marc cuts the ribbon. The mayor holds open a wooden box containing a skeleton key, apparently to the city. Marc and the mayor pose for photographers and shake hands, baring their perfectly white smiles to one another.

I watch Marc, picturing how it would feel if he and I were together. Butterflies zing a lightning bolt through my body as I flashback to his mouth on me. I swallow and try to clear my head. What would our day-to-day together be like? Would I always be this attracted to him or would I eventually see him as a farce, a sellout? How would he see me?

When our float finally makes its way back to the parking lot and everyone disembarks, chatting and laughing, I feel a tap on my shoulder.

"I'm so embarrassed! I had no idea..." Emily says, suddenly shy. "Can I have your autograph?" she asks, blushing purple. "Why didn't you tell me you are Penelope of Ida Bella?"

"Sorry," I say. There's no good reason why I didn't tell her. I smile and take her parade program and marker, signing the outer edge and handing it back.

"My sister is friends with Marc's sister and she said you're going to be playing at the concert later. Is that true? I had no idea Ida Bella was touring," she says, speaking so quickly I struggle to keep up.

"Yes, I'll be there. But it's just me, not Ida Bella."

"Oh," she says, her brows knitting together. "You and Seth didn't break up, did you? Oh my God, I hope not. I'd kill myself!"

I shake my head and laugh. I had no idea anyone else was more invested in the state of my marriage or career than me. The good news is that my reaction never included suicide, so at least I've got that going for me.

"Thanks!" she says. "See you tonight!" She bounces off again, brandishing the program overhead as she approaches a pack of girls her age.

I smile to myself, then pull out my phone and dial Seth's number.

Chapter 35

Seth's phone sends me straight to voicemail. About to retell the parade story, I'm smiling. When I hear the beep, I reconsider. I hang up, realizing I can't just call and share a simple anecdote anymore. The scariest part about contemplating life without Seth is being on the outside. No longer being an insider in one another's lives. I'm still not sure if we're separated or just existing separately. The nature of separation becomes apparent—being apart is slowly becoming reality by default.

It's an awful, horrible, terrifying thing. And yet ... I'm still here. I don't know how to feel about that.

At the concert, I'm surprised to realize I've become accustomed to having a stadium filled with people waiting for me (well, Marc) to entertain them. The adrenaline rushes through me as I step from the side of the stage to the front, but I'm no longer paralyzed when I play those first notes.

This hometown crowd is antsy to see Marc and I smile to myself as I turn around, knowing he's heading out to join me for the end of my set. I play the musical interlude, as per usual, but he doesn't make his entrance. I play it again— sweating halfway through when he still hasn't come out. I can't play it a third time so I play through and sing the first verse solo. I close my eyes and play an intricate solo through what would normally be Marc's part. The crowd cheers enthusiastically. For half a second I'm in love with them. But it continues and I open my eyes, sensing a presence onstage with me. He sings his verse and together we finish the last chorus.

I sing to Marc, who leans in, whispering in my ear.

"We're going to play my new song."

My smile fades. I can't challenge him here onstage, but

everything in me is screaming "No!" I've only heard the song once. This is a terrible idea. Granted, it's a three-chord song that won't be hard to follow, but it's not like him to improvise, especially not with me, especially not with this song.

I love that he wants to play the song, that maybe he still feels something for me. But anger bubbles beneath my happy veneer at being put on the spot like this. I strum away, hoping to mask the annoyance in my voice.

I yield the mic, letting him introduce me, bowing to the crowd, thanking Marc by blowing a kiss. A glimpse of a familiar face in the front row catches my attention and I give a quick wink to Emily. She bounces up and down as I focus on her alone.

It's enough to distract me as Marc takes a seat on a stool that has miraculously appeared out of nowhere along with a second mic.

"It's good to be home," Marc says to a rowdy cheer from the crowd. "And I thought, if I'm going to try out a little something new, I should do it here, in front of my friends and family. So what do you think, do you want to hear a new song?"

The applause is deafening and the pulsing beat of a kick drum paces us in. Marc counts, "2,3,4" and strums the first chord. I'm surprised to see the whole band, and I realize they have rehearsed this. He planned this! It's hard not to feel like I've been set up to be the fool. And I don't appreciate it.

I follow along, singing harmonies where I think they fit. The song has a really nice build into the final chorus, one that I didn't notice the first time I heard it. It's folky, but with a solid pop structure. It really is a great song.

"You like that song?" Marc probes the audience. They erupt again. He grins. "Good! Because that was the first track off my new album," he says, cheers thundering him on. "And I'd like to thank this talented lady," he points to me, "for inspiring me to try something new."

I'm sure my eyes are bugging out of my head. Lips and

teeth part into what I hope looks like a smile to the audience as I clench my jaw to keep my internal dialogue to myself. He flashes his professional smile one more time and I do the same, but for a fleeting second I see a flicker of the earnest eyes that told me he wanted me and that he didn't want to share.

Chapter 36

"What the hell?" I say, bursting into Marc's green room after his encore.

His eyes widen for a moment and he motions for me to sit. Chris is sitting at the table, working on paperwork, but at my tone he looks from me to Marc. A look passes between them and Chris gets up, not making eye contact with me as he goes, the door clicking softly behind him.

"Problem?" he asks, all innocence.

"I didn't appreciate being ambushed."

"It wasn't an ambush. It was a surprise. There's a difference." He leans against the counter, arms crossed over his chest. I hold my ground by the door, shaking my head.

"I'm sorry. It was meant as a compliment. A sort of thank-you-for-the-inspiration."

God I wish I could read his mind. Is he being passive-aggressive, or does he really not see how messed up that was?

"Look," I say, trying for a calm voice, "I love the song." I close my eyes, biting my bottom lip. "But that was really unprofessional. I felt like an idiot, trying to come up with stuff on the spot, when the rest of you had obviously rehearsed."

"You were amazing." He takes a small step toward me. "But you're right, I didn't think about it like that. I'm sorry," he says, his face softening. "I wanted you to know ... not talking to you has been killing me."

It's not fair, deflating my indignation like that. Robbed of righteous anger, I'm left confused, flattered and frustrated. And those pesky butterflies flitter around his last statement that perfectly mirrors my own thoughts.

It was sweet of him to play the song, especially if he intended it as a grand gesture. And thanking me in front of his audience can only be good for my sales. Damn him! I've been miserable since we haven't been speaking, but left inside my own head, I could talk myself out of any feelings I have for him. Or at least pretend to. Being reminded that he isn't an asshole, but actually sweet and thoughtful (albeit a little misguided), makes it impossible to write him off. And where does that leave me?

Here he is, without a hint of reciprocation, letting me know how he feels. I inspired him? That's pretty awesome. He wrote a song for me and exposed his vulnerability to a stadium full of people. How could I not be moved?

"It was sweet," I concede.

He rewards me with a gleaming smile, full twinkle reaching his beautiful blue eyes. "And they loved it, pandering and all," I say, happy to feel a glimmer of our normal banter.

"I knew you'd appreciate that," he grins.

I relax and beam back at him. He closes the gap between us in one long stride and pulls me to him. I allow myself to be embraced, wishing I didn't love the feel of his strong chest beneath my cheek. Sometimes, no matter how much I resist, the universe throws up a roadblock that there's no way around. The only solution is to wait or keep moving.

Maybe he and I can move forward. Maybe there's no other option.

Emily is in line at the merchandise table when I show up for my meet-and-greet. She spots me and waves so enthusiastically she hits a guy in line on the side of the head. He glares at her, but she's oblivious.

"Hi Emily, what did you think?" I say, rounding the edge of the table to give her a hug.

"Ohmigod! It was so great!" She squeezes the air from my lungs.

"Thanks, I'm glad you enjoyed it." I smile, pulling myself free from her constrictive enthusiasm.

"Oh! That song you did with Marc? Best song ever!" She covers her mouth, eyes wild.

I laugh—her excitement is infectious.

"Not better than the new Ida Bella single, though," she says loyally.

"What new single?"

"'Chagall's Carnival?' Came out yesterday? You don't even sound like you. Isn't that weird?"

The air catches in my chest.

As quickly as I can, I sign autographs, smile for photos, and get out of there. I run to the bus. Luckily the party must be elsewhere because I'm the first one on. Safely ensconced in my bunk, I snap the curtain closed and pull down the shade. I flip my laptop open and try to breathe around the pressure building in my chest.

I search "Ida Bella" and just as Emily said, there's a new song posted on our YouTube channel. I hit space bar much harder than necessary. It starts out pretty in a melancholic way. I hear Seth's mandolin and distinct guitar style, trying to squelch my disbelief that he released a song under Ida Bella's name that I've never even heard before. In the lyrics of the first verse there are a couple references to going separate ways. There's a great line about nostalgia, "Are we elemental or sentimental?"

My heart beats heavy in my chest, picturing him writing and recording without me. And then the second verse comes in and I hear it: another woman's voice. Not just any woman either. Freesia Jones! Anger and despair erupt simultaneously in my brain. But he hates her!

I can't process any more of the lyrics. All I picture is her strutting around our house, playing my instruments, comforting my husband. I bet she loved spending late nights in the studio with Seth. And what, was he just pretending to hate her when he really wanted to fuck her? Trying to remove the visuals from my mind I squeeze my head in a vice grip between my hands.

Here I was thinking that Seth was being quiet because he was giving me space. Being the bigger person. A person I couldn't believe I ever contemplated leaving. And now I discover he just replaced me with the first woman to come along. Gah! And not just anyone: Freesia Fucking Jones! Apparently I'm nowhere near as special as I thought. And Lolo … how could she keep this from me? She must have known.

At least my confusion about Marc is based on an emotional connection. A chemical reaction I have no control over. I'm not being spiteful and hooking up with someone I despise. Hell, I'm not even hooking up!

Even worse than that, he asked her to sing a song so obviously about us. That's more of a betrayal than if they'd slept together. Oh God, have they? The thought makes me nauseous. I put a hand to my mouth, just in case.

I replay him getting upset that I was changing the rules of Ida Bella, making me feel guilty. Ha! What I suggested isn't even on par with what he's done.

I don't know what to do. I definitely can't listen to another note of this goddamn song. I can't sit still. We're supposed to drive overnight, leaving as soon as Marc and the band are all rounded up. The last thing I want is to lie here listening to them talking and laughing—or worse, sleeping—leaving me alone with my thoughts.

I can't get off the bus fast enough. As soon as the fresh air hits my face I realize what I have to do if I expect to get any rest.

"Hi," I say, gritting my teeth at the sound of Seth's hello. Even his greeting sounds smug.

"Hey Babe," he says, calm as ever.

"Don't call me that."

"You heard the song?"

"Did you do it just to hurt me?"

I can't believe this is the same person I chose to spend my life with.

"Of course we didn't," he says, sighing.

We! Did he just say 'we?' The voice in my heads screams.

"Are you and Freesia a 'we'?"

"No," he says.

I wait for some kind of clarification and when I don't get

one I ask more specifically, "Are you replacing me in Ida Bella?"

"Are you coming back?" he counters, the cool giving out just a bit.

"Are you sleeping with her?"

"You didn't answer my question," he says, his anger audible.

"Who are you?" I say, pulling my hair by the roots with my free hand. "Never mind. Don't answer. Doesn't sound like it's any of my damn business." I hang up, grabbing at my hair with both hands, just barely keeping myself from screaming at the top of my lungs, teetering close to the edge of crazy lady on the street corner.

It's a terrible, horrible, awful idea. But I go to Marc's bus anyway. I knock, and when he answers I step inside. The buses are growling and ready. We'll be leaving any second now and I know what I'm doing by stepping onto this bus. I am a terrible person.

I look into Marc's face, full of concern. Justifiable, considering my haggard crazy lady expression. I look deep into the navy blue depths of his eyes and realize I'm not that girl. I care about Marc, maybe too much. More importantly, I'm not vengeful.

There is a part of me that wants to sleep with Marc. A big part. I want to feel better—comforted, desired. But I want him in other ways too. I want to talk to him, to joke with him, to share little pieces of the day with him. And if I do that right now, I'll never forgive myself.

He's already made it clear that despite his desire, he doesn't want to share me. Which is all kinds of sweet and sexy. I take a deep breath to calm my raging hormones and force myself to turn around.

I am not going do this to Marc.

He rests his hand on my shoulder. And then he says the one thing I have no defense for.

"Are you okay?"

I feel the tears burning, willing them to go away. I bite my quivering lower lip, trying in vain to stop the waterworks.

"What happened?" He wraps an arm around my waist and pulls me into his body. I let out a few hiccoughing sobs, and step back to look at him.

"It doesn't matter," I lie. "I'm sorry. I shouldn't have come here."

"Hey," he says, making room for me on the couch. He puts his guitar away. "What are you talking about? I'm glad you're here."

"You've been," I sniff. "Honest with me. And now," I draw a deep stuttering breath. "I'm here and I'm crying and it's not fair." I wipe my eyes and work to control my breathing. I feel him watching me but I'm not ready to open my eyes.

"Drink?" he asks.

I bob my head, giving him a grateful smile.

He brings over two beers and sits beside me, clinking his bottle to mine.

"I heard about the song," he says, eyeing me. His jaw tightens as he says it and I can tell he's holding something back. "You deserve better. I hope you know that."

Aww, that's cute. And sweeter than I deserve.

I want to tell him I have feelings for him too, but I can't. I want to kiss his beautiful mouth and wrap myself in him.

"I should go," I say, picking at the corner of the beer's label.

"Okay," he says. It's completely irrational, but a small part of me feels rejected that he doesn't want to sleep with me right now.

I look up at him and watch his brows furrow and unfurrow. I stand to leave and he grabs my hand. He looks up at me and says, "Don't." The look in his eyes tells me he's not asking for my sake.

We drink our beers and revert to safe conversations, for which I'm grateful. The more time I spend with Marc, the more I find we have in common. If I could have described the man I'd end up with when I was ten years old, it would have been him.

I've never felt intimacy like this without sex. The weirdest thing is that it happened organically. It sounds all kinds of cuckoo crazy, but I can't pretend it isn't there. I'd never believe it if it weren't happening to me.

That little ten-year old girl grew up to become someone else though. Married someone else. Built a life with someone else. And now the changes happening in me threaten that someone else. It's a new age full of questions and uncertainties. I guess the one I have to answer is: who is the real me?

Setting aside my romantic confusion, I evaluate the less daunting aspects. Like seeing Dad. That felt good. And playing my songs to all those people. I love that they appreciate the words I wrote. I love being in control of my professional life and making my own decisions. I love connecting to a part of myself I never knew existed.

So yes, I like the person I am right now. Despite everything, I feel like I've found me. Am I the kind of person to give up on my marriage—even with its troubles? Maybe Seth has already made his decision. But if this were reversed, how would I feel in his shoes? Maybe too much has happened for us to go back. More importantly, I know now that I have to be me, whatever the consequences.

"What's going on in there?" Marc asks, touching a finger to my temple.

I must have been staring off. I watch him watching me with care. I am overcome with an emotion I recognize. It scares the hell out of me. But I know, deep in my heart, that it's true.

"I love you," I say.

"Is this because you had a fight with—?"

"No," I say, locking eyes with him. "I just realized it … and I wanted to say it out loud."

He looks wary and that makes me sad. I never meant to put him through all this. I thought he was a different person when we met—shallow, egotistical. It wasn't even a possibility that I could feel this way about him. And I would have laughed in the face of anyone who told me Marc Justin would care about me.

"I am a mess," I clarify. "But I love you. I love hanging out with you. I love talking to you. I love that I think of a thousand things a day I can't wait to tell you. I love making you laugh. I love that you give me butterflies." I don't know what else to say. My heart is filled to capacity and I'm afraid I might cry—again. I refuse to cry so I smile instead. "You deserve to hear me say it."

He closes his eyes, giving me a moment of terror. I feel exposed and raw, primed for heartbreak and humiliation.

"I love you too," he says, gazing intently into my face, not moving even a millimeter towards me.

Magnetized to him, I lean in, breaking the statue stance, and he pulls me roughly to him. We collide in an embrace that holds the promise of passion, the warmth of friendship, and the comfort of love. Electricity hums through my body, intensifying with every stroke of his hands on my back. I know he feels it. It's palpable. It's a tangible entity, existing of its own accord. This is intimacy. With or without sex, I'm in deep.

Fully clothed, I spend the night in his bed. I'm too chicken to start the conversation I know we should have. I wish I knew what was going on in his head, but I'm not going to ask. Holding me, his front spooning my back, our bodies don't allow any space between. It's shocking that I can fall asleep this way, and even more so that I'm rested in the morning.

When I wake up, I nuzzle my face into his neck. "Good morning," I whisper.

He grunts and squeezes me, rolling me on top of him.

"Hi," he says, his forehead on mine. We gaze at each other with Cyclops-like proximity. His heart beats against my rib cage as our breathing synchronizes. Aware of every patch of touching skin in excruciating detail, I'm pretty confident I could orgasm from the slightest touch. He seems to sense it, keeping his arms wrapped around the small of my back. Again, I really wish I knew what he was thinking.

I pull my head back to inspect his face. He bites his lips together and I feel his pulse quickening on me. So it's not just me. The thought makes me smile.

And now I know: I could be happy with Marc.

Chapter 37

"I'm taking you out," Marc says, slipping an arm around me, his back to my front as I admire the view from this ridiculously incredible hotel room. When we arrived in Seattle, Marc told me he booked a hotel room for the few days we're here.

"Presumptuous, much?" I quipped.

He grinned and kissed my shoulder. "Maybe," he said, resting his head on the spot he just kissed. I closed my eyes, enjoying his warmth and proximity, turning me in his arms so that we're face to face, my back against the glass.

"Where to?"

"It's a surprise."

"Well then, how will I know what to wear?"

"Your sexiest dress," he says, holding my hips, his body pressing against mine.

"Oh really? The attire is specifically 'sexy'?"

"Okay, maybe that's just for me. To see you in it. And help you out of it." He kisses me gently, pushing off the glass when I try to deepen it.

A flutter of excitement shoots through me, making me hyper aware of my lady parts. And unless he's got a microphone in his pocket, he's feeling the same.

"What time?" I ask.

"I'll pick you up at 6:30." He leans his forehead to mine, his hands resting on my hips.

"Kay," I say with my eyes closed.

Over the next few hours I move around the bus rushing through my to-do list—sneaking out to pick up some new lingerie, showering, shaving, trying on every dress I brought with me, and trying to avoid talking to anyone else. It would be impossible to lie in this state, but I don't exactly want our date to be public knowledge.

At 6:30 exactly, Marc raps on the door and mouths "wow" as I step off the bus. The dress I chose is a slinky black knee-length dress with a slit up my right thigh. It's form-fitting, with a boat neck top that creates little cap sleeves. I opted to keep my hair up in a simple ponytail, and I smile as his eyes take in the view.

"You look beautiful," he says, kissing me on the cheek and opening the car door for me. His driver smiles at us in the rearview mirror and I watch Marc watching me as we drive off. He's not smiling, but his eyes dance with mischief and desire. Oh boy. I'm in trouble.

He takes me to a restaurant that looks closed. I try to get a closer look and he squeezes my hand and helps me out of the car.

"My good friend's new restaurant," he says by way of explanation. "It hasn't officially opened yet, but I pulled a few strings."

His friend, Carver, is unsurprisingly a world-renowned chef whose restaurant is booked solid for the first six months before even opening. He's prepared a menu just for us this evening, and I get my first real glimpse at how different celebrity life can be.

And what an evening it is. Our usual banter has returned and we eat, talk and laugh all through dinner. At one point I become aware of his eyes on me, and I think I sense a slight melancholy, but it's gone almost immediately.

"You don't have to go home, but you can't stay here," Carver says with a smile. He pulls Marc into a one-arm man hug and hands him a to-go tote bag with dessert and a bottle of expensive-looking champagne.

"Thank you. That was the best crab I've ever had," I say, letting him take my hand between both of his. He grins and kisses my knuckles. He pulls me into a hug and whispers, "He's like a brother to me. I've never seen him so happy. Be good to each other." He holds my gaze in his until I nod my assent.

Marc opens the door for me as we leave, keeping his

hand at the small of my back. As soon as we climb back into the limo, the energy from my exposed nerve endings bounces like sonar waves, assessing the exact distance between he and I. I don't know what he's thinking and I want to break the silence with some bit of brilliant banter, but my mind is completely blank.

He doesn't say anything for an unbearably long time, but finally, as we're pulling up to the hotel's main entrance, he turns to me.

"I want you," he says, watching my reaction carefully.

I swallow, not sure what's about to follow.

"And I want to do all sorts of delicious things to you the second we get upstairs," he says, his eyes hooded with desire. Electricity radiates from my chest, my pulse quickening at the thought. "And I know you want me to."

Cocky bastard. But also true. Damn it.

"But I need you to tell me that you can do this. That you won't regret it." His pupils return to normal and I know in that instant that no matter what else happens, I won't regret it. I want this too.

The elevator dings at the top floor and we enter the suite side by side. I walk to the windows while he sets the tote bag down. I turn around just in time to see him stride toward me, and in that moment I know. I'm going to sleep with him, consequences be damned.

He kisses me with a passion that sends rays of tingling fire from my core to every nerve ending. He presses his whole body against mine, pinning me to the glass. Instinctively my hands slip under his shirt, needing to touch him. A moan escapes me and he pulls back, revealing dilated eyes that don't bother to hide his animalistic desire.

I lean my head back so I can run my tongue along his jawline, nipping slightly. He lets out a groan and turns me around, my body pressed against the glass, Seattle's skyline lit up below me. He sweeps the hair off my neck, the warmth of his mouth trailing across my skin. Without being able to see his face I focus on the ragged sound of his breath, the squeak of glass beneath my breasts, the draft between my legs where he hikes my dress up above my hips, exposing my lacy thong.

I want to rip his clothes off but he keeps me where I am, leaving just enough room for one arm to snake around my waist while the other slides the dress up and over my head.

"Beautiful," he says. In the window's reflection he admires my nearly naked body. I let my head fall back on his shoulder, relaxing into the compliment.

Pushing myself far enough away from the glass to slide my thong down, I kick it away with one foot. He moans as I push against him, his hands on my hips, directing me, showing me how he's feeling about me right now. The fingers of his right hand walk around my hip across my belly, and find their way South. It feels so good I barely register the sound of his zipper as he rids himself of clothing.

"Do you want me inside you?"

"Yes," I whisper.

"Now?" he says, his fingers increasing their speed, then stilling.

"Ah!" I exclaim, as he slides in, filling me. Slowly. Deeply. Deliciously. It takes a second for me to relax around his girth and he rocks back, deliberately taking his time.

"You're so wet," he rasps.

"Mmmm," I moan, unable to use actual words. As he builds me up with his hand, his cock slides deeper inside me and I cry out, the intensity of sensations bringing me close to climax.

This raw exposed feeling unhinges me and I push against the glass, arching my back so that it changes the angle of him inside me. The guttural sound he emits tells me he likes it and I push further, then back, over and over, losing myself in the rhythm.

"Uh-uh," he says, cupping me in one hand while the other stays on my hip, controlling the pace. I might protest if it didn't feel So. Damn. Good. But I don't have that kind of self-control and he knows it, making me come for him, his cock still hard inside me.

"God you're sexy," he says, pulling out of me. He turns me around, smiling at me in a way that I swear, is the actual picture of how every girl wants to be seen. I press my lips to his, separating them with my tongue, kissing him with everything I have to give.

Without breaking the kiss he directs me to the bed, laying me down gently, and for the first time I get to really see him in all his naked glory. Wow. There's really no other way to say it. And although I wouldn't have expected to be so turned on again, I can't help it. How does he have this effect on me?

He smiles, running hands down my body, absorbing every detail of my shape as his mouth explores my nipples, belly, thighs, calves. He keeps his kisses just off the mark. It's driving me crazy and I love every second of it.

When he gets back to the very top of my inner thighs, right when it starts to tickle, he takes me in his mouth, exploring my clit with his tongue. He grabs onto my hips, pulling me tighter to his mouth, and looks up at me from between my legs. I prop myself up on my elbows, eyeing him hungrily. He smiles and slides a finger into me, my head tipping back involuntarily. I hear a moan that I think must have come from me because it elicits a deep groan from him that vibrates into my core, nearly sending me over the edge.

My legs are shaking as I near orgasm and I'm overwhelmed with hormones and emotions. A tear leaks from one eye as I come in his mouth. I swipe at it as my body stops convulsing and he stays where he is. Once I've relaxed, he pulls back, peppering my inner thighs and belly with soft kisses, running his hands up my torso.

"I have wanted to do that since the first time I saw you," he says.

I grin. What's a girl to say?

Instead, standing on my knees, I pull him to me, running my hands across his chest, letting my fingertips wander down his sides and then up his back, grabbing onto his shoulders, pulling him down to me. I trail my fingers from his spine out to the edges of his shoulders feeling his muscles twitch beneath my touch.

"My turn," I whisper in his ear, pulling his earlobe into my mouth. Grasping his hard cock in my hand, I push him onto his back and watch him watch me take him in my mouth.

I don't get to have him long before he pulls me up, mouth to mouth, my legs straddling him. He lifts me up and plunges inside me, stilling as I clench around his cock. "Ah," he says into my mouth. "I'm going to fuck you hard now."

"Yes," I moan, our bodies already in unison. His breathing, ragged in my ear, gets more erratic with every thrust. Inadvertent "ah's" escape me as he fills me up, stretching me nearly to the point of pain. This electricity between us crackles, intensifying to a degree I wouldn't have believed possible.

Afterwards we collapse onto the zillion thread count sheets, our limbs tangled together, my head resting in the nook of his shoulder.

"Holy shit," I say, tipping my head to look at his face.

"Fuck," he says and kisses my forehead.

And then he does the only other thing that could make this night any better: he brings back dessert and champagne.

***

The next morning we have scheduled off. Marc kisses me awake, and I smile as he nuzzles my neck. "I want to take you somewhere today," he says.

Out of nowhere, something Seth said once about Marc having enough money and fame to lure any woman haunts my thoughts. I've never thought of myself as a materialistic person, but am I falling for it? The Puget Sound looks spectacular from his penthouse suite, the purple haze of the mountains blending seamlessly into the grey blue water, atop which sits a translucent layer of fog. This is no place to get perspective.

"Okay, but I have one stipulation," I say, sitting up. His naked body is on display and he smiles as I appreciate it openly. It's absurd how attractive he is.

"You can't spend any money," I say.

"Why not?" he asks, flipping me onto my back, his erection pressing into my belly. Momentarily flustered, I pull myself together and twist out from under him.

He grins, clearly amused by me.

"Because it's easy to be wooed by all the fancy private meals and drivers and stuff, but I want to go out with you. Not your celebrity," I say, sitting up on the pillows.

He narrows his eyes and leans in to kiss my neck but I hold him at bay. "You know, most women think it's romantic, especially when it's directed at them." His lips quirk in a sexy half grin and he runs his thumb across my nipple, taking it in his mouth. I close my eyes, goose bumps covering my bare breasts. "I'm not most women," I say. "Get creative."

"A challenge. I like it," he says. "But you're going to come first."

This is my kind of negotiation.

***

Since this is my first time to Seattle I expect it to be miserable and rainy, and filled with suicidal people wearing plaid. To my surprise it's a bustling city populated by the usual morning coffee drinkers, hurrying off in suits and ties to their downtown office jobs, with the typical ratio of crazies to regular folks I'd expect to find anywhere.

Marc wears his best Seattle disguise—faded jeans and flannel with the sleeves rolled up to his elbows. He adds a dirty baseball cap and sunglasses. It's not his best effort, but it'll do. I opt for jeans and a tank top, with a thin knit wrap sweater, because if there's one thing I've learned on tour it's layering. You can never tell how the day will go and you've got to be prepared.

Marc leads me out the double doors of the hotel to a coffee shop around the corner. I give him a look and he smiles, pulling two stamp-covered frequent buyer cards out of his pocket.

"See?" he says, pleased at his ingenuity. "Free coffee."

"Mmmhmm." I'm skeptical as to how he procured a frequent buyer card from a coffee shop I doubt he frequents (or has ever been to) but I let it slide. What can I say? I like my coffee in the morning.

We sit outside, drinking our coffees, watching people go by. I nudge him with my knee and he smiles. "What's next?" I ask. Outside there are two matching bicycles to greet us, leaning against the side of the building. I raise a questioning brow and he shrugs.

"Borrowing is free."

To explain the difference between borrowing and stealing is tempting, but he points to a hulking figure in a nearby doorway. It's his bodyguard and, as Marc nods to him, I realize these were made available for us to "borrow."

"Cheater."

One side of his mouth lifts in a smirk. Immediately I regret my word choice. We take off, pedaling through the city. I follow him, not concerned with where we're going. The word "cheater" rattles around inside my brain and I can practically feel The Scarlet "A" burning into my flesh. I wish I'd kept my big mouth shut. Not that I'm actually cheating. I don't think. I mean sort of, but it's more of a grey area.

Exercising to exorcise the thought works for me, spurring me to pedal faster. The feel of wind in my hair as we wind our way through city blocks and across parks transports me back to the present. Under a bridge with a giant sand troll holding a car in its hand, we take a break. We wait our turn and pose with the troll, asking a random passerby to take our picture. Marc picks me up, pretending to feed me to the hungry creature. I jump down and thank the stranger, checking out our photo. There are three images—my favorite of which catches me looking at the troll and Marc watching me, a look of longing on his face. That look makes me melt.

We go from the troll down to the river lock, where we watch salmon jumping and swimming upstream. There aren't too many tourists out today because it's the middle of the week, but plenty of people meander along the waterfront paths.

"Technically," he says, looking guilty, "this costs money." I quirk a brow at him. He holds up his hands. "But I didn't buy these today so I think maybe they're exempt from your rules?" He pulls out two passes for the ferry from Seattle to Bainbridge Island.

I don't want to set a bad precedent, but I've always been fascinated by ferries and I've never been on one. I'll give him a pass for this one. And just to make the point that I'm not totally caving, I make sure we ride the whole way to the ferry terminal, which admittedly is a lot farther than I thought.

The ferry trip isn't particularly long and I'm glued to the bow to the whole time. I put my arms out, letting the wind whip my sweater around like a plastic bag in the wind. The force is strong enough to keep me at a forty-five degree angle to the ground. Marc stretches out his arms too, and I laugh because he's completely upright. It's hard to ignore that we look like we're re-enacting the iconic scene from Titanic, but I prefer not to think about epic boating disasters while on a boat. Marc apparently feels otherwise, shouting, "I'm king of the world!" into the wind. I shake my head, embarrassed for him.

The sun threatens to break through the high clouds, creating a metallic glow that illuminates the water. It's spectacular in the truest sense of the word. I snuggle into Marc's arms, relishing the surreal. I can't help it; I'm enjoying the cheese factor.

The ferry docks at the island, and Marc suggests we go to a winery that offers tours and tastings. I can get behind that plan. He smiles, a little suspicious I think, but seems to be enjoying himself so I don't dwell. I squeeze his hand, nuzzling into his side.

We walk, getting to the winery just in time for the tour. The wines are amazing, as are the assortment of cheeses, grapes and bread they serve for lunch, and I swear the soundtrack to a Meg Ryan movie is playing over the speakers. My attempt to keep Marc from using his fame and money has backfired so thoroughly I have to laugh. I cannot imagine a more perfect day. I'm lucky to have this, even with the complicated context.

Down by the dock, awaiting our return ferry, Marc takes a call and I wander down to the water's edge. I imagine the lives of the people who own the sailboats I see in the marina. Where do they live? Where do they work? Are they happy? I think I'd be happy on a boat, sailing wherever my heart desired, sleeping under the stars as the ocean rocked me to sleep. I look across the Puget Sound toward Seattle, the now blue sky mirrored by the water, an unending blue expanse broken only by the jagged edges of skyscrapers and the Space Needle.

Less than a year ago I'd been talking to Seth about our next steps together when he told me to slow down, enjoy life as we live it. And now, here I am on tour (and in love with) with one of the biggest pop stars in the world, exploring a new city and preparing to play my own music to another packed stadium. It's hard to believe how much has changed. How much I've changed. And the funniest thing of all is that for the first time I am enjoying life, moment by precious moment.

"Sorry about that," Marc says, jogging to catch up with me on the boardwalk.

"No problem."

"That was Beth. They need us back for a last-minute radio show."

"Why don't I wander around while you do that?" I say.

"No." He faces me. "They want to interview both of us. And to play a song together."

"Why do they want to interview me?" I ask, barely giving it a thought.

Marc looks at me like I've grown a second head. "Didn't Beth tell you?" I shake my head, no idea what he's talking about.

"They're adding our song "Entangled" to rotation. It's

being played on every major radio station across the country!" he says.

"What?" I say, eyes wide. My hand flies to my mouth and I take a step back.

"When I played them 'Falling to Pieces' they loved it. They agreed that it's the perfect lead single for you."

"Are you messing with me?" I ask, ready to push him into the murky marina water if he's messing with me.

"No!" he says, raising his hands protectively. "You suck at hearing good news." He grins and I glare back at him. He's right. I do.

"It sounds too good to be true. It's like the naked dream. At some point I'm going to be exposed as an untalented fraud and everyone'll point and laugh," I say. Apparently I have some self-esteem issues to work through.

"You can't fake talent," he says.

I attempt to absorb this information. Nope. Can't compute. There must be a mistake. This is the kind of stuff that happens to other people. Not me. I shake my head. Marc leans against the railing, grinning at me.

We walk the rest of the way around the marina, finally making our way back up to the ferry dock. I don't feel much like talking. I don't know why. I just had an amazing morning and got the best news ever, but somehow it's morphed into something oppressive. Something about him suggesting they add "Falling to Pieces" leaves me unsettled. The mist settles in and has morphed from magical to cold and dreary as we settle into seats inside the ferry, looking out through filmy windows.

Chapter 38

To make this day even more bizarre, when I stop by the bus after the radio interview, I get a voicemail from Sal, asking me to get back to him as soon as possible.

"Hey Sal," I say when he picks up.

"Great news!" he says.

Fan-frickin'-tastic.

"You know that video we did?"

"Mmmhmm."

"They want to use your new single for the intro. I can send over the license now. They've asked if you will perform the song at the Grammys! They heard you perform it in San Diego and think it could be great publicity if you had Tyrone sing the backup harmonies. What do you think?"

I have never heard Sal say so much all at once and I'm completely bowled over. Un-fucking-believable. I should have read my horoscope today.

"That's amazing," I say to Sal, trying to improve my reactions to good news.

Maybe it's just my time. Everyone grows into themselves at some point and perhaps this is that time for me. I need to stop kicking positive news in the face.

"Great, I'll talk to Tyrone and send the contract over. Get it back to me as soon as possible, okay?"

I assure him I will and hang up. In my bunk, my mind reels over the incredible day. In my thirty years of life, no single day has ever been so filled with good luck and positivity. Is this the result of years of hard work? Or is there something else going on that I'm missing? Maybe that's the balance: easy professional success in equal opposition to a confusing and upside-down love life.

I check my email and see the new message from Sal with the sync license attached. I sit back against my pillow in my teeny bunk space, contemplating how much this will do for Tyrone. The thought brings a smile to my face, instantly transferring my skepticism to elation. Everyone needs an open door to walk through and, despite being dealt the short stick in life he's been given the winning lotto ticket with this shot. And I get to play a part in that.

I handle a few other administrative tasks in order to keep myself occupied and then grab a change of clothes and head to Marc's bus, where he's waiting for me.

It occurs to me how often he's stayed on his bus this tour. After seeing his hotel suite I realize that's probably more what he's used to. I wonder why he doesn't do it more often?

Just in case inspiration strikes, I grab my songwriting notebook and guitar. I take one last look around my bunk, and find my cell phone lighting up underneath the covers. Beth's name appears on the caller ID.

"Hello?" I say.

"I'm not sure how you got to him, but you need to be careful what you ask Marc to do on your behalf. He has a brand to protect and right now you're threatening it," Beth says, in her typical blunt way.

"What are you talking about? What do you think I asked him to do?"

"Oh, let's see … write his own music? Stop being seen with other women? Put your silly little EP in the hands of Clear Channel radio execs?"

I am stunned into silence.

"That lost little girl act doesn't work on me so don't condescend us both by denying it. Just stop. Leave him alone and go back to your husband where you belong."

The phone goes dead. I gape at it, trying to comprehend what the hell just happened. It's true that I suggested Marc write his own music. And I see how although I didn't ask him to stop seeing the skank flank that could look like my doing as well. The largest radio conglomerate—the Uncle Sam of radio, according to Seth—does Marc favors? And I'm the favor? What, because I don't deserve it on my own?

I know exactly what Seth would say about all this—and it wouldn't be good. But how do I feel? Am I selling out if a famous friend introduces my music to powerful people? Or is that just how the world works—everyone vying for those powerful connections to link them to the gatekeepers?

Everyone needs a break. Isn't it the same thing Sal and I are doing for Tyrone? Why is my situation different to Tyrone's? *Because Tyrone isn't sleeping with his connections*, my conscience pipes in.

Is that it? I want to say there is no truth to the accusation. It's my own fault. I wanted to sleep with him and now I'll never know for sure what role that played. Aside from any ulterior motives, I'm angry because I don't understand why he wouldn't have been honest about wanting to help me. I would have told him no, but still, going behind my back feels condescending. Because it doesn't get to be my choice. I don't get to be involved in a huge decision in my creative life. Again. It's like he's saying, "Just leave the business stuff to me." And isn't that why I'm upset with Seth—for leaving me out of the decision making process? Well, it's enough! I intend to handle my own business, thank you very much.

I shove my backpack under the shelf at the foot of my bunk. I snatch headphones from the shelf, plug them into my phone and turn it up as loud as possible. Music is the only thing that makes sense to me right now and I am in desperate need of grounding. Beth was wrong about at least one thing though. The "lost act" as she put it, is no act. I have never felt so unsure about so much. I worry I'll drift along forever like a balloon abandoned by its child, catching breeze after breeze until I'm finally discarded for good.

Chapter 39

I manage to avoid Marc the rest of the afternoon, but he comes to the stage early during my sound check. I can see the worry etched in his face and I feel guilty for a second before I remember why I've been avoiding him in the first place. I need to stay focused on the business at hand.

"Can I talk to you?" he asks as I strut off the stage.

"Now?" I say, hoping that if I just stall, I'll have time to sort through my feelings on my own.

"Yeah," he says, following my fast clip, jogging a couple steps to keep up. "Beth told me she talked to you," he says.

From my peripheral vision I see that he's trying to get me to look at him. I maintain my race walk and look forward. "And you didn't show at the radio station."

I do feel a little bad about that. I'm not a flake. I just couldn't go.

"Are you mad at me?" he asks.

I spin, stopping when we're face to face. I bite down hard, a ligament in my jaw twitching, unable to find words simple enough for him to understand.

"I'm sorry I flaked. That was unprofessional and it won't happen again," I say, sighing. "But yes, I am mad at you. I get that you wanted to help me."

"Yeah, I did—I do," he says, resting his hands on my hips.

"But you should've talked to me about anything to do with my career. It's important to me that I direct my own career." I step back and his hands fall to his sides.

"The only reason I didn't tell you was because it was a long shot and I didn't want to get your hopes up."

"A long shot because they'd never play it if they didn't owe you a favor?" I say, knowing I'm veering into unreasonable territory.

"I'm not going to apologize for what I did," he says, shaking his head.

That phrase, delivered in that I-know-what's-best-for-you tone I've heard Seth use so often sends me into full-on Crazy Town.

"You think it's okay to fuck with someone else's career?" I say. I know it's too harsh, but I'm too stubborn to take it back and all of my misplaced anger fills the space between us.

"Giving someone an opportunity hardly constitutes 'fucking with' your career."

"You're right. But it was condescending. And I expected more from you," I say, frustrated and inarticulate.

"I disagree. Friends help friends. You're being unreasonable."

"Is it too much to want my success to be based on talent and not on who I'm sleeping with? I just wanted to do this on my own!" I say, finally looking him in the eye.

"Is that why you think I wanted to help you?" he says, clearly hurt. He shakes his head again, stepping back from me. "To be clear, I sent that track the night after we recorded it at my studio."

My mouth opens but no words come out. I don't know how to respond to that.

"And I'm not Seth. But it kinda seems like we're interchangeable to you. Or am I just a little fun on the side to spice up your failing marriage?"

"And I'm unreasonable?" I mumble.

"I told you I don't want to share you. I've always been honest with you." He closes his eyes and takes a breath, keeping his temper in check. "I was offered help in my career early on and I wanted to pay it forward. Success isn't selling out," he says, his eyes a piercing blue. "And they wouldn't have played your song because I told them to. They don't have to pander to artists."

I stand there, not sure how to continue. I'm calming down to a reasonable simmer, but his eyes flicker angrily. Apologizing would make me feel weak, which is not something I want to feel right now. So I stare back at him while he glares at me.

"Congratulations," he says tonelessly.

A sound engineer comes over. "Mr. Justin, you ready for sound check?"

Marc doesn't look back at me. He turns and follows the man down to the stage. I stomp off, wondering if he's right about everything.

As the day's last sunlight spills onto my head and shoulders, I cross the giant parking lot to where the buses are parked. I look from Marc's to the band's and back again. I don't want to talk to anyone right now. So I do the only other thing I think might help. I walk giant laps around the fenced area, replaying the conversation again and again.

I hate that the more I replay Marc's words, the more I realize he was right. He has been honest with me. I'm the one who lied—or omitted—about being married. And it makes sense that he didn't want to tell me about Clear Channel until he knew it was happening. There are so many disappointments in this industry and he wanted to protect me. It's sweet, really. But I still can't let go of the feeling that he wanted some kind of control over my career. I see where that's unwarranted, or me projecting, but it's just a feeling deep in the pit of my stomach that I can't shake off.

Worst of all though, is what he said about being some fun on the side of my failing marriage. Does he really think that? I want him to know that I meant what I said: I love him. But does that mean I don't love Seth? And if I do still love Seth, then is Marc right? My head spins with the possibilities, each worse than the one before.

Onstage everything makes sense. I play my songs, feeling like I've been doing this forever. I lose myself in the melodies, reliving every lyric as I sing. I tap into a part of my inner performer I've never before accessed. I barely register the audience spread out before me. Where I used to feel terror— fearful of rejection or being misunderstood—I now find solace. Who knows how I'll sift through the mess I've made of my personal life, but at least I know how to sing these songs the way I intended for them to be heard. For the first time, maybe ever, I sing with an open heart, exposing my deepest vulnerability.

When Marc joins me for my last song "Falling to Pieces"—my new radio single—I keep connected to that deep thread, following it from the fearsome dark into the light. It's like being outside myself looking in. But at the same time, I've never felt more grounded. This is what I've been looking for. This is me.

After my set I find a quiet corner backstage—no easy feat with all the people milling about, getting props, wardrobe, sound, hydraulics and a million other details of Marc's performance ready. I need some serious alone time. Where's an invisibility cloak when you need one?

Back to the wall, I sink to the floor, knees to chest, head crumpled on top of folded arms. I close my eyes, trying to recapture the empowered vulnerability I tapped into during my performance. The downside to that honest kind of performance is coming back to reality. This—the skin crawling discomfort—is the feeling people stifle with booze and drugs. Unfortunately that's not my style, so I just hide out, hoping it'll go away soon.

Deep down I know I'm the only one who can make it go away. But I choose to sit, waiting for an all-knowing entity to illuminate the answers and show me what is most important. Where's my goddamn fairy godmother?

Nowhere to be found, that's where. I don't get my moment of clarity, but I do hear a familiar voice say, "Hey Babe."

Chapter 40

Why me? One night to myself. Was that really too much to ask for? I squeeze my eyes shut. Maybe if I don't look up, he'll go away. He doesn't. He slides down the wall next to me, his shoulder next to mine. I count to ten in my head and, when he hasn't said anything, I give in.

"Hi."

He offers a weak smile. "Hey."

"Hungry?" I ask. He nods.

***

"I heard your song on the radio," Seth says between bites.

He's eating a burger and fries, drinking a local microbrew. I brought him to this little pub, hoping to keep him away from everyone I work with every day on tour. There's no need to fuel their gossip or attract any unsolicited advice either. The familiarity settles my nerves even though I've dreaded this encounter for nearly two months. This part feels normal.

I sip my water and move salad around on my plate. I set my fork down, deciding to take control of the conversation. I inspect Seth across the table, studying him.

Dark skin encircles his eyes, standing out against his pale complexion that looks like it hasn't seen sun in weeks. His shirt hangs loose on his shoulders and he seems smaller than I remember.

Suddenly I see him in a way I never have before. The man sitting in front of me is human—fallible, broken, confused and scared. I've always seen him as larger than life, impervious to the imperfections the rest of us face.

After all our time together maybe I took his strength and assurance for granted. I never considered that my growing as an artist and person might scare him. He's always been certain of the answers while I stumbled along trying to discover bits and pieces. Did I see him that way because he wanted me to or because I chose to? When I first heard Freesia's voice on Ida Bella's new track it hurt. I thought he was intentionally hurting me. But he was like a child acting out. Trying to get my attention.

"I listened to your new song again. The lyrics are great," I say, realizing I mean it.

"Thanks," he says. "It's about us."

"I know." I lean back against the hard wooden booth, stabbing a piece of ice with my straw.

His posture alternates between defeated and eager, hunched and leaning. I can see he's out of his depth emotionally. And I thought I was lost.

"I'm so sorry," he says.

I scrunch my nose, thinking about how to explain my own thoughts. "I'm not."

He looks away and takes a long swig of beer.

"Don't get me wrong, I hate how complicated everything has become. But singing my own songs makes me happy. It's like all the disparate pieces of myself came together for this one puzzle. I've found something in performing that I've never felt connected to before."

The way he stares at me I can't tell what he's thinking. He looks down, peeling a corner of the label off his beer.

"I'm sorry. I'm not saying that to hurt you."

"I know. I saw your set tonight," he says, glancing up at me. "You've never looked so comfortable or sounded better."

"Thank you." I smile. "That means a lot—coming from you."

It's his turn to be pensive. He seems to be organizing his thoughts. His brow furrows and unfurrows. I sit back and take a sip, giving him time.

"I'm sorry about Freesia," he says without looking up. I sigh, not sure which part to address. I'm aware that I'm in no position to say anything one way or another. But he goes on, "I asked Lolo but she said no. She told me she wouldn't do that to you, and I shouldn't either."

I smile, picturing her face. I feel a wave of gratitude knowing I have a friend I can count on. And I'm relieved he's talking about singing.

"Why did you do it? Why not just sing it solo?" I ask.

"I ... I'm not as brave as you," he says studying his beer.

"Brave?"

"You were always the one who made me feel like I could do anything," he says. "I don't know how to do that for myself."

This is news to me. I never saw our relationship—personal or professional—like that. I always thought I was the little puppy following Seth around wherever he led. He made all the big decisions, controlled the creative direction, produced our albums, everything. How could he think otherwise?

"That's not how it felt to me," I say, putting my hand over his on the table. He looks up at me. "From where I sat, you were in the driver's seat. I was along for the ride."

His eyes widen in surprise.

"That's why I needed to take this step on my own," I say.

"That's plenty clear," he mumbles under his breath. Then he sits upright, setting his beer on the table. "All you needed was space from me to get in touch with yourself. And find someone new." He watches me with shining eyes and my heart breaks.

He takes a deep breath. "I knew he'd fall in love with you, but I hoped you wouldn't fall for him."

I don't know what to say to that.

"Me finding myself was never about us," I say, tackling the easier of the two.

"How could it not be? Everything I have done since we met has been for us. They're not separate."

"When we met, I didn't know myself yet. I took on your likes and dislikes, your opinions and tastes. I followed you down a path toward your dreams while running away from my parents' dreams for me. That's not the healthiest way to live."

"You had your own opinions," he says.

I shake my head. "Think about it. It's part of why we got along. We thought the same way ... about almost everything."

I see the truth of it sinking in as he leans back in the booth seat.

"Either way, I've lost you. And you know the worst part? I set you up. I have no one to blame but myself," he says.

"You haven't lost me," I say. He sits forward, eyes focused and attentive. "But I'm not sure you're going to love the new version of me. And if you don't, I can tell you right now, this is the version that's here to stay."

"I thought you were with Marc now," he says.

I shake my head.

"So you haven't ... had sex with him?" It looks like it causes him physical pain to say it out loud.

I don't respond. He sucks in a breath, downing the rest of his beer in one gulp. He closes his eyes, bobbing his head, obviously trying to get a grip. I can't watch. I watch ice cubes melt in my empty glass.

"Did you sleep with Freesia?" I ask, unable to lie to him, but unwilling to be the only horrible one.

He drops his focus to the table, folding and unfolding his napkin. Even with that telling silence, I can't imagine him getting past me sleeping with another man.

"I'm not going to say I'm okay with it," he says, straightening his back. "But I don't blame you. I was holding you back." He looks at me with a look I've never seen before. This is not the Seth I've been married to. This is new. "I want you, Penelope. I won't blow a second chance," he says, his green eyes on my brown ones. "I'd like to get to know the new you, if you're okay with that?"

Wow. This is the last thing I expected him to say. And I feel the sentimental pull, mixed with something else— something I'd like to get to know.

"I don't know what to say to that," I say.

"Let me prove it to you," he says.

Don't we owe it to ourselves to get to know the new

versions of one another? But if so, what about Marc? I can't just dismiss my feelings for him. I don't want to.

Chapter 41

Seth walks me back to the bus. It reminds me of the early days, making awkward conversation, laughing at each other's jokes even when they're not funny. It's nice after all that's happened recently to feel some sort of forward movement.

I stop in front of the bus and jerk my head toward it.

"This is me," I say, holding my purse in my hands in front of me.

"So it is …" He lingers, scraping his foot along the asphalt.

"This is weird," I say and we both laugh.

He steps forward, his hands on my shoulders and leans in for a kiss. The contours of his mouth are so familiar and yet so foreign now, too. I kiss him back, standing on tiptoe.

"So that's it, you're pissed at me and back with him?" Marc says.

I have no idea where he came from. I didn't see him when we walked up.

"Wha—?" I start, but Seth cuts me off.

"I'm her husband," Seth says, and takes a step toward Marc, chest puffing out.

It feels like he's been waiting for this confrontation. Who knows? Maybe Marc has too.

"Yeah? You asked her lately if that's how she sees you?" Marc counters.

Seth's eyes fire arrows as he looks quickly at me then back to Marc.

"Enough!" I say, stepping between them, holding them at arm's length.

"This is ridiculous," I continue. "You don't have a problem with one another," I look from Marc to Seth and back. "You're both upset with me, for different reasons. So just walk away and I will talk to you both … separately."

"You're wrong," Seth says. "And he knows why."

"You don't deserve her," Marc says.

It's like I'm not even here.

"Oh, what? And you do?" Seth says, brows shooting up.

"Yeah," Marc says.

"You think she wants you for you?" Seth shakes his head, disgusted. "But hey, you got her right where you wanted her, right?"

"It's not my problem she wasn't happy with you," Marc says.

That's all it takes for this testosterone-filled pissing match to combust. They lock onto each other, twisting and struggling to gain the upper hand. Marc seems to have the advantage, and Seth goes for a body shot, punching him in the side. Marc breaks his hold and lands a right cross on Seth's cheek.

"Stop it!" I shout. Considering they are fighting over me, you'd think they might actually listen, but no. This has nothing to do with me, really. So I do the only thing that makes any sense at all. I walk away, slamming the bus door behind me.

I don't see how the fight breaks up. I assume Marc's security won't take long to interfere. I hear whoops and hollers from the entire dancer-musician crew that have been watching from the bus window. They're amped up like they just witnessed the best cage match of all time and fire questions at me from all directions. I ignore them, heading straight for my bunk, where I shut the curtain, silencing them the best I can. They boo me but I don't care.

I close my eyes and go straight to sleep.

Chapter 42

In the morning I find Chris and Beth to tell them about Sal's offer, explaining that I will be performing at the Grammys. Beth grudgingly respects my handling of this news and my ideas for promotion. I ask if they have any producers they'd recommend. I am going to include Tyrone on the final song. I can pay it forward, too.

They give me their opinions and promise to contact a few people and let me know. I thank them for their time and get ready for the show tonight. After so many cities blending together over the past weeks, it's strange to be in one for so long. We'll leave Seattle tomorrow, but I need to clear my head. I don't have any promo today and I don't want to talk to either Seth or Marc so I've decided to go shopping and find a new outfit for the show.

Voicemails and texts light up my phone from both of them, but I don't feel like listening or reading. I know Marc will be at sound check. And I'll talk to Seth eventually. I just need some time to myself right now.

I wander into a part of the city I haven't been before, meandering in and out of shops, picking out items that speak to me. In a record-breaking hour that would make Lolo proud, I have a new outfit, including accessories and shoes. For the first time in my adult life, I am not interested in any opinion besides my own and I relish the extra time I'd usually waste soliciting others' opinions.

I get back in plenty of time for sound check. The sound guys, who usually don't give me enough bass in my guitar, are more attentive. I tell them I want more bottom end. They give it to me. I need more volume in the monitors for my vocal. Okay. It goes smoothly and I finish in plenty of time to give Marc as much time as he needs.

We pass each other in the hall as I'm leaving and I nod cordially. His face is expressionless and I see the ghost of a black eye beneath concealer. I check my phone and see that I have two voicemails: one from Beth, one from Seth. I listen to Beth's and scribble down a name and number of a producer she spoke to about me who is interested in the project with Tyrone. I call her back and thank her.

Then I listen to Seth's voicemail. He's sorry. Doesn't know what got into him. Wants to meet me to talk about things. He's coming to the concert tonight. Super. I turn off the phone.

After his sound check, Marc spots me from across the parking lot and jogs over. I stop, letting him catch up to me.

"Hey," he says, catching his breath.

"Hey," I say. "How was sound check?"

"'Really, that's what you want to ask me about?" he says. "Come on, I want to talk to you."

"All right."

"First, I'm sorry I hit Seth. It was immature and we behaved like Neanderthals."

"It's not me who deserves the apology," I say.

"Okay, if you want, I'll apologize to him."

"It's not about what I want."

"No? I think that's exactly what it's about. We both want you, all to ourselves. Don't you see that?"

I make an effort to keep a neutral expression.

"I don't get in fights. But I did. For you. I'm driving myself crazy, waiting to find out what you want!" He rakes his hands through his hair.

"But that's just it. I'm not a piece of property. I can't be won in a pissing contest. You might think you want me, that you want to know what I want, but the problem is that you each want me for yourselves. That's proprietorship, no question," I say, spinning on my heel, heading into the bus.

Chapter 43

That night, I play the show of my life. I own that stage. And I am rewarded beyond anything I could have dreamt. So many people in one space listening and connecting to my music creates energy unlike anything I've ever felt. It's a bond—a contract—built from beginning to end, building and slowing, cultivating the mood. It cuts through the debris of life outside this building, connecting us on a wavelength where we, as a collective, for a short while, live and breathe as one being. It is perfection.

After my set I head straight back to the merchandise table, signing CDs, meeting fans, offering hugs. I spend at least an hour talking to people, some who tell me how my songs affected them, making them feel understood. Some want me to know that they're sure I am on the brink of stardom. Some just want to say hi. They all have one thing in common: a connection to my music, and therefore, to me.

Back in my greenroom I call Sal and tell him my idea about the producer I've been talking to. He loves the idea of Tyrone on the single. We iron out the details and set a date to meet with Tyrone and make a plan to get him ready for the event.

By the end of the night, I should be exhausted. I'm not. Being myself is less tiresome than anything I've ever been before. I'm exhilarated. So much so that I want to talk to someone—a friend.

I call Lolo.

"Hey girl!" she says. I don't know if she knows about Seth and Marc fighting or even that Seth flew up here in the first place. I don't want to know.

"Hey Lo," I say. "Guess what?"

"What!" she screeches when I tell her about Sal and Tyrone and the Grammys. She shouts the news over her shoulder to Jeff and he shouts a "congratulations" loud enough so I can hear. It's nice to have a normal conversation.

"Guess whose song I heard on the radio today?" Lolo says.

"You heard it?" I ask. I've made peace with it. After all, it's what I want to do for Tyrone. I just hope she gets it.

"I was getting coffee when I heard it. I busted through the line and cranked that shit!" she sáys.

"Then climbed up on the counter, screaming, 'That's my girl!'" Jeff's impersonation of Lolo's excited voice is hilarious, and spot on. I can totally picture it. I smile, wishing I could have seen it.

"Shut up," she says, partially covering the mouthpiece. "You totally deserve it," she says to me. "You know I want that contact, Chickee." I hear her smile through the phone. "Hey, and I'm coming to the Grammy's with you, even if I have to fit in your purse. Just so you know."

"So you don't think I'm a sellout?" I ask.

"Hell no! You've found the friggin' Holy Grail! You got your original acoustic song on national radio. Fuck. You're the bombest person I know," she says. I can hear a scuffle and then Lolo pacifying Jeff, assuring him that he, too, is awesome. I can picture Lolo pushing him away, rolling her eyes, and turning back to the phone.

"How are you?" I ask.

"You figured out who you want to be with?" she says, not letting me change the subject. The tension is audible in her voice.

"I haven't. But Lolo, I better go. Thanks for being such a good friend," I say. I hang up before she can answer with a flippant response. She sucks at compliments too.

As I step outside into the cool night air and walk around to the front of the stadium my phone lights up with another text from Seth.

I'm sorry. I meant what I said. Can we talk when you get home?

I sit on a bench on the sidewalk, just looking at the marquis, watching the cars and people disperse like ants.

Okay. I type.

So much weight rests in such a small word.

Marc's hotel is visible from where I'm sitting and for the first time since we fought, I really want to talk to him, to get back to a good place. I dial his number.

"Hey, are you at the hotel?" I ask.

"Not yet. Give me five minutes."

I need him to know that my feelings for him are real. That this magic between us is real. That I don't believe he wants to own me. And that I'd like some time to settle into this new skin I've grown.

"I don't think you want to control me. I'm sorry for how I treated you," I say to him later at the hotel. "I need some time to figure out who I am now and that means I need space. Can you understand that?"

He nods and kisses me. I feel the same fire as before, but this time it doesn't control me.

"I don't like it, but I understand. I can't just wait around for you though, you know that, right?" he says.

"If there's any way for us to be together, I have to be myself. And to be myself, I have to take that risk."

Tears spark the backs of my eyes, but I force myself to leave. Whatever happens or doesn't happen at some future point will be for my future self to deal with. All I can concern myself with is the present. And presently, I have to go.

Chapter 44

These last couple months in the studio, working with Tyrone and Sal have been busy. Since the tour ended, I've been helping get the music room set up for the boys in South Central. Now that they have funding, Sal and I are organizing a great new music teacher and the acquisition of enough instruments for all the kids to learn on and borrow.

This past year has taught me so much. As I prepare myself for the Grammy stage and plan the details of my first solo headlining tour, I can't help but reflect on it all. From the time I was a little girl, I wanted a life full of adventure. Without hesitation, I can say my younger self would be proud of me now.

And the rest? I dreamt of an extraordinary life from the safe shelter of my limited girlhood experience. But life cannot be planned or bent to my will. And I think that's a good thing.

If it had been up to me I wouldn't have two Billboard top 10 singles or be co-writing with three new artists. I wouldn't be learning to produce my own music. And I wouldn't be nearly so fulfilled with what I'm doing.

There is a lot less drama in my love life since accepting that I can't control the future, and I have to say, it's a nice change. I've got a home life I can relax into. I get to be myself and make music—my own and with Ida Bella. Of course, nothing is perfect. I'm still figuring things out as I go.

But from up here, on the Grammy stage, in front of the entire music industry, I'm looking into the audience at my plus one, smiling. Life is good. Tears have been cried, decisions made, lessons learned in painful authenticity, but it's all part of the journey. My very own adventure.

Acknowledgements

Novel writing is a heck of an undertaking that requires a lot of patience and understanding from those surrounding the author. I would like to thank my husband, Lee Coulter, for indulging my particular brand of crazy while I've gone through draft after draft, always giving me the extra time and support I need, not to mention being my first reader and story editor. Thank you to Kai, my favorite human, for being my little super hero—catching a major error in the cover before it went to print! Good eye, kiddo. Thank you to Donna Watts for her story edits, writing dates and friendship. Thank you to Susanna Rosen, my copy editor, for her keen eye and kind words. Thank you to Cindy Lynch and Kiki Corbin. Thank you to Josie Brown, author extraordinaire, for mentoring me. And, in particular, THANK YOU! My readers. You are amazing. And more encouraging than I could have ever dreamed possible. You make my job an absolute pleasure and I love you all!

Also by Sharisse Coulter:

Jenna Jax-Anders hit rock bottom in high school. Or so she thought. From rock star heiress to knocked-up has been, she turned it all around, marrying the punk rock baby daddy love of her life. The perfect Hollywood fairytale. Until the day she walked in on him kissing her best friend.

As she struggles to find herself and redefine the world around her, she faces the challenges of raising her over-achieving teenage daughter, the heartbreak of losing her best friend (backstabbing aside), and emerging from the shadows of two famous last names to find her own identity. Oh, there's also the tiny issue of her husband's record label, backed by an anonymous mogul whose morally ambiguous creative direction may ruin them all.

But she doesn't know about that yet.

About the Author

Sharisse Coulter, originally from Lake Tahoe, started with a smidge of college in Paris (not Texas), a dash in Australia and, voilà! A master's degree in Anthropology framed and placed lovingly on a shelf, never to be dusted off again. Instead, she took the clear path to success, marrying a musician, becoming his manager and touring the country playing gigs, taking photos, and making music videos. Finally, she had a son (and subsequent identity crisis), which fueled the completion of her first novel ROCK MY WORLD. Soon followed by A Novel Music Tour: a 5 month 55 city national music/book tour. THE BIG IF is her second novel. She lives in Encinitas, CA with her husband and son and enjoys learning to surf and drinking lots of coffee.

www.ingramcontent.com/pod-product-compliance
Lightning Source LLC
Chambersburg PA
CBHW020603180626
46810CB00007B/2626